KU-053-151

AN ENGLISHWOMAN IN FRANCE

Wendy Robertson

Severn House

This first world edition published 2011
in Great Britain and the USA by
SEVERN HOUSE PUBLISHERS LTD of
9–15 High Street, Sutton, Surrey, England, SM1 1DF.
Trade paperback edition first published
in Great Britain and the USA 2011 by
SEVERN HOUSE PUBLISHERS LTD.

British Library Cataloguing in Publication Data

Robertson, Wendy, 1941-
  An Englishwoman in France.
  1. Extrasensory perception–Fiction. 2. Murder victims'
  Families–Fiction. 3. English–France–Fiction. 4. Agde
  (France)–Fiction. 5. Love stories.
  I. Title
  823.9'14-dc22

ISBN-13: 978-0-7278-8031-4 (cased)
ISBN-13: 978-1-84751-344-1 (trade paper)

All Severn House titles are printed on acid-free paper.

Severn House Publishers support The Forest Stewardship Council [FSC],
the leading international forest certification organisation. All our titles that
are printed on Greenpeace-approved FSC-certified paper carry the FSC logo.

Typeset by Palimpsest Book Production Ltd.,
Falkirk, Stirlingshire, Scotland.
Printed and bound in Great Britain by the
MPG Books Group, Bodmin, Cornwall.

PART ONE

ONE
Starr

England 2009

My name is Estella, sometimes known as Starr. I'm thirty-two years of age and my partner Philip thinks I'm barmy. No, seriously, he thinks I'm mad. In fact I'm very normal – or as normal as any of us ever is. And the older I get the more I realize no one is really normal. Aren't we defined by our abnormality and therefore normal in our own way?

Of course, like most people, I have my own play on what is considered *normal*. There is this family tradition of seeing the dead. My grandmother's sister, Great-aunt Lily, was a medium – you know, one of those people who stand in front of a crowd and call up the dead. Me, I see the dead in the more ordinary way of things. I just see people who *shouldn't* be there, in that place at that time. For me this is the ordinary way of things.

These visions can appear in the most ordinary places: the park, for instance, where I used to walk hand in hand with my mother and once saw a soldier in full First World War battle gear. In fact I saw right through him to the dusty privet hedge behind. Then there was that time, in the Spar shop on the corner, when I saw this woman standing *behind* the woman at the till. She was very old and wore a red sari with gold edges. I could see through her to the serried ranks of cigarettes on the wall behind her. She was like smoke in the air.

And I would regularly see my father standing behind my mother in the bathroom. Not so unusual, you might say. But *he* wasn't there either. She and I subsequently decided the person I saw must have been my father, but she wasn't sure who that even was. It could be one of four men, she said. 'There were those four wild weeks in 1977 on this campsite in Brittany. They were all nice guys. But, you know . . .' she added vaguely. 'Ships that pass in the night and all that.'

My mother often relished our shared gift, but she taught me very early on to keep it a secret. 'That kind of thing used to happen to me, love, when I was young,' she said. 'But it kind of faded away.'

When, in the early days, people showed their concern for me, she would explain away my first visions as 'imaginary friends' – a normal part of childhood. But then one day, when I was eight, she sat me down and suggested I should keep my observations and descriptions to myself, as my strange habit unsettled people and made them think I was odd. 'Anyway, Starr, it's kind of bad manners. Makes people uncomfortable. Like talking to poor people about how much money you've got.'

She said I should even give up sharing my visions with Mae Armitage, my best friend. It seemed that Mae's mum had talked about it with my mother and said that all this stuff had to stop. Apparently it gave *her* nightmares, even if it didn't bother Mae. Of course Mae and I took no notice of her mum. We still told fortunes with the cards. Mae was usually better at it than me, because she could make up exotic and bizarre stories. I just told what I really saw – which was sometimes quite boring stuff.

Once when Mae was sleeping over and my mother was away we chalked an ouija board on our kitchen table and had a go. But we quickly scrubbed out the chalk letters when the air started to smell of incense and the room started pulsing like a bomb.

But really, my mother's ban started to wear me down – effectively turning me from a bubbly, wide-awake child into a quiet, reserved one. This ban started to make me feel odd in my own eyes as well as the eyes of others. Mae was my only relief from this. We still shared some secrets that bound us together. But to tell the truth even Mae herself didn't really want me to go on seeing these dead people. In the end I thought it best to keep it a secret, even from her.

Tib: Good Fortune, 301 AD

A warm, salty breeze lifted the bright reddish hair of the boy, sometimes called Tib, who was sitting with his legs dangling from the flat roof of the house of his father, Helée, governor of this city which was now laid out below the boy like a map.

In front of him the neat road – square blocks of basalt – led straight down to the busy river harbour, widening halfway where it joined with both the straight road down from the barracks to his left and the narrower road to his right that led from the graceful temple of Venus. The clusters of houses on either side of the road were laid out in a grid, their black stone walls relieved by clumps of wild fig and straggling, bulging garden plots.

Tib raised his eyes and watched closely as the elegant ships hauled down their sails and resorted to the power of muscle and oar to manoeuvre their vessels into the teaming river port finally to squeeze into spaces alongside vessels already drawn up at the long harbour wall.

But however fast or elegant the ships were in reaching and tying up at Good Fortune, they had to wait their turn to be unloaded by the labourers and slaves working for the long-haired man – looking more like a pirate than a harbourmaster – who goaded them on with a combination of roars and threats which they answered in good measure. Even up here on the hill Tib could hear the deep, gravelly sound of their throaty curses.

Tib felt proud of the order and efficiency of hundreds of years of harbour routine that drove the port to such success. His father's tax scrolls were witness to that. Now he watched the shouting workers on one part of the dock heaving ashore great jars containing fine goods – silverware, spices, pottery and wine imported into Gaul from lands across the Great Inner Sea. Then he leaned sideways to see slaves manhandling racks of equally tall earthenware jars now containing wine and grain, salt and oil, ready to take them in the other direction, to the Imperial City of Rome.

TWO
Siri

True to the family tradition, my own daughter Siri was the outcome of a rather arresting one-night stand. Not quite ships-that-pass-in-the-night, but something similar. (More about that anon.) In fact by the time Siri was born my mother was living in Scotland, married to a very steady teacher she'd met on the Internet. The two of them grew vegetables and kept pigs and were very Green. Siri and I sometimes went up there for Bank Holidays. On occasions I left Siri with them for the long summer holidays so that I could bank up a pile of work to make both of our lives easier.

In those days I worked as a kind of dogsbody on a women's magazine and by the time I was pregnant with Siri I'd actually managed to turn my strange habit of seeing the dead into a saleable commodity. One day the regular journalist went on maternity leave and they added her astrology column to my more mundane tasks. I took a deep breath, did this lump of research into the nitty-gritty of astrology and – using those conventions – wrote some pretty inspired copy which entertained the editor, even though she thought it all nonsense. Then when the proper astrologer had twins and didn't return, the job was mine. Perhaps that was something she hadn't seen in the stars.

I even posted my astrology column right through my very short maternity leave, to make sure I kept the job. Then, when Siri was three months old, I came back into the office to do the astrology columns and the other usual running-around tasks at the magazine. But of course the cost of childcare in London swallowed up half my salary, so after seven months I began to take Siri into the office with me. It was nice having her there, first barricaded in a corner with chairs and then beside me on the desk, her fat legs swinging. Later she would sit under my desk playing with shiny kitchen utensils from the props cupboard. But then we got this new editor who was very edgy about Siri being in the office. You'd have thought women working on a women's magazine would be more understanding, wouldn't you?

In fact, the column was very successful with advertisers and readers, who relished its quirky tone. In the end, my editor – marginally embarrassed – told me perhaps I should write the column from home. 'Such good feedback on the piece every week, with your kooky slant on all things stellar, darling, but . . .' Her glance dropped to Siri who was on the floor, chewing a corner of last month's edition. 'Perhaps from home? Easier for you I'd think?'

The woman must have felt a bit guilty because she got me this contact on a men's magazine, where I became 'Joe Black', who could see into the future for a whole band of men who liked luxury and had mundane, if expensive, tastes. Then the column – appropriately modified – was syndicated in a series of magazines here and abroad. So in the end I actually made a better living working from home.

You might think it was an isolated life working alone with Siri in our little flat, but it was fun, creating columns, filing them, then going to the park and the play group, having coffee in cafés and thinking up new takes on Saturn being in the ascendant. The two of us lived on our own, on our own carefree island, in our own world.

Then, late one night when Siri was four, we ran out of milk so we went to our local twenty-four-hour Spar. That was the night we met Philip Crabtree. Those two took to each other and that was that. They were entranced.

To be honest, despite being entranced with Siri myself, I was just a bit lonely, Philip was kind and funny, and Siri was entertained. In no time at all we were a little family in his house south of the river. I still did my astrology columns and kept my independence. Philip went to the office, and Siri eventually started school.

So far, so ordinary.

Then one day my dear mother died very suddenly in Scotland. She'd been picking up sacks of food for the pigs. Brain haemorrhage. Pouf! She was gone and I never saw it coming. Isn't that strange? She left me two distinct legacies. First, that joy, that sunny sense of freedom that shone from her in rays. Second, a rather substantial lump of money from an insurance she'd paid into since I was born. Oh! And her special gift of insight, of course. That's three legacies, isn't it?

I only saw her once after she died. I'd mourned her in a catatonic fashion, feeling wooden and strange at her absence. It was as though my whole world – even Siri – was now rendered in sepia. I only slept two hours at a time. I often woke up, left Philip and climbed into Siri's bed.

Once, I woke up in the middle of the night, clasping my own neck with a strangling grasp. I blinked and there was my mother beside the bed in a bright yellow dress, watching me in that same close, thoughtful way she'd had in life. 'It's all right, Starr,' she said. 'You can let go, you know.' Her voice sounded so normal. I have to tell you that was the first time I'd ever heard one of my visions speak.

My hand loosened from my neck and I glared up at her angrily. She nodded and smiled. I could see right through her to Siri's bedroom door. Then she was gone.

'What is it, Mummy?' Siri, beside me in the bed, opened a sleepy eye. 'What do you see?'

'It's nothing,' I said. 'Nothing at all. Everything is all right now.'

And so it *was*. Then.

Tib

The boy raised his eyes further to where the sun-silvered water splashed up against the bright hulls of the ships on the far shore, then spurted into the air, each drop a sparkling world in itself. And now his eye was drawn to a smaller, neater galley painted in Imperial colours, as it manoeuvred itself onto the Governor's private landing. A smart seaman jumped ashore and secured it with stout ropes which looked fresh and new.

Tib jumped as a hand dropped on his shoulder. A voice murmured in his ear, 'A fine sight, son, eh? The best in the world d'you think? Finest goods from the East coming through our port to trade in Gaul? How about that?' His father's tone was proud, affectionate but still seemed to the boy to carry a warning note, like a stone in a clod of earth that a friend throws at you in a fun-fight.

Tib wriggled, uneasy as ever in his father's clasp. He released himself by swinging his legs back over the parapet and standing up straight in front of his father, in the soldierly fashion he'd been taught. 'So it is, sir. The best in the world.'

They turned and watched together as a man disembarked from the Imperial boat and jumped across two boats to reach the governor's landing. 'There he is,' said the governor. 'The Corinthian.'

The man, who was now getting directions from the piratish harbourmaster, wore dark flowing robes of a foreign cut, a round hat on his head and carried a heavy pack tied with leather thongs slung over one shoulder.

'Who is he?' asked Tib. 'Does he visit us?'

'Aye, he does, son. Well, he visits you. He's to be your teacher. Some of our distinguished guests have returned to the court with tales of your talents. It seems that the Empress was intrigued by these tales, so she sends you a teacher to test your wits. This Greek is her man. A freedman. Said to be very clever, a doctor of many arts.'

Tib sighed. Talk of his cleverness was always embarrassing. Since he was very small he'd endured the required ritual of performing for his father's guests like a Barbary ape – spouting poetry, playing his flute, showing off his calculations and inventions. In his eight years of life many great men had patted him on the head and many gracious ladies had given him sweetmeats. He thought of one woman, black haired and wild eyed, who'd given him a pomegranate. He had liked her. He wished she'd come again.

'My education is sufficient, Father,' he said now in desperation. 'With the documents and instruments you've had brought here, and my mother's help . . .'

'No, no, son! Your mother has the brain of a pea.' His father was firm. 'You need further food for that thinking miracle you have inside you. The message from the Empress says that this doctor has unique knowledge of the medical arts. Armed with those arts, and your great wisdom, one day you'll be of service to the Empire.' He examined his son from head to toe then back again. 'You never were going to make a soldier, Tibery. And because of your pea-brain mother you are too tender in the mind to be a leader. But . . .'

Tib had heard the story many times of how the Empire and the Emperor had served Governor Helée well. Here was an empire where a man like him, the Gaulish son of a mere blacksmith-turned-soldier, could rise from the ranks to the high Imperial position he held now. In this modern world anything was possible. And like many veterans, Helée was relishing the rewards of his life's loyalty to the Empire.

Father and son stood watching the tall man make his winding way through the harbour-side buildings and the clusters of dwellings, then on up the straight road to the gate of the Governor's house.

'What is he called, the Corinthian?' asked Tib, giving in, as he usually did, to his father. 'Apart from Corinthian?'

'His name is Modeste,' said the Governor. 'And do not be mistaken, Tibery, he'll be your teacher. The Empress has made up her mind and that's that. You remember the Empress? She once brought you a pomegranate.'

THREE
The Great Bear

Now you're asking yourself how, years before, I came to find myself alone with Siri. Well, I can only say it was love at first sight. He was a great bear of a man: tight blond curls and a face that was slightly too long; shadows under the eyes. He had the look of a fallen angel and looks don't lie. My friend Mae pointed him out – well, I thought she did – across the length of the Three Stars, our first stop on our Friday night flight into the town.

Locally known as The Stars, it was a rare pub where drinking was the real business and the business of food was only secondary. The fire at the end of the bar blazed a century's welcome. No cheap beer or half-price cocktails here: just crooners like Nat King Cole – already old-fashioned – undercutting the chatter in the bar and lounge. The only choice of drinks was one of three beers on the pumps, or unnamed red or white wine from boxes.

On this crucial night Mae shouted into my ear, 'New face!' She nodded towards the crowd by the fire. She gulped her red wine quickly, thirsty for that first hit of the night.

I peered down the bar but failed to see the man she was interested in. My eyes were stopped by those of *another* man at the end of the bar. *He* raised his glass and nodded, as though we were old acquaintances. The sound in the pub receded for a second, then surged up again.

'You know him?' said Mae, still concentrating on the man by the fire.

'Never met him,' I said in her ear, meaning the second man. She gulped down her wine. 'Let's go!' I was only too happy. I wanted to get away from this man. Even then I knew he was too powerful, too right for me. Mae grinned, grabbed her handbag and dragged me out of the pub, ready for action.

Mae and I always went out like this when I came home from London. It was a sentimental journey – reliving our young days when everything was a truanting adventure. Mae still did the 'Saturday night out' thing but my life, since I deserted the North for college in London, had moved on. I soon learned that in London every night could be Saturday. Every night could be party night.

When we were young, Mae was always the leader of our escapades. But these days I was more sure of myself – living and working in London had seen to that. But tonight the sight of this fallen angel had shaken me. I wondered whether he was real. Mae knew I was fleeing, but she thought I was fleeing the man by the fire. I'd learned to be careful now, kept quiet about seeing people who weren't there. Despite, or because of, making my living by astrology I'd come to know my gift as ordinary, even mundane. So far in my life this skill, these insights, had never managed to knock me sideways like this.

That Friday night our second pub call was at the White Swan – just called The Swan – where the music was post-punk. As usual it was packed with people and humming with the subdued roar of talk – twenty-somethings speaking on broadcast over the music and battling to be heard. We always went there to meet our friend Spelk, whom we'd known from primary school as a tiny mewling spelk of a boy and who was now, as Mae always said, a six-foot-six mewling log of a man. Spelk was meeting us at the Swan before we went on to the Blue Lagoon, known simply as the Lagoon, the best place to dance in Priorton on Friday nights.

Metamorphosed from the ballroom of the Marlborough Hotel, the Lagoon had been turned into a hot disco when the otherwise snobbish owners realized that disco was where the money was to be made. Now they turned a blind eye to the plethora of drugs that were part and parcel of the Lagoon experience. There was money in it, after all.

Spelk had rung Mae to say he'd be late, so we perched on stools at the bar and ordered a drink. Then I felt hot, and my skin burned. Heat was radiating from my left-hand side. I turned to see the tanned face of the fallen angel. 'All right?' he said. So he *was* real. Not dead. I didn't smile. I just nodded and turned back to Mae.

I felt a tap on my shoulder. 'Don't you know it's rude to turn your back on people?' His voice in my ear. No anger in it.

Mae's painted brows raised behind her fringe. I blinked,

took a breath and turned back again to face him. His eyes were very, very blue.

'Can I buy you a drink?' he said.

'We're waiting for someone,' I said, standing back to include Mae in the conversation.

'Well,' he said, smiling, 'have one with me while you're waiting.' He nodded at the girl behind the bar, who obligingly brought two new glasses.

'So, who might you be?' asked Mae, scowling slightly.

'I'm Ludovic,' he said.

'Ludovic?' she said scornfully. 'Isn't that a board game?'

'My father wanted Charles and my mother wanted Ludovic.'

'And your mother won!' said Mae, laughing now.

'Not really,' he said. 'I ended up with both names. People call me by both names.'

I relaxed. How ordinary was that? You couldn't have a fallen angel called Ludovic Charles. Too silly. 'I'm Stella – Estella really,' I said.

'But very honoured people call her Starr,' Mae put in.

'Hey, you two!' Here was Spelk, six-feet-six of arms, legs and spiky hair. 'Sorry . . . late . . .' he gasped. 'Spilled paint on the floor. *She* made me clean it up.' *She* was the sister-in-law in whose house he was forced to live. He punched me on the shoulder and kissed my cheek very hard. I could smell beer. 'Cool, Starr! Home again is it?' he said.

It turned out that Spelk wouldn't stop for a drink.

'What I want is to get down the Lagoon, to score, and to dance. I want to get *her* outta my head.' Spelk was known for throwing shapes that were out of this world. The long arms and legs helped.

Mae gulped down her drink and jumped down from her stool. 'I'm in,' she said.

'Let Starr stay and finish her drink,' said Ludovic. 'The two of us'll come on to the Lagoon after.'

'Spelk!' I said. 'This is Ludovic. He's *not* a board game.'

Mae put her arm through Spelk's. She looked at me, then up at the stranger. 'Right then!' she said. 'We'll go. See you there.'

We watched as Mae and Spelk made their way out of the door before turning back to our drinks. 'You live in the town?' he said. 'Can't remember seeing you here before. I've seen your friend and her giant at the Lagoon. But not you.'

'I always used to come here,' I said carefully. 'But I work in London. Not been home since Easter.' I caught sight of myself in the bar mirror. Hair too dark, ironed flat and shining. Long eyes – at Mae's insistence – over painted. Skin too white, bones too sharp. 'But you were never here then, as far as I can remember.'

'Recent arrival,' he said. 'After Easter.'

I looked at him through the bar mirror. He was thick-set, a full head taller than me, and his curly hair was too long for the present-day fashion. But the bones on his face were finely drawn and his blue eyes were smiling. His skin was weather-beaten without being ruddy. He was older than me – perhaps as much as thirty. Then I could smell salt and hear somewhere the jingle of boats bobbing in a harbour. 'Are you a sailor?' I said suddenly.

He laughed out loud at this. 'Not bad! I'm no sailor but I do sail. I love sailing. My father was a sailor.'

'What do you do, then?'

'Funny thing, isn't it?' He shook his head. 'How people always try to pin you down by what you do. Like they need to put you in a frame before they really see you?' His voice was soft and deep, definitely not local. South-west, perhaps.

I turned to look away, across to the table under the window where two couples were tucking into scampi and chips. Behind one of the men I could see the shadow of an old woman standing with her hand on his shoulder. In fact I could see right through her to the street outside. There was no reflection of her in the glass.

'Well?' I insisted. 'What *do* you do?'

'All right,' Ludovic said. 'I have this unit on the Oak Tree Estate. I build narrowboats.'

This got my attention. 'A unit? Narrowboats? Here? But we're miles away from the sea.'

'These babies are not sea-going. Well, not generally. My boats are for rivers and canals.'

'How can they get to a canal? From here?'

He laughed. '*Very* big lorries. Low-loaders.' He made a wide gesture with his hands, like a man describing a fish he had caught. 'We even sell them abroad.'

I scowled at him. 'You build them? Do you paint them? Don't they come with pictures on?'

'Well, I don't do it all myself. I have a lad to help me with the build. I get painters in to paint them. The decorative stuff I do myself. Like tattoos.'

'Tattoos?' I was still scowling. 'But why here? Why build boats here?'

'I wanted to do it. Thought I could.' He shrugged. 'And it's cheap here. It's what they call a special area. They give you good allowances for setting up.'

I couldn't think of any response to that, so I finished my drink and jumped off my stool. 'I'll have to go. Mae and Spelk'll be watching for me.'

'The Lagoon? Do you *really* want to dance?'

'When I come back home I *always* go dancing with Mae at the Lagoon. We always have.' I paused. 'Anyway. You come as well if you want. The disco's good.'

He shrugged. 'Don't dance, Starr. It passed me by. Seems really strange to me, dancing. Out of control.'

That got my interest. Everybody dances, don't they? 'So you don't like that? To be out of control? Doesn't fit, somehow. Someone who paints boats, not being able to dance.'

He shrugged. 'You build boats on your own. It can be a one-man job. I like it that way.'

I picked up my handbag – black patent, borrowed from the prop room at the magazine, very much envied by Mae – and slung it over my shoulder. 'Gotta go. Mae'll be waiting.'

'Stop!' he said, putting a hand on my shoulder. 'I want to show you something.'

'What? What will you show me?'

'It's a surprise.'

I ignored the alarm bells that jangled right through me, resounding from my pelvis right up into my throat. What did I know about just how far this angel had fallen? 'Go on then,' I said. 'I like surprises.' The words just popped into my mind. In truth, I didn't like surprises, not then. Despite my tendency to see dead people, my life – apart from reading the stars for money – was full of comfortable predictability: nice boyfriend on the lower echelons of London law, nice nights out at mid-price restaurants, nice weekends with croissants and the newspapers.

What was I doing, saying I liked surprises?

'Good!' Ludovic took my arm and his hand seared my skin.

He led me out of the pub into the market place with its lollipop lights, its newly planted trees and cobbled thoroughfare. Priorton was a funny old place. At weekends the market place would throw off its daytime elegance, eschew its listed status and become the bawdy centre of nightlife in the district. Pretty, half-dressed girls (Mae and me among them) would totter from pub to disco on towering high heels, trailed by boys, less pretty but luminous in crisp white tee shirts that showed off their muscles. In between pubs and the final destination of the Lagoon, we would pick up a couple of kebabs to keep us going, only slightly uneasy under the bland gaze of policemen – some no older than us – standing in pairs around a big black van.

Ludovic led the way. Soon we left behind the half-dressed girls, the muscular boys and the policemen and came to the ornate gates of Prior's Park. I looked up at him. 'What surprise? I know this place. Anyway the gates are locked. *Unlocked at dawn, locked at dusk in summertime.* See that notice by the gate? Not that you can see it just now. Dark, isn't it?'

He drew me to one side, to a narrower gate. 'But this gate's open. See? People live there, inside the big gates. In the Prior's Hall, and in those little houses. They have to get in, don't they?' The gate creaked as he opened it and pulled me through. He took my hand and walked faster, making me race. Our feet crunched on the gravel as we ran past the Prior's Cottages then made our way alongside the high wall of the Prior's Hall to the broad farm gate that led into the park.

I wrenched my hand from his, breathing heavily. 'Where's this surprise? I've been here hundreds of times.'

He opened the farm gate and pulled me through. 'Ah, but I bet you've never been here in the dark, have you?' He shut the gate behind us. 'And you've never been here with me.' He took my hand again. 'When I first came here I thought this place was magic, full of surprises. The park may be no surprise to you, but in the dark, I'm telling you, it's total magic.'

I looked around. The lights in the town were in the dim distance and the wooded park before us was enfolded in the dark. I could feel the great age of the massive trees in the fore-ground as clearly as if I were counting their rings. I could hear the murmuring river below. I used to play here when I was small. Tonight I could sense the great ridge beyond the river where as a child I'd once watched the roots of great trees on the High Plains reaching down and tangling with the riverside shrubs.

In my mind's eye I could see the greensward winding through them, leading onto the high road beyond. I remembered a time when I was eleven, blackberrying there with Mae and I could see this very old road, buried beneath this greensward. It was on this unseen old road that I saw a carriage with horses. And a cart hauled by an old horse with a pony tied on behind. And a man trudging along with a backpack. I told Mae that this was a road from *olden times* and she told me that it was just a bit of green and I should get lost and stop being such a mad hen.

Now Ludovic's hand tightened round mine. 'Well? Are you game?'

I let him lead me onwards. We walked through the park to the Deer House that stands on a promontory above the river: a hollow colonnaded structure with a tower at one end. Now, with the light and the sounds of the town almost gone, I could smell the dried, burnt-off smell of the autumn and hear the occasional flutter in the undergrowth.

'Here we go!' said Ludovic. He opened the battered wooden door to the tower and pulled me in.

In all the times I played here with Mae as a child, I'd never been inside this place. As children we found it forbidding, like a witch's castle. Inside it was pitch black and smelled of rotting leaves. But looking upwards in the roofless tower I could see the belt of Orion the Hunter, in the bowl of lighter night sky.

Halfway up the tower wall was a platform. 'That's for us,' said Ludovic.

'You must be joking,' I said.

'I'll show you,' he said. 'It's possible. I tried it. You do it rock-climber style.'

He made me face the wall and stood behind me. I could feel his chest against my shoulder blades, his thighs against mine. Then he took my hands and made me reach up and curl my fingers into stone crevasses. He reached down and slipped off my shoes and showed my feet where to grip. So we went up the wall, he like a crab's shell on my back. He smelled faintly of sweat and turpentine and his breath was like honey on my cheek.

After some hauling, gasping and giggling we were standing upright on the platform in the darkness. I peered through a narrow arrow slit into the mantle of darkness outside, making out the giant trees which were like the very core of darkness. A delicious orgasmic wave rippled through me from my heels to my head and I could sense every living being who'd ever stood in this spot, from eighteenth-century gardeners, back to seventeenth-century revellers, back to Roman camp followers, back to Celtish men in hoods following one after another in a line. The place was teeming with them. My head was aching with their presence on the surface of my time.

Ludovic gripped my arm tight. 'Look! North!' he said. Northwards, where the polluting lights of the town had stopped staining the night, the sky had retrieved its dense black and the stars were intense points of light. Orion, Cassiopeia, the Pleiades and Pisces were all there, shapely in their dispensation. It seemed the Gods were here with us. A privileged audience for the night's events.

I shivered.

He put his arm round me and hugged me to him. 'It's all right,' he whispered in my ear. 'It's all right.'

His cheek was soft against mine, not rough like I'd expected it to be. He put up a hand and combed back my hair with his fingertips. I turned my face to him and kissed the corner of his mouth. He moved his cheek and his lips were burning on mine. He had one hand on my throat, weaving its way under my shoulder straps. 'Such soft skin!' He spoke against my lips and I wanted more, much more of him. So much more.

I pushed his shirt collar to one side and felt his collarbone with my finger tips. His skin was hot, burning. He let out a groan and in a single action, loosed himself from his shirt. Now my fingers were tracing the muscles on his chest and he was easing off my top and we were skin to skin. In that moment I knew my father and my mother. In that moment I knew how I had been made.

In my life up till then I'd made love with quite a few men and relished the experience in a languid fashion, exploring my feelings and satisfying my curiosity. It was a natural, enjoyable process, like having a good meal. And I was often hungry. When I first went to London I even lived with a guy for a month or two. But he was keener at playing houses than playing lovers and soon became very dull. He was quite hard to shake off, however, and went on to play the stalker for a while.

But making love with this man whom I didn't know at all – this Ludovic – was different. Finally naked and shivering, we slipped to the floor of the platform and on a layer of densely packed fallen leaves we made love – once, twice, the energy pouring from us both, lighting us up again and again. And in between we stroked each other and giggled like children. Then, exhausted, I drifted off to sleep and dreamed of my mother and father. At that moment I remembered my father although I had never known him. His face was like mine, only longer in the jaw. I *saw* my father, this man whom my mother didn't even remember.

I woke up covered with clothes – his and mine – to find Ludovic beside me, naked, leaning on his elbow looking down at me. 'You are amazing,' he said, grinning from ear to ear like a goblin. 'Really amazing.'

'I know,' I said demurely. And we both collapsed into giggles, our breath steaming into the cold night. Then he tried to make love to me again but didn't quite manage it, which made us laugh even more.

I shivered and we both sat up with our legs dangling over the edge of the platform. We got back into our clothes with some difficulty. He pulled a flat torch out of his back pocket and flashed it into my face. 'You're all sooty,' he said. Then he launched himself from the platform and landed on the ground, steady as a cat. He held out his arms and said, 'Jump!'

So I jumped into his arms and we rocked together for a moment. It was like being enfolded by a mountain. He kissed me on the cheek. 'You are something, Starr,' he said. 'You are something very special.'

Then we clambered down the steep bank to the river and kneeled down to dip our hands in the water and rub them together to clean them of the scent of the rank leaves and the sticky outcomes of our lovemaking. After that we splashed water on our faces and as I bent down to do this I glimpsed other reflections in the water, illuminated by the stars and the gleaming moon. I looked behind me and of course there was no-one there.

'What is it?' Ludovic said, rubbing his hand down his shirt.

Then I looked across the water and could see a line of men and women, draped in long clothes, their faces in shadow. Some were holding long sticks, others held planks or boards of some kind. They were walking in line, one after another. I rubbed my hand up and down his shirt, front and back. 'Nothing,' I said.

We walked back in a kind of uneasy silence through the park to the narrow gate. It creaked as he pushed it open. 'Do you want to go back to dance?' he said. 'Or would you like to go back to the Swan?'

I looked up at him. 'What do I look like?' I said.

He touched my cheek with his fingers. 'A clown,' he said. 'Your eye-lines have run.'

'I can't go back in there then, can I? I'll make my way back to Mae's. She won't wait for me at the Lagoon. She'll suss out what's happened.'

'Let me take you.' He led the way down a side street to a motorbike, chained like Hercules to a bollard. He flipped open the box and handed me a helmet and a big leather coat. 'Here, put those on.' He grinned. 'Going home in style!'

The cold night air burned my skin as we made the short journey through the streets of Priorton. The journey was too short. At Mae's house he jumped off, removed his helmet and took mine. I slipped out of his coat, folded it over and handed it to him.

He held it to his face. 'It smells of you. Can I come in?' he said.

I was already shaking my head. 'Mae's mother and brother are in there. Impossible.' I waited. 'Perhaps we could meet tomorrow.'

He coughed. 'Well, the thing is, I'm riding out at the crack of dawn. Big meeting back home with a supplier. Four o'clock start.' He took my hand.

That was when I felt the wedding ring. I thrust his hand away. Why had I not felt it before? On the ledge? There'd been no ring then. Had there?

'I'll be back up here early next week,' he said.

I was already shaking my head. 'I don't live here. I live in London.' I waited, then, for him to tell me that he got up to London. Sometimes.

In the dingy porch light I saw his face change. 'I thought, after this, you would . . .'

I was sorry for him. I picked up his hand again and very deliberately ran a finger over his ring. 'It was a time out of time,' I said. 'No past, no future.' I kissed his cheek and ran inside.

I stood there with my back to the door, listening to his motorbike roar away. Then Mae's mother popped her head round the door. 'You all right, love?' she asked.

'Yeah. Fine,' I said.

'Our Mae not with you?'

'No. I came away early. She's with Spelk.'

'That's all right then.' Mrs Croft had known Spelk since he was indeed the little spelk that got him the family nickname.

Upstairs I lay on Mae's bed and stared up at the stars she had pasted on her ceiling. I should have felt foolish, but I felt happy. It had been a perfect night. The Deer House. The stars in the heavens. The faces in the water; the Celtish funeral procession. And this Ludovic, who built and painted boats. Ludovic who? I didn't even know his name. Perfect night, though! It was the perfect night to make a baby, because that was when my Siri, my own precious girl, was made.

When Mae got back home an hour later she demanded details. I gave her a much edited report. She shook her head. 'You must be mad, going down the park with that big galoot. Could have been murdered. Could have been murdered by him. Idiot.'

'I was safe enough,' I said. 'He's married.'

May stopped slathering cream on her face. 'Married?' she said. 'Worse than a murderer, then,' she said gloomily.

'Anyway I've to go back to London tomorrow.'

'Tomorrow? I thought you were staying till Monday.'

I shook my head. 'Gotta get back,' I said. 'Just got to get back.'

The next day on the train, watching the landscape fly by, I imagined Ludovic, that big bear of a man, on his motorbike roaring down the roads parallel to the railway. Even now, deep inside, I was humming with delight, going over and over again the events of that perfect night. I knew I'd never see this man again but at the same time I knew this matter was not finished. Perhaps I knew – even then – that Siri was with me. Otherwise

why should I be so happy when I had just met and lost – in
the space of four hours – this man who could have been the
love of my life?

You might ask why I didn't pursue Ludovic about Siri.
Perhaps it was my mother's strange but successful example
of single parenthood; perhaps it was the gold ring on his finger
that had given me such a jolt. But I didn't tell Ludovic about
Siri.

Mae told me later that he'd come back to the Swan several
times looking for me. But she obeyed my strict instructions
not to betray my whereabouts. And even she did not know
about Siri until my daughter was born. By then she failed to
make the connection with the big boat builder, thinking Siri's
father some guy I'd met and dropped in London.

I'm not quite saying it was all in the stars, but that's at least
one interpretation of events. After that night I came to think
about Ludovic when I looked at the night sky and saw Ursa
Major, the constellation known as the Great Bear.

FOUR
Blue Murder

I t took them just six days to find the boys responsible. The younger one, Kerry, was finally forced – by nightmares and unwarranted vomiting – to confide in his sister, who told their mother. The family, not unused to concealing more petty crime, considered the problem. Then they decided this secret was too large, too terrible, to keep and went to the police.

At the first court hearing, even through my own miasma of grief, I felt sorry for the mother of this younger one who had been Siri's classmate, her friend. The woman was white faced and confined in clothes too small for her. There was a strip of white flesh where her tank top did not meet her jeans.

It seemed that this family blamed Pete, the older one; called him the ringleader. They told how, on the intervening six days after the murder, in between bouts of cider drinking in the park, he'd been riding around the town on a stolen mountain bike. When the police pounced on him he was cocky, defiant. He blamed Kerry, the younger one. 'Looks like an angel, don't he? But behind those eyes, mister, there's blue murder. I'm tellin' yer.'

I discovered all that from the papers much later. At the time I learned some stuff from the police liaison officer, Lily. (Sagittarius. Earth sign – full of desires and creative energies. Optimistic, freedom-loving, good-humoured, honest. On the other hand blindly optimistic, careless, tactless and restless.) Odd in a policewoman, perhaps. I remember she smelled of lily-of-the-valley perfume. Very earthy. This policewoman said there might be something in what the older boy said, but that both boys were to blame. For me, whoever was to blame, *who* drank cider and *who* spewed up, my beautiful Siri could be no more, nor no less dead.

You will know the details. (I think everybody in England knows the details. This kind of death is no private affair.) Twelve-year-old girl, young for her age but clever – according to her headmaster 'a credit to her generation' – anyway, this twelve-year-old girl plays football with Kerry, a boy from her class. His older friend joins them. The three of them follow the kick of the ball into nearby woodland. (How I regretted then, moving to Philip's place south of the river. My inner-city block was much safer than this suburban wilderness.)

Anyway, the three of them played, messed about, had a laugh. Then there was some kind of quarrel and Siri strode off towards home. Pete caught her in a neck-lock and hauled her back in among the trees, struggling. They tied her to a tree and the two boys play-acted a scene of crime and punishment. The younger boy, Kerry, could not remember the words that were said. He said he was frightened but still thought it was a game. He said that Siri thought so too. He said she laughed. At first. Then the older boy punched Siri hard and she screamed.

'It was very loud, her screaming, sir,' the younger boy, Kerry, confided to the policeman who was taking his statement. 'And it got on Pete's nerves.'

Pete said that it was Kerry who filled her mouth with grass and gagged her with her own long socks. Kerry said it was Pete. What happened next involved stones, and does not bear telling. Even here.

I would keep telling myself over and over again that Siri's life ended when she and Kerry were kicking the ball around in the road outside our house. But of course that's just a lie I told myself to stem the nightmares. Counsellors did give me strategies, doctors did give me pills, but I knew that nothing – nothing in this whole world – would fill the hollow, raking, nightmare vacuum. A filthy black vacuum that lodged itself at the centre of my heart, my soul, my life.

This was bad enough, but even worse was the fact that my casual lifetime gift of seeing the dead let me down in this crucial moment. Knowing Siri to be dead I searched for her everywhere – every street, every park, every shop that I knew was familiar to her. More than once the police brought me home to Philip in an exhausted daze. Other mediums wrote to and emailed me with offers of advice and comfort, even contact. But I ignored them. One informed me quite coolly that there was a cosmic law that a mother may not see the spirit of her murdered daughter. Or even worse – that the sudden violent death of my beautiful child had placed her in limbo from where my puny gift could not rescue her.

It might seem odd, but despite seeing dead people throughout my life, I'd never before considered seriously that religious stuff about *hell* and *purgatory* and *limbo*. I just thought that some of us, like my mother and me, could see through time as though the millennia were mere lifting veils that swirled around us.

In truth, my work in astrology was just me playing around in the area between the familiar symbols of my gifted imagination and managing to hit the right message more times than could be explained logically. I never questioned it and as I have told you, it had rendered me a good living.

After I lost Siri time piled on top of me like iron weights with spikes, distancing me from that terrible morning when I had waved my Siri off and told her to enjoy herself. I kept seeing her lift her head and smile at me, in that way she had. Through those first two, then three years, my early raging grief stiffened into a kind of wooden armour. I was still consumed with anger but was too wooden to show it. I continued to be angry with Siri for saying yes to a game of football. I was angry with those boys, now locked away until they knew better. I was angry at the world that had somehow conspired to stage her destruction.

It took me nearly three years to enter Siri's locked bedroom. And when I did and I found nothing of her in there, I loaded all of her stuff – clothes, toys, schoolbooks, posters – into bin bags. I threw out everything except a small attaché case she had begged from my mother. In this scruffy little case I put random pieces, one from each bin bag: some of her baby shoes; a sun dress she wore on a holiday we spent with my mother and stepfather; a battered copy of Maurice Sendak's *Where The Wild Things Are*; her first school writing book; a diary with a padlock that I'd given her on her last Christmas. There was nothing in it. I looked. And the little red hat Siri wore when we met Philip was in the top of one of the bags. That too went into the attaché case.

The room was stripped and the door was locked again.

I went on being angry at Philip for not being angry enough, for not being as crazy with grief as I was. Even so, one slender part of my wild mind sympathized with him. How could he feel like me? Since we met him he had acted the father to perfection – teaching Siri to ride a bicycle, blowing out her birthday candles. He'd done the things any father does. As time went by, when we were together, his family started to note the resemblance between Siri and him.

His mother once showed me photos of Philip at the same age. 'Two peas in a pod, see? Siri's the model of our Pip.' I think she'd convinced herself that he and I'd had this affair in London and come together again later. He did nothing to disabuse her.

Perhaps Philip stayed sane just because he *wasn't* Siri's father. Oh, of course he was upset, incredulous, spluttering. He talked about skewering those boys like (he said) the little pigs they were. But in the many months of the investigation he kept a cool head and a hard hand on any explosive feeling. And finally, when the boys were locked away and the press moved on to another spicy case, he said to me that we should look forwards not backwards. We could be practical and help other families in similarly bad plights. He'd already been approached to do this.

He could be very convincing sometimes. And I thought that perhaps I might help in this way. But I knew that I had to *see* her again – any shade, any shadow of her – before I might move on. Finally I allowed some of my acquaintances from the fringes of astrology to try to help me see her, but in the end they threw up their hands as, one by one, they failed in the face of my scepticism and disbelief.

Then yet again I started to go everywhere where she, or she and I, had ever been – every street, every lane, every alleyway, every bus, every train. I took long journeys to every place we'd been on holiday, to look for her there. I started to go and hang around her school at break times. In the end her headmaster, so kind at first, lost his rag. He came, coat flapping in the wind, and dragged me to his car and drove me home. Now that made Philip *very* angry.

Still, no matter what I did, Siri was never there.

You might find it strange that through all this mad time I still continued to do my astrology columns, recycling old stuff, free-basing new stuff, making new money to prove I was alive, adding it to the stash that came from my dear mother's foresight. I worked through the night and slept through the day, only rarely catching sight of a perplexed Philip. I cut down on my antidepressants because there was the possibility that the numbness might make me renege on my deadlines and keeping Siri alive in my mind. Also I realized that the pills were giving me suicidal inspiration and I wanted to stay alive to see Siri again.

On many nights I would cast and recast Siri's chart for the time then and the time now – for the day of the murder and for this same date – one, two, three years later. And again and again I would stare in the mirror and wonder why, why on that day I should have told her, 'Yes love. You go and get some fresh air!' What I should have done is shackle her to the fridge, the bed, the washing machine. Anything.

I looked at Siri's constellation, Virgo, in the night sky and willed it to bring her through to me from whatever fog she was in, so I could see her. But these days, angry at the man called Ludovic who had started it all, I no longer sought out the Great Bear in the night sky.

Even worse, I was perpetually seething with anger at Philip for just being normal. This anger and my nocturnal habits drove an ever widening wedge between us. Where there had been kindness there was now rancour. Where there had been tolerance there was blame and disbelief. He saw me as crazy and incomprehensible. I saw him as hard and unfeeling.

Then, after another bout of not speaking to each other for days on end, he breezed in saying that – out of the blue – someone in his office had offered him a house in the Languedoc for two months. Seemed she'd rented it but couldn't make the dates now because her daughter in Australia had become pregnant. Philip was very keen on the idea. Perhaps he thought it was the last chance for us. This was why he'd broken his silence. 'Don't you think it'd be a chance, Stella, to get away, to freshen up a bit?' His tone was anxious. 'It'll do you good. You can take your laptop and do your pieces.' He offered it as an enticement.

I struggled for an excuse. 'Two months? They won't let you go for that long.'

'All legit, Estella. My boss thinks it'll do me good. Doc's signed me off. Stress.'

'Stress?' I frowned.

'You know. Siri . . .' His voice trailed off.

I stared at him. 'You . . .?'

'It's not only you, you know.' He was uneasy. 'Well, you being stressed makes me stressed. I explained it to the doc. Feller got it, surprisingly enough.'

I changed tack. 'This place? Where is it?'

'I know it. My family used to go there when I was a kid. Sunshine. Beaches, bicycles. All that.'

Siri on her bicycle. There was a boy on a bicycle the day she went off with those boys. He had scattered the three of them as he charged down the road. But still they went, with their football, out towards the woodland. The police searched for this boy but he was never traced.

Now the blood drained from me and I swayed. Philip put a hand out, touched my shoulder. 'I know, Estella. Siri would have loved it. I shouldn't have said that.'

I threw off his hand as though each finger was a poisonous viper. 'Don't!'

'But when Dot Smith made the offer, it seemed just the thing.' He sounded wretched.

I connected at last to the despair in his voice. My anger evaporated and the blood thumped back into my face. I shrugged. Perhaps it would do him some good. If the doctor thought my stress was bleeding into him perhaps I shouldn't stand in his way.

'If that's what you want, Philip, we should do it. If it'll do you some good that's fine. I'll take my laptop. I can work anywhere, can't I?' I said.

He nodded. 'Could be our last chance,' he said quietly.

I looked at him for a moment and for the first time in years allowed myself to be really sorry for him. Maybe this would be the last chance for him. And me.

My last chance with Siri was long gone, after all.

Wasn't it?

FIVE

Beside the Great Middle Sea

Gaul 301 AD

In their early times together the boy called Tib was very much in awe of his Corinthian teacher Modeste. In his short life he'd never met any person who was cleverer than himself. From the very first time the Corinthian put a hand on his shoulder he was aware of Modeste's power and intelligence. When he noted Modeste's smile and the dimple dancing in his left cheek he knew the Corinthian's great cleverness was imbued with humour and humanity. He liked Modeste's voice – deep and soft, and kind of curling at the edges with his Greek accent. He thought that had Modeste not been clean-shaven with his hair smoothed back under a scholar's band, he would have looked like many of the sailors down at the harbourside who came from all parts of the great middle sea beyond the mouth of their own wide river.

The day after Modeste's arrival two sailors from the Imperial barge hauled two great boxes up the hill to the Governor's villa. These were full of treasures that – though he did not know it – would eventually constitute Tib's curriculum. At first his father Helée would listen approvingly, as Modeste taught Tib about Roman history and glory, about the great taletellers, and the myths of the gods who ruled the universe and the great emperors who in turn became gods. Then, deciding he could trust him, he left Modeste to it and went about the business of being the governor of this busy port.

On fine days Tib and Modeste would walk and ride together through the hamlets and villages out beyond the town of Good Fortune. As they travelled Modeste showed Tib how to find plants and roots and cure them, making them useful for the villagers and farmers they met on their travels. He also showed him how to make maps that were in proportion and could be followed by others.

But as the days grew colder and darker the two of them stayed inside Governor Helée's fine house. Now was the time for Modeste to decant the contents of his boxes and talk to Tib about their magic. The first box was clearly a doctor's box, with instruments rolled in protective linen, and strange dusts and mixtures, stored in horns and vellum packets, all neatly labelled in Modeste's fine Latin hand. Modeste would say, 'This is for . . .' or 'This is for . . . , but only when the moon is in the first quarter. This is for . . .'

Tib, with his extraordinary memory, heard, learned and never forgot. Ever after those early lessons, when he came across an illness or an affliction he need only close his eyes, and in his ears he would hear Modeste's precise recipe for a cure. The admiration between them was mutual. Modeste was impressed by this skill of memory and even more with Tib's ability to connect cause and possible effect.

After a month of being Tib's teacher Modeste was called to Helée's finely decorated chamber to report on the boy's progress. He did so with enthusiasm. 'The boy is as a sponge, Your Honour. But then, not only does he replicate what he has learned from me, the boy then puts it in that great thinking soup of his, and out comes intelligence, wisdom!'

Helée, who had just returned from a very successful tax collecting and magisterial trek around his province, took the flattery personally. 'It is in the blood, Corinthian, it's in the blood. There is no doubt about that.'

Tib's mother, Serina, when she had finished instructing the slaves in their tasks, would often come with her sewing to sit in the corner of the eyrie-like room at the top of the house where Modeste and Tib worked side by side. Their work table was the long plank brought by Modeste off the ship and laid on trestles.

Sometimes, as they were working, Modeste would consult and defer to Serina and her responses were always considered and informed. One day he told her, with some grace, that it was very easy to see where the boy got his gifts. Tib relished this comment. So much for his mother having a brain the size of a pea!

In time, at Tib's excited urging, they got to the second box of treasures. This turned out to be full of scrolls and documents and measuring instruments. So as the winter became even darker and colder they began to pore over these great texts which recounted Greek history, myth and Greek scholar-ship, which came before that of the Romans. Tib began to make sense of the ideas and discussed them with Modeste with a wisdom much older than his eight years. And so he learned that all things did not begin with Rome.

One day he noticed that there was one set of scrolls at the bottom of the box his teacher left undisturbed. 'What about these, Modeste?' he would ask. 'These look interesting.'

'Soon, dearest boy. Soon.'

The days went on and the wind was swirling up from the sea and the sun seemed unwilling to make more than a transit-ory appearance. The howling seabirds were swirling off inland. But even in harder weather, on one day in each seven days, Modeste would borrow horses from Helée's stables and travel with Tib further afield through the villages and hamlets with his bag of cures. Modeste would use these visits to test the boy, to see if he'd really learned his lessons. The villagers were amazed that a child so young could diagnose ailments with such accuracy and even cure them.

But on another day every week Modeste would don his hat and his heavy sandals, take his pack and go off on his own, walking from sunrise to sunset, returning with scratched and dusty feet. Tib was puzzled by this habit and asked his mother where his teacher went on these days.

'I think he walks to *think*, Tib, to gather his thoughts,' said Serina. 'You bleed his thoughts from him and it seems he has no more left. You were the same with me. I felt sometimes you used to use me up. Modeste needs to gather himself up again.'

One evening, from the window of his eyrie, Tib spotted Modeste trudging his way back to the city. Tib ran out of the great gateway to meet him. 'Where do you go, Modeste? Where do you go when you walk like this? I *must* know.' He hung his head and sounded bereft.

Modeste laughed and took the boy's hand in his. 'I am searching,' he said, striding on. 'I go in search of something that was lost.'

'What do you search for?'

'I search for the truth.'

'Is the truth in a place, Modeste?'

Modeste came to a stop and stared down at the boy. 'The truth cannot *really* be in a place, Tib. It's inside our bones, our flesh. We know it when we see it, when we feel it. It is not in a place.'

'So why do you go and blister your feet and tire your legs in all this searching for a place?'

Modeste began to walk along again, pulling Tib with him. 'Perhaps it's a vanity, Tib. I *know* this truth. I've learned it. But I wish, just once, to touch the truth-teller with my own hands. It may be possible here in Gaul. I've learned that this may be possible here.'

Now it was Tib's turn to stand still. Then he spun round and round until the horizon became a single thing, a line in his head. 'Here? Here in Gaul?' he said. 'You could touch the truth with your own hands?'

Then Modeste was laughing, his voice full of joy. 'Yes, Tib, here in Gaul! This is why I persuaded her gracious majesty to send me here. To touch the truth. Is that not wonderful? One day, perhaps.'

The next morning at very first light Modeste called Tib up to the eyrie and asked if he'd slept and broken his fast well.

'I have, Modeste.'

'And are you full of energy?'

'I am. I am full of energy.'

'Then I will show you something!' He reached into his second box, brought out the last scrolls and laid them on the big table.

Serina slipped into the room. Tib was worried. Perhaps Modeste would not open the scroll with his mother there. But Modeste ignored her. 'You know I come from Corinth, Tib? Before I was in the service of the Empress?'

'I do. My father calls you the Corinthian.'

'Well, hundreds of years ago, in my country, we were once visited by a great man, a philosopher and thinker.' He paused and said the words very distinctly. 'He was a follower of the Nazarene.'

Serina stirred in her chair but said nothing.

'This great scholar stayed with us a while and taught my forefathers many things. Then he left us, but afterwards he sent messages to us about the good way to live and how the way of the Nazarene was the right way to go.'

Tib touched the nearest scroll with the tip of a finger. 'And these are his messages?'

Modeste laughed. 'No, they are *copies* made by my many-times great grandfather from the original messages. They are my family's treasure.'

So it was through Modeste the Corinthian that the boy, Tib, son of Helée the Roman governor of Good Fortune, read the letters of Paul of Tarsus with his teacher and became a heretic, preferring the virtues and the legends of the charismatic Nazarene and his burgeoning church called the Way, to the obligatory propitiation to the old Roman gods and the worship of the Emperors made gods.

SIX

Starr at the Maison d'Estella

It was when we were pulling our cases to the house from the market square up through the crowded, narrow alleyways of Agde old town that it dawned on Philip that we were not so close to the cherished beach of his childhood memories. Instead we were making our way to a bulky house behind a high black-stone wall, with a massive door that looked as if it had been hammered by Richard the Lionheart. I looked along the narrow street and shivered. The high wall was pierced with smaller doors and other windows, which seemed to have been carved into the walls with a random hand. But I knew this doorway on the high ridge of the town had at one time been an important place. I could see the pediment of an arch with an eagle at its point before it melted again into the high wall.

The door creaked open on to an irregular courtyard set around by windows and walls that rose up into a bowl, cradling the blue southern sky. To one side was a stone balustered staircase that led to a blocked-off doorway, going nowhere. Seagulls chirped, chattered, shrieked in French and posed on the topmost ramparts. I breathed in deeply.

The place smelled of time, of layers of life and people. Around me in the deserted courtyard tumbled a whirling smoke of people going about their eternal business of survival, commerce and politics. Their gauzy layers welcomed me. I breathed out. For the first time in months – in years – now, I felt comfortable.

A leaflet on the old heavy table in the big kitchen informed us that the stones on the boundary wall of our house are part of the ancient town wall, built, like many buildings here in pockmarked black volcanic stone, quarried throughout the millennia from the slopes of an ancient volcano.

Philip turned to me. 'No beach then!' he said, making every effort to be cheerful.

I amazed myself by smiling faintly. 'No beach,' I said.

'No matter,' he said heartily. 'We'll hire a car. Beaches only a few minutes away. Dozens of beaches. Great family beaches.' He went red. I guess by now he was really sick of putting his foot in it. 'Sorry, Estella, I didn't mean . . .'

We settled in. I set up my laptop in a top bedroom and spent my nights up there weaving my astrology charts and forecasts as usual. I had to bank them on the laptop ready to take to the town library to file them through the internet. No broadband here in the house. I sat in my eyrie and listened through the day and through the night to the kids playing in the alley outside, yelling at the top of their voices and careering round on motorbikes and mopeds. Late one night I peered through the window to see the spin and spark of fireworks celebrating the new Miss Agde (*on her way to the world title*, the poster said) down at the quayside. The smell of sulphur was in the air. The fireworks crackled and banged, lighting up the night sky in playful echo of the charts I had carefully pinned up on the walls of my eyrie. These bright lights certainly blanked out the real thing. The stars in the sky, on my maps and in my head paled at their brightness.

Mostly I slept till noon, then came down to the courtyard to eat a tray of 'finds' from the fridge in the kitchen and drink the wine Philip had opened. Then I would lie back and try not to think of Siri, allowing the sounds of the alley outside to wash through the door and flow over me. Alongside the sounds of clamouring women and children and the grind of motor scooters I could hear the clatter of horses' hooves and the faint cries of street-sellers from other ages, the urgent murmur of townspeople from other times. They crowded in on me. I dreamed them and saw them, night and day.

Most days Philip hired a car to go to the beach and drive up into the hills of the Languedoc but I encouraged him to do that on his own. He made acquaintances in the town: English people who had packed up and come to live here; French business people he met in bars who spoke his pragmatic language in more ways than one. He read biographies of British comedians, histories of France from the revolution to the Second World War. He watched international rugby in the sports bar, drank coffee and brandy, and played poker with an old soldier he met there.

He would return to the house from his own journeying about five o'clock, having done his marketing. Then he would become absorbed in his elaborate preparations for our evening meal.

All the while I knew he was waiting, waiting for me to get better. Waiting for me to become calm, to lose my madness. He waited for me to forget Siri dying. For him I should only remember her living. He was so very anxious. I knew it was not for nothing that his boss had given him compassionate leave, to cure his wife of madness and save his marriage. Or not. Even through my perpetual fog I knew that this was our last throw of the dice, our last chance to stay together. Still, the way I was, I found it very hard to focus on this.

My nocturnal habits were blighted a bit by the fact that I had to get out of the house at some time during the day to go to the Maison des Savoirs – the rather grand library – to file my columns to London, Australia and South Africa, do my emails for my online consultancies, and rake cyberspace for . . . what? Notices of sightings of Siri? I looked all the time but I didn't know what I was looking for.

Then one day out of the blue I had this rambling email from Mae in response to some jokey card Philip had sent. Who knows? Perhaps he had sent out some coded cry for help. Anyway it seemed Mae had decided to come and stay with us. The children needed a break. Hubby (as she called him) Billy needed a break and seeing as we had all this room she had decided they would come to help us out.

I told Philip when he came back from a ride out to a monastery in the hills. He was delighted at the news. Relief bled from his pores and danced in the air. He'd got on so well with Mae right from the beginning. Her openness and forthright pragmatism appealed to him. As she got older Mae had become more, not less attractive. She watched her diet, became toned and tough. She ran a slimming support club at her doctor husband's surgery. She laughed when Billy told us gravely she was a pillar of the community, but still she believed him. I always asked about Spelk but their lives had diverged. He was now working for some charity, directing the building of a school in Africa.

When we lost Siri, Mae came down to London and flurried around us quite a bit. She let Philip feed her and in return she cleaned the house, which had gone downhill a bit. She tidied

Siri's bedroom without my permission. She tried to approach me with comforting assurances but I wouldn't let her inside my grief. In the end she went home. The last day she looked at me. 'I did what I could, Starr,' she said. 'I tried.'

'I know,' I said. I managed to touch her arm.

'But it would never be enough, would it?'

I shook my head and almost pushed her through the door.

And now here she was in France, trying again. One call from Philip and she was here.

Philip was disappointed at my lack of enthusiasm for Mae's visit. So he set to work himself, sorting bedrooms and buying new sheets in the Thursday market for her and her brood. He swept the courtyard and stocked up the kitchen with things like Diet Coke and crisps *ancienne et naturel*. As he was a stickler for healthy food and authentic cooking, this was quite a concession. He spent all that week marketing, chopping, planning and fettling.

As it happens I'd had a very bad night the night before their arrival. I'd sleepwalked down the steep wooden stairs and ended up on my back in the courtyard babbling to the stars.

So, the next day Philip decided that it might calm me down to take a boat trip on the famously beautiful Canal du Midi. It would take the best part of the afternoon, so he could finish his shopping and get some decent food on the table for Mae and her family.

Somewhere, fogged up in my soul, I think I agreed with him. My sign was Pisces after all. From water we came and to water we shall return. The water of the canal might just dissolve the lava lump of pain that sat inside me.

When I got up in the morning I felt very unwell. Philip took my arm quite tightly and said, 'You don't want to be here when they arrive. I'll get them settled in. I know it. You *are* going on this trip, Estella, if I have to carry you there. I'll tell the people on the boat to take care of you. But I tell you, Estella, you're doing that trip!'

SEVEN
The Boy on the Boat

I feel a silent gliding in my body even before I get to the side of the canal. A crowd of people jostles around the landing place. Will they let me on? Philip has spoken to the captain. *Make way for the invalid!* The French respect the ill and the invalid. The way parts before me like the Red Sea divided. The Captain's helper – a *gamine* in black jeans – sets me against the side of the boat like a pot plant. Even wedged as I am in this genial crowd it takes a mile or two of gliding for me to feel safe, stuck as I am in the here and now. The hubbub of the travellers fades, as one by one we're hypnotized by the silver-green water and the trees standing to attention every ten metres, clawing the banks to make them safe.

Now my mind slips backwards and I can see old men in dingy clothes about their business, steering their barges loaded with coal and tin, bales of cloth and racks of wine. Then there's only the limpid beauty – silver, green, slate grey; gleaming water alternating between the elongate shadows of trees and the bright reflection of the southern skies.

We're one hour into the journey when I notice the boy: narrowly built with orange hair and eyes too wide for life. He's leaning backwards, staring at the Wedgwood-blue helmet of sky, his long hair dripping towards the water like strands of fire. At his side sits a youngish man in a crew-necked sweater, his long nose in a worn black book. Even in repose the dimple on his cheek gives his face a benign look. His black hair is slightly long, but short at the front, combed across his broad brow. When he raises his eyes to gaze at the canal I see they are bright, cornflower blue. Now and then he puts out an absent hand to stop the boy tipping back into the water. These two are an odd pair. Father and son? No. The older one's too young. Brothers? I have to settle for brothers. But there's no resemblance. Absolutely none. The colouring is wrong.

Suddenly I have this prickle of unease. I know when things are not quite right, in this and other worlds. I close my eyes and have another glimpse of them but now the boy has his hair tied back in a kind of cue and the man is wearing a hooded jacket.

I blink. Now the boy's sitting upright and leaning across to speak into his companion's ear, making him laugh, bringing that dimple into full play. The man's teeth gleam in a flicker of sunlight. The man cuffs the boy on the shoulder and they dissolve into conspiratorial giggles. I know now that things are all right with these two and the black cloud that has been sitting somewhere in my head all morning starts to shred itself.

Oh! Now the boy has climbed up and is balancing on the rail, arms out straight, like a tightrope walker. He makes his way, dancing on light feet, towards the prow of the boat. A mutter ripples through the crowd and a woman nudges the arm of the boy's companion, making him drop his book. He stands up, just in time to see the boy launch himself off the prow of the boat and sink like a stone under the grey-green water, creating ripples that surge towards the bank, swilling the roots of the great trees that hold the canal safe, soaking the bright yellow irises sitting there on the verge. The muttering swells into shrieking and the canal boat's engine putters into silence.

At last the boy's head breaks the surface of the water and the shouts turn from panic to relief. *Dieu merci!* The boy swims to the bank and hauls himself out, water dripping from his whipcord muscles. He grins a crooked-toothed grin and holds his clenched fists above his head in victory. The people are cheering. *Bravo!* Everyone cheers the boy except me. And the boy's companion. *He* shrugs, leans down to retrieve his book, and starts to read again.

The sky darkens and rain begins to patter on the boat's awning. Of course this is not like English rain. It does not cool the warm air. The boat's engine starts up again. Now the boy is jogging on bare feet along the towpath. We race the boy the last half mile to the jetty. He's fleet footed and wins the race, but the boat is not far behind.

My Philip is standing under a big golf umbrella in the rain at the jetty. He searches my face anxiously. I take a deep breath. As I've said, my state of mind these days is Philip's big nightmare. He's always been so afraid of my agitation. His myth is that I just need to *calm down* for me to get better. His recipe is afternoons in shaded rooms; platefuls of his gourmet food; more wine than is good for me – anything to *calm me down*. You'd think a murdered daughter was an illness visited on a person by natural processes. And by similar natural processes you will eventually become *calm* and thus be cured of her death.

He's well intentioned, is Philip, but he's the mad one, when you think of it. But he wouldn't know, would he? Not knowing could be a sign of his delusion.

When we moved into the Maison d'Estella two weeks ago I tried to tell Philip I actually *liked* the house – not least because it had presences. I mentioned the people walking through the rooms.

'Ghosts?' he said. 'Sweetheart! You are so funny. Imagination getting the better of you again!' Then he smiled in that special inward way he has, complimenting himself on his tact with this woman whom he loves, but who is rather inconveniently crazy. What he first thought charming he now finds wearying.

And now today as we splash our way through the traffic across the bridge and up into the old town, he scoffs at my tale of the red-headed boy. 'I was there at the landing, sweetheart! No saturated boy, no man with a black book got off the boat! I assure you.'

But there was. The people on the boat cheered the boy's safe emergence from the water. The woman nudged the man. I *saw* them.

And I've seen the boy since. Walking on top of the town wall, and then in the alleyway behind the Promenade, legs astride, standing upright on the pedals of his mountain bike.

Now I'm getting ahead of myself. First I must go home to the Maison d'Estella and greet my guests.

EIGHT
Entertaining Mae

I look up at the old door, a solid and safe haven even after living here only two weeks. As usual Philip struggles with the key. The door is massive – heavy hinged, peeling and weathered with time. I stand for a second out in the narrow alley and reflect how the house has grown on me. I've felt safe in this house, roaming the rooms at night, standing on the terrace after Philip has gone to sleep, looking across the shadowy, eternally crimped roofs to the black mass of the cathedral and then – always, always – on up into the sky, dense as blue-black ink. Virgo is so alluring, so seductive that I feel I can put up a hand and very nearly touch the constellation. Some nights I come down from there making my way down the wooden staircases to the courtyard where I lie on the ground and look up through the cupped hand of the old building into the night sky. As I've said sometimes I do this in my sleep and end up in the courtyard still unconscious, which rather upsets Philip.

Today we open the door to the sounds of Norah Jones singing 'Feelin' the Same Way' and to the sight of Mae dancing around the courtyard, a glass in her hand. Her husband Billy is at the wooden garden table, the *Observer* close beside him and a beer beside his hand. The geraniums are nodding in their pots. Surfboards and beach chairs are tumbling from the space under the grand *escalier* which leads to nowhere.

'Stella!' Mae puts down her glass and flies across to me. I hold myself stiff as she hugs me to her. Her body feels like a bunch of sticks. She smells of Coco by Chanel, of cigarettes and of that stuff people use to dispel the smell of cigarettes. I must smell of . . . what? The air? Wine? The garlic in the *cassoulet* that Philip made last night? Misery? What does misery smell like? In my experience we all smell of our feelings – right through from desperation to elation, unhappiness to euphoria. This fact used to help me a lot when I used to do personal readings. People would clap their hands at my insight and say 'How did you know? How did you *know*?'

Mae strokes my upper arm. 'Phil was saying you've been down the canal on a boat. I don't know how you could do that, me! Go on a canal in this foreign place, among strangers. You might catch something.' She hugs me tighter – wanting, I know, to say more than that, to call up our early days, before she was thin and before I was crazy. In my head I can hear Mae say it. 'Things were so much simpler then, Starr.'

Her accent has smoothed off through the years, evolving into that middle-England speak that echoes a person's home region but has rounded itself out, become more distinct, more articulated. It happens to us all, I suppose.

I stand away, rescuing myself from her close clasp. 'I'm as you see, Mae. Here and in one piece.' The words come out more crisply than I intended.

'Estella!' Philip says sharply.

'Great to see you, Mae. Really.' I make amends. My eye moves across to the table. 'And you, Billy!'

Mae's husband holds up his glass in a toast. 'Now, Starr.' Billy always called me by my nickname since the time I told him (having drunk too much) that my mother called me Starr. 'I fear we've brought our northern weather with us.' Billy always starts his conversations with the weather.

I smile at him. 'Perpetual heat here in May is a myth. But Nyrene, the lady who owns this house, tells me she loves this time of year. There might be rain, but because it's cooler and greener the flowers by the canal are a spring miracle. She's right. I saw them today from the boat. Flag irises, clover, carpets of vetch, lovely grasses. And birds.'

I wonder what Billy would think if I say I saw ghosts on the canal today. I want to keep talking to him because I like him, and also for some respite from Mae's attention and Philip's surveillance. 'Nyrene rides along the canal path every day on her bicycle. She knows about flowers. And birds. She says there are nightingales in the evenings. *Rossignols* in French,' I add.

His eyes brighten behind his round glasses. 'Bicycles? Can we get bicycles?'

'Yep!' I say. 'You can borrow them from the landlord. He's a good sort.'

Billy puts his head on one side and looks at me. His eyes are much kinder, less searching than Mae's. 'Sea air's doing you good, then?'

I like Billy. Sturdy, uncomplicated GP. Ex rugby player running to fat; easy-going and quite content to let Mae push him around. I've also thought that's how he manages her. He has this chubby face and wears round glasses; he smells of cornflakes and, very faintly, of that antiseptic wash doctors use. I think the cornflake smell is because he's around the children a lot.

Suddenly there is shrieking and a strange thumping inside the house.

Mae laughs, her bright white, well capped teeth gleaming. 'Terrors on board!' she says easily. 'Playing trampolines on the beds.'

I wonder what my stylish landlady would think of that. The beds are big wooden carved wonders from the last century. Philip tells me the *brocante* shops here and in Pezenas down the road are full of them. Visiting them is one of his regular lone jaunts.

Come to think of it, these antiques will probably survive the bouncing better than the Ikea beds at home.

Mae catches my thought. She lights another cigarette. 'Go and get them, Billy. Can't have them getting into *Madame* here's bad books, can we?'

Billy vanishes through the glass doors into the house and at last Philip comes to my rescue. 'Estella needs a bit of a rest, Mae.' He gives me a gentle push. 'Go and lie down, Estella. I'll sort the meal.' He usually calls me by my Sunday name. I've never asked him why.

Billy comes through the glass doors, hung about with George and Olga, four and six years old respectively. George is a small roly-poly version of his dad. Olga is tall for her age, just into little-girlhood. Designer jeans and tee shirt. Bare feet. Hair up in bunches and round red-framed glasses. She holds out her hand. 'Hi Auntie Starr.'

Oh Siri!

'Olga!' I fold her small hand in mine and feel the shadow of the thousand or so times I had done this with Siri. I feel sick.

'Hi Auntie Starr,' squeaks George just behind her.

I take his hand too and smile. 'Hello, love. Haven't you grown!' My voice is crackly like a bad record.

I hurry past them and, looking back, I catch a knowing glance between Mae and Philip, before charging through the glass doors and up the wooden stairs. I throw myself on the day bed in my top-floor eyrie. I'm angry at their knowingness – knowing that I am sliding away to some place where they can't reach me, exasperated because they can't help.

I close my eyes and concentrate. Now again I can feel the slight sway of the canal boat. I can hear again the chatter of the people as the boy jumps, his hair streaming behind him. The dark man is there and he leans down again to pick up his dropped book. This time, though, he looks at me directly, his eyes locking on mine. *'Travelling through, just like you.'* His tone resonates in my ear. Manchester? Edinburgh? No. That doesn't seem right. His voice is accent-less. Timeless.

My heart stops, then falters on. *Siri!*

I can't sleep. I jump off the daybed, go to my work table and check my list. I bring up a chart on the screen and start to make notes. This work is the thread that has kept me this side of the sanity gap since Siri was taken from me. It can fulfil its sanity task for me today and all this week while we're entertaining Mae and her family. How can I relax or sleep with the sound of a small girl's laughter in my ears? I know that if I sleep I'll dream again of Siri kicking around a football with her friend Kerry then waving goodbye. Smiling.

NINE
Healing Processes

One day, in the spring of the year after the Corinthian came to Good Fortune to teach Tib, when he was off on his regular wanderings, a woman with running scabs all down one side of her face came to the great iron gate of the Governor's house and sent a child running, asking for 'the boy doctor'.

Tib picked up his leather pack (a new gift from his father) and went to see her at the gate. He put his hand on the woman's shoulder and smeared her face with ointment from a horn he had in his bag. Then he said the prayer Modeste had taught him and made a mark of the fish on her forehead. He told the woman to keep the ointment on her face for five days and afterwards wash her face in running stream water from above the town twice a day for twenty days.

'Above the town!' he said firmly. 'Don't forget!'

Within two days the whole district knew the woman's face was clear of these chronic sores for the first time in five years.

There was another time, down by the harbour, when Tib came across two men holding down another, whose arms and legs were flailing around like a windmill. Small as he was, Tib hauled them off the man. Recognizing their assailant was the son of the Governor, the men stood back. The madman leapt to his feet and began to set about Tib, who tried in vain to keep him at arm's distance. Suddenly the flailing stopped and the man stared at the boy. Then he smiled and knelt at the boy's feet. Tib put one hand on the head of the man, then, with the thumb of the other he made a sign on his forehead. The man sniffed, wiped his nose with the back of his hand. Then he stood up straight and strolled away, a picture of calm.

After that people started to trickle to Good Fortune from all across the region to be cured by the boy doctor. Tib applied all he had learned from Modeste in terms of both medicine and method. But the Corinthian observed that, in addition, the boy had this strange ability to calm people down, to right their disordered brains, to reduce their inner torment – all with a touch of his hand. The more observant patients and onlookers noted that his cures were always accompanied by some kind of invocation and a special touch on the forehead.

But Tib's growing reputation was not a total success. He failed to cure the harbourmaster's son, who was suffering from a throat infection that seemed to have closed off his throat entirely. Despite Tib's and Modeste's efforts over a whole week, the child died, and the harbourmaster was heartbroken.

At first Governor Helée looked on his son's emerging healing powers with benevolence. It was his job to keep the local population settled and happy, safe from brigands and not too upset about the taxes. Things were going well – after all, he himself still had Imperial ambitions. There were whispers of a move to Rome itself. He was in the habit of discussing this with eminent visitors long into the night, urging them to plead his cause to the Emperor. His wife Serina, in her quiet way, suggested that perhaps Helée might be seen as too keen on preferment. He should not pin all his hopes on such a vague possibility, she said. This extreme agitation was not good for him.

Then, one day, Helée woke up and couldn't see. He rolled out of bed and charged around his room, bumping into basalt columns and carved stools that stood by his bed. He roared for his servant, who went running for Serina. Serina calmed her husband down and got him back to his couch where he rocked backwards and forwards, praying to Jupiter to give him back his eyes. Had he not made the sacrifices? Had he not given the gods respect? Had he not made libations to the Emperor Gods? What reward was this for a man who had shown valour in the field of battle, to take away his eyes?

Serina sent the servant running for Modeste and Tib. She held his hand while Modeste did his usual thorough examination. Modeste shook his head in her direction. 'There is nothing here, Madam. There is no sign on his body that His Excellency may not be able to see.'

Helée moaned out loud.

Serina and Modeste both turned to Tib, who came forward nervously. He put both of his hands, first on the crown of his father's head, then over his ears, and then on his brow, and then over his closed eyes. As he repeated this series of actions, under his soft boy's hand Helée became calm.

Then, still with his hands on his father's head, Tib closed his own eyes and muttered the prayer he had learned with Modeste. He made the mark on his father's forehead. Then he stood back, and stood up straight at his mother's side.

They all waited.

Helée breathed in deeply, let out an enormous sigh, leaned his head back on his cushions, and seemed to sleep. They stood there waiting for half an hour. An hour. Then Helée sat up, opened his eyes and blinked. He turned his head left and then right. He blinked. He could see! He stood up beaming and clapped his son on the shoulder. He even embraced his wife. 'I said to you many times, my son. The Empire will be proud of you yet.'

Modeste and Tib went upstairs to a tiny corner room off the eyries where they did their work and gave thanks to Jesus the Nazarene for the curing of Helée, who, even though a pagan, was a man of virtue and common sense.

TEN
Madame Patrice

Having worked at my charts half the night, I drag myself from my bed earlier than usual the next morning. As I make my way down two flights of winding stairs at the Maison d'Estella the bell of St Etienne informs the whole town, as it has for hundreds of years, that it's eleven o'clock. Hedged around with the chitter of swifts and the occasional faux-baby wail of the seagulls, the house itself is silent. It's bright and hot today. Billy must have been pleased when he woke up.

I know that my visitors woke much earlier today. At eight o'clock I sat bolt upright in bed, groggily aware of the rumble and shriek of the voices of men and children. I threw myself back on my pillow and stayed where I was. I finally made it downstairs to find a note in Mae's scrawling hand on the kitchen table. *Off to Sête to suss those fab beaches! And look for bikes. Mmmmmmmmmm.*

Philip has left me my breakfast covered in a cloth – croissant, cheese, ripe pear, coffee in a flask. I sit down and eat it as though he's still here, watching me, calling me Estella. At one time I used to hide the food he made for me and not eat it. I got very thin, but started to eat off very small plates and kind of grew out of that. It seems now that the last fragile tendril of our relationship is his making food and my eating it. But these days we rarely eat together, just as we rarely sleep together.

Last night he and Mae and the others ate their supper together in the courtyard. Billy brought my food up to my eyrie – some kind of mussel stew with green beans in a vinaigrette dressing on the side. On the tray beside it was a lovely crystal glass with a small *pichet* of *rosé* wine.

Billy had put the tray down on my work table, stood watching as I pulled up my chair, then he stayed there, massive rugby arms folded. 'I bet you're sick of being asked how you are,' he said.

I poured myself a good slosh of wine. 'You bet!' I replied with some feeling.

He hesitated, then took off his spectacles and wiped them. They must have steamed up as he laboured his way up all those stairs with my tray. 'You know you shouldn't put pressure on yourself, Starr. It takes people years to get over . . .' He caught my look. 'Of course I know one never really *gets over* these things. Perhaps the most one can expect is to get back on some kind of an even keel. Get some kind of basis to start over again, you know.' He hesitated again. 'One has to do that, merely to survive.'

I was already shaking my head. 'I don't want to start over again, Billy. Not without her, my Siri.' I like Billy and I was trying really hard not to sound soppy. But my heart still hurt so much. 'Look! I need to *see* her, then I may be able to start over.'

He looked at me quietly for a moment. 'I do respect all this stuff of yours, Starr, but . . .'

'You think it's a load of old sewage.'

'Not exactly.' He stared at me for a moment. 'But wishing for something you can't ever have could stop you going on at all, Starr.'

Somewhere, somewhere in my soul I felt he must be right. I've been looking for Siri for so long now. 'But if I don't see her what reason is there? To go on?'

He watched me, his eyes troubled. Finally he said, 'So . . . how's the medication helping?'

I smiled faintly at him. 'I'm down to the minimum, seeing as you ask. You don't have to worry that *they* be my chosen method.' I was seeing again the boy diving into the water. 'I am Pisces. Water is my medium.'

'You won't do *that* on my watch, I'm telling you, girl.' He pantomimed scowling grimness but there was no doubting his seriousness.

I shovelled some food into my mouth. 'I was on the canal, you know, today.'

'I know love; I was here when you came back with Phil. Remember?'

'I saw this boy jump into the water.'

He blinked. 'Christ, Starr! You're not thinking of jumping, are you?'

His perplexed tone made me smile. 'I wouldn't say that. But there was this boy on the boat with red hair and he jumped. And he had this man with him. I saw them clear as day. I saw it! But Philip said I *hadn't* seen them. He insisted they weren't there.'

Billy shook his head and sighed. He put his arm round me and hugged me then turned to go. 'Remember, Starr, we don't *all* see the same things. Remember that. Just forgive the rest of us for the things we don't see.' He stood there and finally the words came out of his mouth. 'So you're *really* all right?' I gave him a look. He defended himself. 'Sorry! Mae said I had to ask. The old girl feels hurt that you're blanking her. I told her you must be basically OK because at least you're still working.'

I shrugged. 'And even that's only possible because I work on my own. Me and my machine and the sky above.'

'I can see that.'

I dug my fork into the green beans. 'You can tell Mae I'm all right. I'm as all right as I ever will be. With all this . . . *stuff.*'

I waited until the door shut behind him, pushed the plate away and started on the cheese. Billy's a true Taurus – *a builder and restorer, a self reliant caretaker of the people around him, restoring them to health and well-being. Kind and honest as the day is long, easy to be with, very touchy-feely.* Mae wrote me a letter when they met, saying he was a roaring bull on the rugby field and gentle as a lamb off it. There's no science in what I do but when I see as good a match as this, I think there may be something in it.

But all that was last night. This morning I am alone and the house is peaceful. I'm not being watched by anyone, even Billy. In the kitchen here it's cool, although the clear blue sky above the tall house opposite tells me it will be warm today. The clouds have gone.

Now fully awake, I decide I'll go earlier down to the library, to use their broadband to file my copy. I want to leave time later to walk by myself down to the canal. The alleys are cool canyons folded under the bright, hot blue of the sky. Some boys kicking a ball shoot it in my direction and call out for me to stop it. I step to one side and let it roll past me. I have reason to hate footballs. Further along, I step into a doorway to avoid an oncoming motorbike which – with scooters – is the only transport that works in these narrow ways in the old town.

At the end of the alley I step from the cool of the buildings to the oven heat of the market square. At the corner is the sprawling Café Plazza. I sit down at an empty table. I can't remember the last time I stopped anywhere for coffee, here or at home. My seat is at the back. No-one will notice me here. The café is crowded, busy. I sit there with the sun on my neck, my head shaded by the canopy. It feels familiar. I might have sat here a thousand times before. I even call up some French. *'Un café et un verre d'eau, s'il vous plait.'*

'Oui Madame!'

The waitress is young and shapely, with a wide gold belt that clinches her tight black tee shirt. Then I do this other thing that I've never done since Siri was taken. I start to watch the world around me, to attend to what is being said. Now I have one skin less and I can see, hear and feel all of it at once.

Some local men at the bar behind me are arguing and talking in the deep local accent; in front of me are three generations of a Spanish family with dark strong looks, the grandmother heavy and slack on her chair. They gesticulate and talk as they watch their children play football in the square. Local Gitan people – gypsies – from the old town are deep in conversation, looking serious about their business; an affluent looking couple in designer sailing gear are eating what looks like a mountain of ice cream; three young women share confidences over glasses of wine that glitter in the sun, their toddlers in strollers beside them and tumbling about their feet.

The waitress brings my coffee, with the bill on a saucer beside it. The coffee is strong and full of flavour.

An elderly couple, well dressed in the *bourgeois* fashion, sip red wine. On the table beside them are oysters in a smartly labelled box. On top of this is a fancy wrapped cake, ready to take home for their afternoon treat. I notice a small girl with hair so shiny that it's slipping from its ribbon. Her brown feet are tucked into glittery sandals. *Siri! Oh my Siri.* I clutch my coffee cup too tightly.

I notice a man with an orange leather crossover bag carrying a poodle in his arms like a baby. It strikes me how well the young French women walk – straight backs, hips jutting slightly forward. I wonder if they have deportment lessons in their *lycées*. I have a vision of a line of girls walking on tiles, with books on their heads.

These images whirl together, hitting me all at once; the clatter and noise swells and recedes in my ears. That's when I notice this old woman sitting at the next table. She has a straw boater planted straight on top of her grey-blonde pony tail and wears neat blue jeans and a battered white linen jacket. She's pointing to a little white dog beside her feet. I can't hear her words but she's pointing at the dog, chastising him the way people do when they don't really mean it.

The dog ignores her and wanders across to lift up his story-book face to look at me. I've no idea what you do with a dog. I lean down and scratch his neck. 'Now then, doggie!' I say, my own ridiculous statement ringing in my ears.

The old woman catches my glance and smiles. 'English?' she says.

I nod and smile back. She's not so easy to read. Her neatness, her composure, her nut-brown skin are all distinctly un-English. '*Et vous?*' I say politely.

'I am English also.' She allows a trill of laughter to escape her small neat mouth. She sounds French. 'But in France forty years now so I sound neither one nor the other.'

'Forty years?' It's been so long since I've been curious about any stranger.

'I came here in sixty-eight to Paris, to demonstrate with the students. I never managed to leave, I'm afraid. We had such a smashing time, despite the throwing of stones.' She's right about her accent. It *is* neither one thing nor another.

'But you live here in Agde?' I say. 'It's a long way from Paris.'

She nods. 'It's a long story, I'm afraid. After the *démonstrations* I sailed a boat down here on the rivers and canals with two of my new French friends who were also at the *démonstrations*. I married one of them and he became a *professeur* here at the Lycée. So I stayed and taught here as well.' She shrugged. '*Hélas*, he is gone now, my Etienne. But we were a long time together.' A small smile crosses her face.

I want to lead her away from her sadness. I look through the café crowd at the square with its heroic statue. 'This is a very mysterious place,' I find myself saying.

A smile lights up her face. 'Ah, you see this? Everyone does not see it. Agde is a place of all the ages. It is simply lovely. Do you know that they're digging down near the quayside just now? You will not believe it, my dear. A very large hole which shows you five cities layered down there, one on top of the other.' She counts them on her fingers. 'The Greek city, the Roman city and the layer of charred wood where the Spanish – I think it was the Spanish – burned the town. All time is here, my dear, right back to six hundred years before even Christ walked the earth.'

I sit there relishing this old woman's love for her town as it purrs through her strangely accented voice. My whole body is tingling like a struck bell at what she is saying. My glance moves behind her across the square to the road at the edge of the *promenade*, where the traffic is slowly moving down to the roundabout.

Suddenly a boy on a mountain bike charges on to the square in front of us and makes three circuits of the statue, finally making it rear, like a horse. Then he stands up on the pedals and bumps it down the steps on to the road, his hair streaming behind him. Men shout at him and cars beep their horns.

I stand up and catch a flash of red hair before he vanishes down a side street opposite. I sit down with a thump and turn back to the old woman. 'Did you see him? Did you see the boy?' I demand.

She raises a brown pencilled brow. 'Who? *Le garçon aux cheveux rouges*? Riding the *bicyclette* like a stallion? Of course I saw him.' A smile hovers around her thin lips. 'A boy of adventure. Like *Swallows and Amazons*. Do children still read those books in England?'

I could hug her but I don't. 'You really saw him, Madame?'

'Of course I saw him, my dear,' she said quietly. '*Un garçon aux cheveux rouges. Riding une bicyclette.*'

I feel happiness, exultation running through my veins like quicksilver. If this is mad I *want* to be mad.

Now she stands up and picks up her wicker basket. 'We have to go to the market, Misou and I,' she says, pulling on crocheted gloves. She shoulders her basket, scoops up the dog and walks across to her bike, the old sit-up-and-beg type, manacled to a bollard. Something scratches at the back of my mind, begging to be remembered: something about a bike and a bollard. But I can't reach it. She puts Misou in the basket in front and ties her basket to the back pannier. Then she stands astride the bicycle, her eyes shaded from the bright sun by her small straw hat. Despite her nut-brown skin she looks now as English as Miss Marple.

I go to stand beside her. 'Thank you for the conversation, Madame,' I say. 'It was interesting.' I hold out my hand. 'I'm called Starr.'

She takes her hand from the handlebar, leans across and squeezes mine. 'Patrice Léance,' she says. 'Around here they call me Madame Patrice. You may call me that, my dear. Now Misou and I go to the market.' She puts a foot on the pedal and pushes off, her legs in her English tee-bar sandals flexing their muscles.

I watch her leave, then I walk across the square and down the side street where I had seen the boy vanish. There is a mountain bike thrown down outside a tattoo parlour. I peer through a window and a muscular man shoos me away as though I'm a stray cat. He reminds me of Siri's headmaster, containing his anger as he drove me away from his school that morning and had words with Philip about me frightening the children.

Siri . . .

Giving up the ghost, I go to the library, file my copy, return to the house to dump my laptop, then make my way down to the quayside to look for this five-city hole in the road that Madame Patrice told me about.

Later, when I get back to the house they are all there in the courtyard, a tangle of bicycles against one wall. Billy's face is bright red from the sun. Mae has her hair under a tight turban.

Philip's face lights up when he sees me. 'You've been out, Estella?' he says. 'Walking about in the sun?'

'Always good at the obvious, our Phil,' says Billy heartily.

I nod, keeping cool. 'Must have been out, Phil. Here am I coming through the gate.' They're all looking at me. 'I give in. I went to the café and wandered down by the harbour.'

Mae examines me from head to foot.

I put up a hand. 'If you ask how I'm feeling, Mae, I'll sock you,' I say.

'There's fresh coffee,' says Philip. 'Shall I pour you one?'

I look warily round the courtyard. 'Kids are siesta-ing,' says Mae, lighting a cigarette. 'Don't you worry your little head about those two!'

'No need for that, Mae,' says Billy.

She laughs, ruffles his hair, and leans across to pull me down into the seat beside her. 'Come in, Starr! Sit with us. I've missed you. I've missed my dear old Stella.'

Now I can feel her, the old Mae, plump, naughty and sparking, telling fortunes with the cards and sneaking round the back of the labs at school for a smoke, making me laugh about the gross impossibilities of the diaphragm we'd just been shown in a sexual health lesson in school.

Philip thrusts a pot of coffee at me and I take a sip.

I shake my head at Mae. 'You shouldn't be smoking, Mae.'

She shrugs. 'Billy tells me that once a day, every day. Now I've got prim Miss Olga telling me off. But do I take any notice of these experts? No siree! Of him? Of her?'

Billy rolls his eyes. 'My girl's got a death wish!'

So for a short time, until the children wake from their siesta shrieking and wailing, it's just a bit like the old times – the four of us sitting round talking in a desultory fashion about odd things in the news and Mae's battles with the Town Hall over her council tax.

Even from the other side of the table I can feel Philip relaxing. At one point he looks across at Mae and she winks at him. She thinks she's cheered me up. I leave them to their winking and go on explaining to Billy how the syndicating of the column works, and how those astrology gurus say my style makes the column a 'one-off' and that makes it sell in the strangest of places.

But all the time, inside myself, I can feel this singing, this fizzing. All three of them are sitting there thinking I'm calming down, forgetting about Siri, but it's quite the opposite. Haven't I seen the hole in the road now, that shows the lines of five cities? Haven't I seen the boy who swam in the canal? What's more, my new acquaintance Madame Patrice saw the boy too. And that means something. I'm certain of it.

ELEVEN
Nightingales

Next morning I wake up as usual with Siri in my head and this gnawing, terrible space in my stomach. But then this strand of wonder creeps into my mind that Madame Patrice might be there at the café and I get out of bed.

I open my window to the explosive chirruping and dive-bombing of the swifts, as they greet the day outside the window of my eyrie. I straighten my couch and make straight piles of the notes on my table. I pick up my little clock and shake it. It's only eight o'clock. So I find myself getting up when the house is still full of people. I make my way down the wooden stairs. Philip, filling the dishwasher, smiles across at me. 'You coming with us, Estella? We're going to Vias Plage. Good chance to try out the surfboards.'

'We've got surfboards,' said Olga, eyeing me carefully through her red-rimmed glasses. 'Auntie Starr. We've got surf-boards and we're going to try them out. Did you know that? Then, guess what? We are going on bicycles.'

I take a breath. 'Sorry, Olga. I've got this work to do, see? And after that I'll have to go along to the library and send it away to London on the Internet.' Look at me: I'm talking directly to a child for the first time in nearly four years. But I'm no less raw inside. Olga stares at me for a moment, frowning. Then she turns to her mother and asks if there will be ice cream.

Now I want them all to go, to get out of the house. I want to have my own breakfast and make my way back to the Plazza to see if I can catch Madame Patrice before she goes to do her marketing. The three of them joke about and talk too long, so I just go off on my own, leave them to it. Mae and Philip exchange glances but make no attempt to follow me.

I see Madame Patrice's bicycle outside the café tied to its bollard. But the café is packed. It's Thursday, market day, and even now the Plazza is a kaleidoscope of people. The sun is glittering on the bright awnings and glancing off brown limbs.

Madame Patrice is at the same table at the back. Before her on the round table are a small cup of coffee and a cognac. She gestures towards me, says something to Misou, who is sitting at her feet, then pushes back a wicker chair for me. '*Bonjour* Madame Starr!' she says cheerfully. 'You are well, today?'

'Very well, Madame.' I sit down and Misou puts up his snubby snout for a rub. *Very well!* That's the truth today, and that's the difference. Being *alive* is well, compared to being a block of wood. I have been a block of wood for such a long time.

Madame glances across at the waitress and she brings across a small coffee, the same as yesterday. 'And how are you, Madame?' I say politely.

She beams. 'I am well as always, my dear. And today is good, as I have a visitor for tea. I will buy small cakes and set my table with lace. So rare these day to have a visitor.' She sips the cognac and sets it down again beside her coffee cup. 'And you, Madame Starr, what do you do today? Are you here for the market?' She waves a hand at the market stalls which now stretch right down from the library in the square called Jeu de Ballon, around the fountain here in the square, right along the *promenade* and round the old battlements, nearly down again to the river. The place is heaving with people, a swirl of colour in the bright sunshine.

I shake my head. 'No. I'm on my way to the library.' I take my USB stick from my pocket and put it on the table. 'I use the Internet to send some work to London.'

She frowns. 'That small thing?'

'Sometimes I bring my laptop, but today just this. It's like a letter going through space.'

She sighs and flutters a hand in the air. 'Computers! One must just accept such things on faith these days.' Another sip of cognac. 'And your work, my dear. What *is* that?'

I try to explain about the astrology and the newspapers.

She nods. 'Ah, we have these things here also. They can make one smile, *absolument*. And you live by this? This star-telling?'

'I do. It's convenient. It's truly interesting. I can work at it at home.'

'But you have insight, true insight?' she says, her voice suddenly quite sharp.

I don't know quite what to say. 'Well it's very technical, there are many programmes you can follow. But yes, I couldn't do it without some kind of insight. But more than that, you need imagination, language. That's what they pay me for.'

Beside us a woman wrapped in an orange *hijab* pushes a buggy with two babies in it up into the old town. I need to change the subject. 'Do you live here in the centre, Madame?'

'Just a little way from here, near the quayside.' She sees my questioning look. 'The quayside this side of the river, where the fishermen have always unloaded their catch. Further along the harbour they used to ship fine goods from the east. But no longer.' She looks into the distance for a second.

'And you live in a house down there near the harbour?'

Her laughter tinkles like a bell. 'It is not a boat, Madame Starr, though sometimes I wish it were. I so loved the boat of Etienne that brought us here to this wonderful place. Where I live *was* a house. Now it is a house of many homes. Etienne and I once had an apartment there. Now I have a little studio by the front door, just for me and Misou. I have a passage where lives my *bicyclette*. It is convenient and cheap. The rue de la Poissonnerie is not expensive. Through many years there have been big floods down there and people will not buy the house, even these foreigners who are sweeping through the south these days.' She glances at me. 'Sorry, Madame Starr, I do not put you among these people.

'So the poor gather down on rue de la Poissonnerie. And I am one of them. Bad things are said of them but they are wonderful people. And they look after their children, you know. That is always a good sign.' She sounds tranquil, not bested by her circumstances.

She drinks off her cognac, little finger in the air, and moves on to her coffee. 'And after the library, my dear? What then?'

I answer without thinking. 'I will walk by the canal.'

'Ah. *Bon!* It is good down there. The creatures in the water. The flowers. The birds. You will hear so many birds down there. Even nightingales. Those magical birds.'

'Nightingales?'

'I don't really know whether they are nightingales, but Etienne always insisted they were. They sing at night and in the early morning. Perhaps this gives them magic. They make songs when all around them is in the dusk.' She pauses. 'Sometimes I think there are people who do that thing? Make songs in the dusk?'

'Perhaps you are like that yourself, Madame?' I don't know where that came from.

The clumsy compliment seems to fluster her. She drinks up her coffee and pulls on her lace gloves. We talk a little more about her journey, sailing by boat to Agde all those decades ago with two companions, but then she seems eager to get away. '*Bonne journée*, Madame Starr. Enjoy the water. It will be a good day for you.'

Today it takes me longer to make my way to the canal without Philip at my elbow hurrying me on. I take my time, walking through the old town, across the wide bridge, down by the little *canalet* that leads to the circular lock and on to the main canal. Then I make my way along the canal path down under the railway bridge where the cars wait obediently while the double-decker TGV charges on like a dragon, swinging through on its way to Nîmes, or Carcassonne. Then on the *aucluse*, the circular lock where boats are also standing in line, waiting to go through the lock.

I remember Madame Patrice's tale of traversing lock after lock through France as – steered by herself and her two young men – their boat forged its way to the Mediterranean. Now her voice chirrups in my ears as I bring to mind our earlier conversation. 'And then, dear, we found Agde! We'd run out of cooking oil so I jumped on my bike and cycled up into town. And here it was, a city buried in time! Unchanged since hundreds of years. The land that time forgot. My dear, I was so very excited that I cried, there in the street.' That was when her voice became more English. 'I raced back to tell the boys about it and Etienne raced back with me. He loved this city in a moment. Wanted to stay here forever and this was what he did, Madame Starr. Etienne was a scholar and here became a *professeur*. And I found our apartment on la rue de la Poissonnerie.' She laughed. 'And now I am back there although the room I live in is much smaller than our apartment.'

'And the other one? The one who came with you?' I sensed

the three of them had been *very* together, very intimate on their journey. 'The other boy?'

'Auguste?' she frowned slightly. 'Ah, Auguste, being such a modern boy, he did not love the city. He thought it old and called it a rubbish dump. He picked up a new crew in a café at la Place de la Marine, and sailed on to the Camargue. So then it was just Etienne and me.' She smiled. '*C'était très sympathique.*'

Sitting there with her yesterday I had seen very clearly the slight young girl with the fair pony tail and rope sandals, embarking on this life, so full of the past, present and the future.

But today I make my way alone along the narrow pathway beside the canal. For a second the water soaks up all the sound around me, but then the silence is broken by a muscular man with a strimmer, scything down the grasses on the banks where yesterday they had been nodding their feathery heads in the sun. I feel thankful that the man leaves the bamboo to survive, rustling in the slight breeze off the water, a screen against the *bru-umm* of traffic above.

I know that yesterday I wouldn't have felt this, not have noticed any of this. I wouldn't have noticed the way the grey-green water laps up against the winding roots of the trees, I wouldn't have seen the squawking duck scattering the pigeons hovering over the water, sending them up to roost in a forty-foot plane tree.

I walk carefully along the narrow path, watching out for the ribbed roots of the trees that offer the canal its dappling shade. Then I jump at a muttering sound behind me as a young man – first a silhouette, then a figure in the light beside me – draws abreast of me, talking to himself. He's tall and bearded and sports dreadlocks in his rusty blond hair. Hung about with a sagging rucksack, he carries a bulging supermarket carrier in each hand. A dog is tethered to him by a loop round his belt. As he passes me he ducks his head. ''*Jour, 'dame,*' he says politely. His dog looks up at me and the man pulls him on, away from me. The pair of them are soon out of sight.

I watch him go ten paces, then I set away again, glancing down at the water, now a sheet of silver in the sun. And now, swimming right down the centre of the canal just below the surface, I see this green turtle. His movement is lazy, unhurried, as though he has a thousand years to make his way. I trip on a root and look down. When I look up again he's gone. For a second I feel bereft, cursing the root that had lost him to me. Of course, feeling bereft is my default state. I'm used to it.

Then a bolt of electricity charges through me and I lift my eyes to the opposite bank to see the red-haired boy, standing astride his mountain bike. He's grinning and waving his arms above his head, making sure I notice him. Today his hair is tied back with black tape and I can see his wide eyes, his high, hard cheekbones, his less cherubic demeanour. He looks older.

Then I blink and the boy is gone. But suddenly I know I don't have to worry. I know I'll see him again. I feel certain. I *will* see him again.

My legs are tired with all this walking so I find a bollard that doesn't have a boat tied to it and sit down. I look at the rows of boats tied up here on both banks and let the sounds filter through. Now the silence, just marked by the twitter of birds and the roar of the distant train, is supplemented by the sound of bilges pumping and people murmuring. One woman swills a deck; another brushes down an awning. A man in a business suit jumps off his small boat and goes to a modest car. The churring and chirruping of the birds escalates, attracted as they are by the cool water and the insects whirling in the trees and feasting near the ground among the grasses. Across from me a clump of yellow flag iris celebrate the sun and wish me *bonne journée*. I remember how the wash from the boat the other day swamped irises further along the banks.

My cup runneth over. This intense surge of sound is piercing my skin, invading my pores – the tiniest splash of a waterfowl is expanded a thousand times. My senses are in overdrive. I am hot. My heart is thumping. My head is spinning.

'*You have to arrive rather earlier to catch the nightingales.*'

From behind me the deep voice, slightly accented, nearly blasts me off my bollard. I look up into the face of the man from the boat: the one with the boy. But he too looks older today. His thick black hair is threaded with streaks of iron grey.

'Nightingales?' I splutter, going even redder.

'One needs to get here before nine. When the day is getting underway.'

I remember Madame Patrice. 'How do you know they're nightingales?'

He nods. 'They are nightingales. Believe me, Madame. Listen! It is a long, sweet song.' He smiles and his face is younger again. 'So you returned home safely despite the rain?'

'So you *were* on the boat?'

He lifts his shoulders. 'You saw me there. On the boat.'

'With the boy?'

He shrugs again. 'There was a boy there.'

'Look!' The heat inside me is beginning to fade. 'I've just seen that boy. On the other bank. He looks different.' I examine him closely. 'And so do you.'

'It's some time since we saw you last,' he says carefully.

I stop myself saying that it was only yesterday, when I saw them.

He stands back from me and makes this strange gesture, open-handed, towards the town. 'You will return to the town? We could walk together?'

I stand up and take some deep breaths to calm myself down. There is no way I can refuse this civilized request.

At first it is a bit awkward, as it always is, when you walk alongside a new person. On the narrowest ways I don't know whether to walk behind or in front of him. Then the man makes it easier; stepping back he holds out his hand to help me over a massive tree root and lets me walk before him. His hand is strong and dry. He asks me how I like the town. I tell him I'm growing to admire it.

I hear his footsteps behind me. 'I know you can feel the time in this place and in the other cities here in the ground.' His murmuring voice is in my ear.

I stop to look back at him. 'I met this woman at the Plazza and she told me to look in this hole in a road by the harbour. I went there but it was hard to tell just what was what. She said you could see evidence of five cities in the lines of the earth.'

He nods. 'You refer to Madame Patrice. She lives in the room below me in the rue de la Poissonnerie. I know this lady. She is an exceptional woman.'

What could I do? I turn and walk again, ahead of this stranger. I walk ahead of him into the town. Something is about to happen but I don't know what.

Something . . .

TWELVE
Pilgrims

This stranger and I finally stand side by side as we wait by the road across the bridge, making ready to dodge through the traffic to get across the road. Here again we encounter the dreadlocked man with his bags and his dog. For a second he stands silently in front of us, barring our way.

Then my companion puts a hand on the man's shoulder and points up the river, which is flowing under the bridge. 'That's the way, brother,' he says.

The man nods and pulls his dog to one side. Then he turns haunted eyes on me and says, "*Jour, 'dame! 'sieur!*" and goes the way he has been directed.

We walk. 'You know him?' I say, curious.

'I've met many like him,' he says. 'He's just another pilgrim.' He stops and turns to me, smiling slightly. A dimple deepens in his left cheek. His eyes are bright blue. 'We walk together and we have no names,' he says. 'My name is Louis. And you?'

'Estella. But some people call me Starr.'

He laughs, his face full of merriment. 'Ah. A good name, Starr. Bright and shining, and showing people the way in the dark.'

I want to tell him that his comment reminds me of Madame Patrice, but I don't know how to say that. It seems too intimate, too knowing. This man knows Madame Patrice. Perhaps he's the one having tea with her this afternoon.

Now we're on the quayside and I stumble on the uneven lava blocks that pave it and – quite naturally – he takes my arm. I can hear the jingling of boat tackle and the shout of seamen's voices but there are no boats drawn up on the quay these days, just waiters and waitresses setting out cutlery and napkins in the smart pontoon cafés huddling here in the place where ships once docked, drawn up side by side, ready to unload. Madame Patrice said that, didn't she?

'You know Madame Patrice? You said you knew her,' I say.

'I think I probably do. I knew her husband Etienne from another time. He was a great scholar. And I am acquainted with Madame Patrice. But I've not been here so long, this time.'

'So why are you here now? In Agde?' This is more direct than I've been for years.

'I come from the University of Toulouse, and before that the Sorbonne, and before that, Rome.'

'What is it? Some kind of research?'

'It's my mission.'

It's an odd thing to say but now I am distracted. The quay-side has opened on to a pretty tree-lined square with a huge carved globe of the world at its centre. The man called Louis pauses at a café table. 'The Place de la Marine is always a good place to stop. It's where the fishermen landed their catch in the old days,' he says. I look around. This neat café – a scattering of tables under the dappled shade of trees – is different from the bustle of the Café Plazza.

Sweat is running down my back from the exertion of the walk and the intense heat of the afternoon sun. He pulls out a seat for me. 'We rest a little here,' he says. 'You look tired.'

I take a deep breath and smile. 'I haven't walked this far in some years.'

'You're pale. You've been confined?' he says. 'Shut away?'
Siri.

'Something like that.'

'You've been very sad,' he says.

'Heartbroken,' I say. My own boldness makes me blink. I can't stop my eyes blinking. Then suddenly they stop. I feel calm. He glances away, across the river, taking the pressure away from me. We leave it at that and wait for our coffee. I try to guess his star sign. Libra. I bet it's Libra. *A thinker, a problem solver. Good mediator. Bit of an extrovert who loves teaching, can share his ideas in a very natural way.*

I fill the air between us with polite words. 'So, this research of yours. What is this research?'

He shrugs. 'Some people would think it's very boring. My study is to evaluate the nature of being a Christian when to follow the Christian way was to be a heretic. In the time before the great Roman Emperor Constantine. In the time before the

Roman world took it on itself to define Christianity and convert
the world.'

It's hard to know what to say to that.

He catches my blank look and laughs. 'I know! Who cares?
It is of the past. I should be studying how to make the world
a greener place, no?' He nods at the waitress – a sturdy girl
in dungarees – as she puts coffee down before us. 'But you?
Why are *you* here in Agde?'

I smell the round warm smell of the coffee. 'It's a kind
of . . . accident. I was brought here by my partner because I
have a sickness. He thought it would make me well.'

His close, forensic gaze reminds me of Billy. 'You look
tired, Starr, but not sick. You're sick in the heart, perhaps?'

Even I know it's a mistake to talk to a stranger like this. I
look around. 'I have to get back to the house, I think.'

'And where do you stay here in Agde?'

'On the rue Haute. The house is called Maison d'Estella.'

His look sharpens. 'Ah, I know this house of Pierre d'Estella.
It is very old. On the high citadel. By the Parthenon.'

I have to smile. *'Parthenon!'*

He nods vigorously. 'There was a temple to Aphrodite there
on the high point in the old Greek city. And in the same place
when it was a Roman city there was a temple to Venus. Just
along from the house of the Roman Governor. These two cities
– the Greek and the Roman – would be on the lower levels
in the hole in the road you investigated at the suggestion of
Madame Patrice.'

I frown. 'How can you know all this?'

He ducks his head to finish his coffee. 'You forget, dear
lady. Me, I'm a student of those ancient times!' He stands up.
'Now you must go back to the Maison d'Estella and look out
again over this city, whose layers you are peeling like an
onion.' He pauses. 'You found that house because of the name?
It is like your name, is it not?'

My turn to shrug. 'A coincidence. Just a coincidence.'

We walk through the town and part at the Café Plazza. He
shakes hands with me and then, to my surprise, kisses me
three times on the cheek in the way I've noticed here. Left,
right, and then left again. *'Au revoir,'* he says. And somehow
I know this is a message as well as a farewell. *Till we meet
again.*

There is not to be an end.

When I get back to the house, it's empty. After the heat of the early afternoon outside the shadowy courtyard is cool. I pour myself some lemonade and – suddenly hungry – I butter a hard chunk of bread left over from breakfast and sit outside eating it at the wooden table.

And now Siri sweeps back into my mind like a warm breeze off the river. *Siri.* I reflect on how long it took her to be born and how kind the midwife was, how patient; how I apologized for not being *good* at this thing that some women do so easily.

I remember listening to my mother pottering round my tiny flat, keeping out of the way, just as I'd asked her to. I remember the midwife sitting with me into the early morning hours knitting a jumper for her son, waiting for that fulcrum point where Siri really *wanted* to come and my body felt a proper willingness to squeeze her out. I remember thanking God that my colleague at the magazine had managed to fix me up with a home birth. By now, I thought, in hospital they'd have been doing all kinds of things to haul Siri out. They'd have had instruments out, for sure. But that night my midwife told me that all it took was patience.

Then at last Siri joined me in the world. The fact that my mother was in the next room made me swallow the grunts and roars as, with a final heave, Siri came! She was here, with me in the world, outside my body. She let out this very polite, yelling cry of surprise and the midwife washed her face and wrapped her in a linen cloth. Then she laid my baby on my breast with her face close to mine, squeaking and muttering like a kitten.

'Not hungry yet,' said the midwife. 'Tired herself out getting out of there, poor pet.'

I stared down at Siri's round, pink face and the rim of hair standing up from her head like a black crown. The midwife, busying herself at the other end of my body dealing with the afterbirth, glanced up just as my baby opened her big black eyes and looked straight, straight into mine. My body was engulfed by what felt like waves of electricity as we recognized each other.

'Ha!' said the midwife. 'Been here before, has that one!'

That was when my mother pushed her head round the door. 'That's it, then? Did I hear someone cry?' She came in with a big mug of tea. 'Aren't you a clever girl?' She kissed my sweating brow. Then pulled back the linen cloth. 'And isn't this a very pretty . . .'

'. . . Girl!' I said.

'I thought so,' she said.

Then the midwife, suddenly looking very tired herself, started to pack her bags and baggages. 'Kip for me,' she said, smiling down at me. 'We did well there, kid.'

'What's your name, Miss Clark?' I said. 'What *is* your name?'

'Siri,' she said. 'I know, I know! But my Mum's Swedish pen-friend was called that. You know what mothers are.'

'I do now!' I said, touching my sweating cheek against that of my new daughter. 'I do now.'

THIRTEEN
Punishment

Led by one of the Governor's guard, the harbourmaster made his way through the garden on to the colonnaded terrace that looked down towards the harbour. Helée was sitting on a stone bench, his hunting dogs at his feet. Like many Romanised Gauls, Helée relished the hunt.

The harbourmaster stood, holding his round cap, his face nut-brown under the pale line which marked the place where his hat normally protected his massive forehead. His heavily greased hair was pulled back into a cue.

Helée nodded, gesturing towards a low stool by the bench. When the harbourmaster sat, his knees almost came to his chin. He had to look up to the Governor to make his report. He reported on the weather, the fish catches, the imports and the exports, the markets and the census. Behind him, by the wall, the scribe scratched away on his tablet.

It was all good news. The Governor nodded his dismissal. The harbourmaster sat on, turning his hat in his hands.

'And was there something else, Harbourmaster?' said Helée. He'd learned early in his army career that a kind of tough courtesy got you quite a good way with such people, who – being only a hundred years from barbarism – were as jumpy as a startled hind, only rather more dangerous.

'Well, your honour. I did hear that your honour's son is becoming very popular with these cures of his and all. News of it is shouted right across the province. I hear he cured your honour of a very bad affliction.'

Helée bent his head. 'That is so, Harbourmaster. He is becoming a fine doctor.'

'So many fine arts are at his fingertips, your honour.'

Helée stood up and his dogs got to their feet, ears pricked. 'Was there something of concern for you, Harbourmaster?'

'He did attend to my own dear son, your honour, but to no avail.' The harbourmaster squeezed even harder on his hat.

'Well, your honour, a certain thing does concern me. It concerns me that these wonders are performed alongside invocation to the Nazarene, the one some of the Greek lads down on the dock call the Christ. The young master makes the mark of these Christians when he performs these miracles.'

Helée scowled and moved to grab the harbourmaster by the folds of his cloak and up off his feet. The dogs growled, their tails low. Then he dropped the harbourmaster, brushed his hands, one against the other and shouted for his guard who were lounging outside the door. 'Here! Kick this fellow down to his hovel at the harbour and kick him on to a ship where he may cure his concerns with a bit of hard rowing. He resents my son for not curing his son and he blasphemes against the Emperor and blasphemes against my house.' Helée stood there and watched his guards kicking and pushing the harbourmaster all the way down the hill. Then he shouted at the door for someone to bring his son. '. . . And the Corinthian!' he bellowed. 'And while you're at it you may request that my wife attends me.'

Later, standing before a red-faced Helée, neither Modeste nor Tib denied that they invoked the Nazarene to aid them in their work. Helée moved in closely to Modeste who took half a step backwards. 'Is this what you do, Corinthian? You take my son and make my very blood blaspheme against the Emperor and our god Emperors? Our great Emperor has toiled to purge the army of these savages, putting them down like the vermin they are. They're like the monster whose head you cut off and two grow on its place.' He was terrible in his rage, spitting his words into Modeste's face.

'Messire, the Empress . . .' began Modeste.

Helée put up a hand. 'Utter no more blasphemies, Corinthian!' He turned to the guard. 'Shut away this blasphemer, teach him not to insult his Emperor. He needs a hard lesson. He's only fit for meat for the arena.'

The guard hustled Modeste away, grasping him with a handful of his gown.

'Father!' pleaded Tib. 'Please!'

Helée turned on his son. 'And you! You're in for the best thrashing a boy may endure for doing this in my name.'

'Helée!' murmured Serina, who was standing by Tib. 'The boy gave you back your sight. Remember . . .' The delicate objection in his wife's voice enraged Helée further. Unlike him, she was Roman by birth, and sometimes this sat between them like a drawn sword.

'The spawn of the Underworld possess their magic I do not doubt!' He loomed over her and she shrunk away from him. 'You! You've not been listening to this traitorous gabble about the Nazarene? Tell me you haven't, woman!' There was a keen question in his voice.

She stood up very straight, her gown falling back in its graceful folds, one hand on Tib's shoulder. 'I am faithful to the Emperor and faithful to you, Helée. But the boy and the Corinthian mean no bad things. They cure and help people. The boy is only eleven. He is my son. He is *our* son. I love him. You love him, Helée.'

Her husband's smile was like a fox baring its teeth. 'Then your motherly love must hold him tight, madam, while I will beat this heresy out of him. He must give it up.'

He had his guard tie the boy to one of the columns in the courtyard. Serina placed her head on the stone beside that of her son so he could only see her face. She clutched one shackled hand tightly.

Helée took a whip from the guard's hand. From another part of the villa they could hear Modeste crying out in agony. 'Do not hurt Modeste, Father. Do not!' said Tib in a clear voice.

That was when Helée struck Tib three times with a whip, making the boy grunt with pain. 'Do you renounce this heresy?' He barked the words into Tib's face. The boy shook his head, tears flying down his face, glittering in the rays of the low afternoon sun.

The dogs growled.

Helée handed the whip to his guard. 'Here, make him see sense, will you? Three strokes and ask him the question again.'

Then he strode off, dragging a protesting Serina with him.

The guard, a middle-aged Gaul, who had watched the boy grow up from birth and had witnessed his healing wonders, laid on the whip with a much lighter hand than his master, making sure the snap and crack occurred before the whip flicked the skin off the boy's back.

After twenty-one such strokes he reported to his master that neither the boy nor the Corinthian would recant. 'There is one thing, sir. I have to say the boy's strips are healing up as soon as they are laid. Curious thing, that!'

Helée clapped a hand to his forehead. 'Give the boy to his mother. How will I explain this? How?'

The next day Helée had Tib and a limping Modeste brought to him and pronounced his judgement. The two blasphemers were to be set in a boat and banished from his sight, to be left to the wilderness where the boars and the bears might take their fill of them. 'You are my son. And now you must be an example to others. I will not have this poison in my house.' He turned to the guard.

Helée, from his high terrace, watched as the pair was marched down to the harbour surrounded by a unit of his guard. Tib had to help Modeste, who was badly injured from his beating, although he himself had not a mark on him. Serina and her ladies walked alongside in silence, the skirts of their gowns trailing in the dust.

The tumult and noise of the harbour came to a stop as slaves and the harbour men put down their ropes, left their pulleys and stood in silence watching the little procession. From his terrace Helée's sharp soldier's eyes observed his wife as she embraced both her son and the Corinthian and handed them over to the substitute harbourmaster, who lifted them bodily into a small boat that boasted only a mere slip of a sail and two oars.

Helée made his way out of the house and stood halfway down the hill, watching. He watched as Serina – who had clearly prepared for this – had her ladies put packages of food aboard, along with the leather pouches that they both carried with their cures. Last came a male slave with Modeste's boxes. She glanced up the hill at the still figure of her husband. He bowed his head, acknowledging her small defiance.

The boat pushed off and the man and the boy started clumsily to row upstream, watched by a silent crowd. Then, at a nod from Serina, one of the seamen jumped aboard and another followed him. They took the oars from Modeste and Tib and started to row the boat for them. A cheer went up amongst the watching people who admired the courage of the seamen. Who knew what punishment the Governor would exact for such an act?

His face expressionless, Helée turned away and marched

up the hill. In the house he called on members of his guard to strip down the boy's eyrie of any remaining blasphemous documents and take them outside to burn them. They returned to say that the room had already been stripped and there was no sign of documents or other traitorous items. It was empty.

FOURTEEN
Philip and the Small Red Hat

'm sitting in the courtyard munching strawberry jam on another chunk of breakfast bread when the big door opens and Philip and Mae tumble through, laughing. They look at me in surprise. I might be the turtle I saw this morning, swimming down the centre of the canal. Philip actually looks up at the window of the eyrie, where he expected to find me and now looks back down at me as though I'm the ghost of myself. 'You're eating! My god you're eating, Estella!' He staggers and steadies himself with a hand on Mae's shoulder.

Mae giggles. 'Yeah, honey-Starr. You're eating and *we're* drunk.' She puts an arm round his waist and guides him to a chair. He's the one more worse for wear.

Philip sits back and looks at me through half-closed eyes. 'You're eating!' he repeats, his voice full of dark, self-pitying accusation.

I take another bite. 'It's not against the law,' I say with my mouth full.

'Against Philip's law,' says Mae. 'Our Phil is a man of the law, i'n'he? Rules the table, rules the court, rules the world!' She giggles and busies herself finding a cigarette in her handbag.

Philip's head drops slowly and he closes his eyes. His face is slack and he looks vulnerable. To be honest, it's quite good to see him not in charge. I wipe the crumbs from my lips and look at Mae, who's trying to connect her lighter with the end of her cigarette. 'So what happened?' I say.

Mae sits up straight, takes a long drag of her cigarette and pulls herself together. She's like a dog shaking itself, righting itself when it gets out of the water. Or rather a bitch.

'Well,' she says. 'What's happened is this . . .' Another drag of her cigarette. Then the words come out in smoke on one long breath. 'We go to Cap d'Agde, take a look at the market, and take the kids down around the hurdy-gurdies. Then down on that nudist beach, take a look at a few naked women stretched out there, you wouldn't believe it, Stells. All shapes . . .' She takes a breath. 'Then we have a swim. Then it's too hot so we have a long lunch and Billy takes the kids for an ice cream and Phil and I have *more* lunch. Well, more *pastis*. And more. Then Billy comes back and we're pissed. And he shovels us all into the car, and he's just shovelled the two of us out at the car-park down at the Jeu de Ballon. He's mad at us. Mad! Tells us to get back here and get to bed before he gets back here with them. That we're scaring the kids.' She giggles and takes another draw on her cigarette. 'Not together. Bed, that is.'

Philip opens an eye. 'Estella! You're eating!' he mumbles.

I'm grinning despite myself. 'You'd better do what Billy says, Mae. Get Philip to bed. Not your bed, of course! I'll keep Billy down here.'

She screws out her cigarette on my bread plate, stands up, and gives me a mock military salute. 'Yeah, ma'am! Keep Billy at bay, mind!' She pulls Philip to his feet then pushes and pulls him through the salon and up the stairs. Then I can hear her through the open window in the main bedroom as she pulls off his shoes and tells him to *sleep it off, darling*, before she trips on her high heels through to the bedroom that she and Billy share.

I pour myself some more lemonade, still smiling to myself at Philip's antics. And wait for Billy.

You know that Siri and I met Philip quite by chance. Siri was three or four and we were still living in my old flat and one night it got to ten o'clock and she'd woken up. She was always easy enough to quieten. All it took was warm milk with real chocolate, grated and sprinkled by her own chubby hand.

No milk . . . She looked up at me, shaking her head.

'No worries,' I said. 'We'll go to Mr Patel's.'

She ran to get her small red hat. It was a favourite of hers at the time. Mr Patel's shop, out on the main road, stayed open all night. He used the quiet times to maintain the beauty of his vegetable displays. And he always made great efforts to ensure that whatever customers wanted was available on his shelves. Shelves of Weetabix, Shredded Wheat, loo rolls and kitchen paper sat alongside shelves of daal, olives, dates and spices

– all a person could need, really. Just one thing was missing. Mr Patel had stopped stocking cigarettes due to some local dispute, when his fruit was spoiled by a gang of lads who were trying to buy cigarettes without paying.

His customers ranged from people who lived nearby to late or early workers who called for groceries on their way to or from work, to kids getting their mobiles topped up, to office people from the City on their way to the more prosperous northern suburbs.

Among these city types that night was Philip, neat in his suit, his business case on a long strap over his shoulder. He told me later that he often picked things up there on his way south after work and sometimes he worked very late. 'I never have to worry,' he said. 'I can park outside and Mr Patel is always open.'

Even our being there at the same time in the all-nighter was no guarantee that we should meet. It was Siri who guaranteed that. She ran up to him and showed him her red cap. In fact she offered it to him. I saw him go pink as he took it, and I thought that was touching. He pushed the cap back at her. 'It's very nice,' he said. 'A very nice hat.'

I caught up with her. 'I'm so sorry,' I said. 'She's very fond of that hat, so you should be honoured.'

He smiled. 'Do you come here often?' Then he laughed. 'I didn't just say that, did I?'

Philip was thinner then, and had this gentle face which was made more, not less beautiful by his rimless spectacles. I liked him instantly and so did Siri, who was now leaning on his trolley eyeballing him with the kind of fierce joy that was one of her gifts.

I told him I was not usually out this late. 'It's more usually sixish,' I said. 'We ran out of milk.'

Three nights later Siri and I came in for potatoes and an ice lolly at six o'clock. She saw Philip from the bottom of the second aisle and ran down it to give him her hat. He looked down at her and up at me. It wasn't a *coup de foudre* – well not for me. It might have been for him, but that was a thing he'd never tell you.

He grinned. 'Well, fancy meeting you here!'

I rolled my eyes. 'What a coincidence!'

He returned the red cap to Siri. 'Well, if by coincidence

you mean finishing work early and being at Mr Patel's at six o'clock for three nights running, stocking up on loo rolls for the nation . . .'

'A man of purpose!'

He smiled broadly. 'Well. It's served its purpose. Here you are!'

We stood looking at each other, neither of us sure of what to do, now he had achieved his goal. 'Well . . .' I said.

This was something very different. In my life – so home-centred with work and with Siri – the only men I met were clients who wanted private readings to target their stock investments, to guide some business decision, or scan various houses for investment potential. In any case even most of that communication was on the telephone, not face to face.

Standing in an all-nighter looking into the eyes of a tall, attractive man my own age was rare, to be honest.

Now Siri mentioned the ice lolly and we all relaxed.

'Come with me for an ice cream,' he said.

So, over ice cream at the local *gelateria* we discovered the usual things about each other – names, ages, jobs, favourite films, preferred music. He was a solicitor working behind the scenes doing something about property and the Church of England. 'Dusty, but I like it,' he grinned. 'Leaves time for proper things, like cooking.'

He liked cricket and jazz. He'd married his childhood sweetheart at twenty but she'd run away to America with a shoe designer. His mother lived in Hove but came up to town every three weeks to get her hair done. 'No hairdressers in Hove!' he said. It wasn't very funny but I still laughed. He laughed as well. Siri waved her long spoon and laughed.

When he discovered what I did for a living he said the usual thing – how he'd never met anyone who'd done that kind of thing and wasn't it all – er – telling people what they wanted to know and usually what they knew already?

'Not quite. It's often me telling some sharp businessman to avoid certain stocks.'

'Can you really do that?'

'Seems I can. Sometimes. A bit like remembering the future. I always tell them there's no guarantee. But they come back, so something must be working. The women come back as well – but a lot of them want other stuff. More personal.'

'What are they like, these people? Isn't meeting strangers risky? There could be a few crazies out there.'

'Most of them I never meet face to face. I meet most of them on the telephone, like I say. And yes, there are a few crazies, but they're easily soothed. And they don't know where I am. I could be in Timbuktoo or the Isle of Arran, for all they know.'

He frowned a bit then, keeping back more cynical thoughts. 'Well,' he said finally. 'I know my mother would be fascinated. Never fails to read the stars in the paper.'

For some reason we all laughed at that and then he walked with me and Siri back to our block of flats. He looked upwards, scanning its height. 'You live here?'

'Yes,' I said. 'I like it here. It's central and there are people around. My neighbours are just wonderful.'

He shook his head. 'I'll take your word for it.'

There was this awkward pause then. But I stood there and let him make the move. It would save him buying more loo rolls.

He coughed. 'Look,' he said. 'I'm taking my mother out to tea this Saturday. To the Wolseley in town. Would you two like to come to tea with us?' He looked from me to Siri then back to me.

I didn't quite know what to say.

'Look, it might sound a bit weird, but I thought that might reassure you that I'm not after . . .' He was floundering.

I looked upwards at my building. 'After my wonderful city pad?' I said.

'Saturday!' said Siri who was watching us both closely.

'Well, *she* wants to come,' I said.

He relaxed. 'Shall I pick you up here? Taxi's best, that time of day.'

'We'll come in our own taxi, thank you.' I paused. 'So, when's *your* birthday?'

He looked at me keenly. 'You're not going to try those heebie-jeebies on me, are you?'

'I told you. It's like a cross between common intuition and remembering the future. Nothing to be scared of. And remember it's you who's going into loo-roll overdrive because you wanted to meet us. Remember? This is just another way for me to check you out.'

He held up his hands in front of his face, in mock self-protection. 'OK, I give in. It's July the thirteenth, 1988, ten thirty a.m.'

Cancer the crab. Homemaker. Doing a boring job that gives him time to cook. That makes sense. 'Right. We'll be there.' I looked down at Siri. 'Right, Siri. It seems we're going to tea with Philip and his mummy on Saturday.'

'Best purple jeans?' said Siri.

'Best purple jeans,' I said.

That night, after I'd tucked Siri into bed and listened to her comments about the ice cream man liking her red hat, I got out my books and looked at Philip's chart. It was staring me in the face. We were not really compatible at all. But that was just the charts, wasn't it? My instinct told me otherwise.

It seemed that I was right. His mother was a great woman, large and cheerful, much more extrovert than he was. And I have to say the years with him and Siri were the happiest in my life. It was only now that the incompatibility was gritting its way into our lives, blown up by a random, savage, meaningless act outside any remembering future or past.

Now in this beautiful courtyard I force myself to think of how savage murder can happen in the middle of predictable lives. I've always been sure of the fundamental common sense in the visions I've had in my life and the advice I've offered people. This advice has helped some people to make fortunes and others to make the right decisions in their lives. Women have followed my advice and their own intuition to take up good careers, taken fruitful chances, have successful dinner parties. There is a common-sensical pattern to universal lives and loves.

In the ordinary way of things, death is in everybody's chart. People are born, people live, people die. That, at its most authentic, is what the charts tell. And in that, they tell the truth. But the devil implicit in any murderous act upsets every apple-cart known to man. The murderer is the devil's weapon and – caught or uncaught – he will be destroyed by his own deed.

What has underlined my grief is that ever since Siri was born I'd done her charts in every astrological tradition. All the portents showed a life of light, of creativity and mystery, of the ability to show others the way, to be a guiding light.

No – *no* – violent, ugly death.

But murder, by the ludicrously random act of one boy losing his temper, cannot be foretold. Poisoning, cruelty, vengeance – yes, the charts will show that. But not this . . . this *ludicrous* accident! Perhaps that's why I was not as murderously angry with the two boys as many people – including Philip – wanted me to be. There was one very prominent newspaper which would have given me a fortune if I'd just called these two boys the *devil's spawn*. But I wouldn't.

Because that's not how it was. My Siri being plucked from me like that was like a tear in the fabric in the universe. To say it was down to the evil of those two boys is to trivialize it. What happened to her was against all the universal laws that inform my intuition, that guide my vision and inform my dreams. For the first time in my life I could not reach out into that visionary space and touch her; and that's why she cannot reach me.

Truly I tell you it's enough to drive a woman insane.

And now I am reflecting on my day – the best day in my life since Siri was killed. Haven't I talked to Madame Patrice, who has seen the boy? Haven't I seen the boy again by the canal? Haven't I walked the streets of Agde with a man called Louis who knows time beyond time? Haven't I seen my over-controlled sane, dear, measured Philip in a maze, tumbling with drink? Hasn't he made me laugh, like he did when we first met? Haven't I revived the sheer joy of Siri being born?

Even so my tears are falling, glittering on the table like the silver waters of the canal.

The sound of a girl's voice and the scrape of the big key stop the tears and bring me back to the present. Billy walks through the gate with a sleeping George on his back and Olga brings up the rear, hauling a heavy beach bag.

The house is full of voices again.

FIFTEEN
Billy Asks a Favour

George is slumped over Billy's shoulder, fast asleep, a dirty tide of ice cream around his mouth. Olga's face is just generally grubby, her spectacles smudged.

'Did they get back?' Billy raises his eyebrows in my direction.

I nod, a smile retrieving the last of my tears. 'They put themselves to bed.'

'Not together, I hope!' Billy's wry grin tries to tell me he's taking it lightly, but his mild eyes are angry. 'I'll tuck old George here in with Mae, shall I?' He looks down at the detritus of my impromptu lunch. 'Perhaps you could rub a flannel over Olga's face? She's the dirtiest eater I know. And I include myself in that.' And he's on his way upstairs before I can object.

Olga is staring at me. 'I *am* seven, you know,' she says.

'Right!' I say. 'Right.' But still I stand up and follow her into the downstairs bathroom off the inner courtyard. I lean on the doorpost and watch as she takes off her glasses and fills the bowl nearly to the brim with warm water. She dips in the pink flannel with *Olga* on it, wrings it out and lays it over her face like a shroud.

My heart dives in on itself. Siri used to do just that.

Then Olga grabs hold of the flannel and scrubs it up and across four times, like the sign of the cross. I wait for Siri's face to emerge. But the face that emerges is Olga's, now red as a tomato. She cleans her teeth with four scrubs of the brush, hangs up her flannel and pulls the plug. Then she puts on her glasses. 'There!' she says, eyeing me grimly. 'I told you I could do it myself.'

'So you can.' I unhook the damp flannel and lean across and wipe some toothpaste from her cheek. 'So you can.' My heart is melting with feeling for her. For Siri. I really, really want to cry.

She follows me back into the courtyard and sits opposite me at the table. She eyes me severely. 'Mummy and Uncle Philip were very silly in the restaurant, you know.'

'Sometimes people are like that, love.'

'Mummy kissed this man there. And do you know she didn't even know his name?'

'Oh dear!'

'And Uncle Philip stole this man's hat and tried it on!' The gloom in her voice deepened. 'And he *danced*.'

'Uncle Philip can be funny sometimes.' I'd forgotten that. He used to make Siri laugh till she cried.

'Daddy said they were *a cut*. What does that mean?'

'It means they made a show of themselves. They should have behaved better.'

'Will they have a very, *very* bad headache when they wake up? Mummy always has a headache afterwards, when she's been silly.'

'So she does.' Billy's voice booms from the doorway. He has a can of beer in one hand, and Olga's Gameboy in the other. 'Want to play your game, love? I see Auntie Starr's done a good job with your face.'

She jumps from the chair and snatches the Gameboy from him. 'Me!' she shouted. 'Me! I did the job myself, if you want to know.' And she marches through the glass doors into the salon, the only place where the Gameboy works properly.

Billy sits down. 'Can I get you a beer, Starr? A glass of wine?'

I shake my head. 'And please, Billy, don't comment on the fact that I've made myself bread and jam. I have to tell you Philip couldn't get over it, drunk as he was.'

He pops his beer can and lets out this very big sigh. 'Surprised he could see as far as the table.'

'Bit of an effort, I think. Poor lad was out on his feet.'

'The pair of them,' he says glumly. 'You should have seen them egging each other on. Never seen Phil like it! Just short of dancing on the tables, he was. He practically got a date with the waiter!'

I can feel my lips twitch. I feel sorry for Philip. 'He's just letting his hair down, Billy. He's had a sticky time lately, trying so hard . . .'

He stares at me belligerently, then flushes. 'Sorry, Starr. I'd forgotten. Well, I suppose . . . Sorry, Starr.'

'Philip has tried so hard, you know. I have to remind myself that he's lost Siri too. I think it's all getting too hard for him. I don't know that we can survive all this, him and me. He's *bored* with my grief, Billy; he doesn't want to know about my head or my heart any more. All he can do is feed me like a Strasbourg goose. I get this. He does it because it's the only thing he can do. But it really makes me mad. I can't help it.'

'Strasbourg goose?' Billy stifles a smile. 'Sorry, Starr, but that's a terrible image.' He takes a gulp of his beer. 'You know, I never did find out how you two got together.'

I told Billy about me and Siri meeting Philip at the all-nighter. 'Then I met his mother. Libra. It was love at first sight.'

'You and Phil?'

'No. Me and his mother. She's a doll. He's Cancer, which is much more problematic.'

He grins at that, then goes and gets another beer, has a word with Olga in the salon, and sits down again. 'So. Enough of my dramas!' he says. 'What have you been up to today?'

He's very good, Billy. Never off-duty.

'Well, let's see. I did some work. Went to the Café Plazza. Met this new friend.'

He looks interested. 'New friend?'

'Her name is Madame Patrice. She's English but doesn't sound it. And she has a dog called Misou.'

'She's from round here?'

'No, she's from Stoke-on-Trent. But she doesn't sound that either. She's been here for forty years.'

'Interesting!' He doesn't pursue that, or ask for details. Like I said, he's a wise one, is Billy. 'What else?'

'Well, I tried to go down by the canal and listen for night-ingales. But I was too late. You have to go early or late in the day. So I missed them.'

'Pity, that,' he says.

'But I did see the boy from the boat. You know, the one I was telling you about? Remember Philip said he wasn't there? Well, today I saw a turtle, swimming there in the water. And I saw the man. The man from the boat who was with the boy.'

'Did you, now!' His voice is just a bit too hearty.

I point a finger at him. 'Don't you start humouring me,

Billy-Boy. I get enough of that from your drunken friend upstairs.'

He smiles sheepishly. 'Sorry. I believe you! I do. But I also believe you have visions. Could that not be one of those?'

It's a funny thing that Billy, the rugby player, the scientist, has always been more open-minded about my gift than Philip, who – no matter how he might pay respectful lip service to it – has always put it down to what he sees as my craziness, my out-of-kilter approach to life. That has always been a bit dodgy to handle, even in the best of times.

'No, Billy,' I say firmly. 'I know the difference.' I pause. 'Anyway, promise not to say anything to Philip or Mae. They have me down for mad already.'

'Well, *I* don't. Remember that.' He stands up. 'Sure you don't want a beer? No?' He drifts away.

There is a rumble of voices as he checks on Olga again and he comes out with a bottle of water. He waves it in the air. 'I suppose one of us has got to stay sober.'

'Olga OK?'

'She's saving the world from a three-headed Greek monster.'

'That's all right then.'

He's still keen to talk. 'I hope we haven't come down here and disturbed your peace, Starr. We got a bit of an S.O.S. from old Phil but we might just have made it worse.' He paused. 'Mae can be a bit strong, I know. But she thinks a lot of you. Always has.'

I nod. 'Always mutual. Sometimes when I see her I think she's changed too much. But sometimes . . . Oh! We were such friends when we were young, Billy. Even here and now I see glimpses of that old Mae. I get a peep of it and it makes me smile.'

'Of course you've both changed,' he says quietly. 'Haven't you? That's life.'

Now I have to force a laugh. 'I suppose you might say I've changed more than she has, really.'

'But that's not surprising, is it?' he says. 'London and . . . all that.'

I start to panic. I can hear him thinking hard, trying to find some useful words to say.

'You have to watch old Mae a bit, Starr,' he says finally. 'She gets these crushes on people. Starts by trying to be

Florence Nightingale, then gets too involved. It can be messy.
I always think she needs to prove herself again and again. I
can't imagine why.' He coughs. 'To be perfectly honest just
now I think she's getting a crush on old Philip. I can see the
signs.'

I look at him, weary now. 'What do you want me to do,
Billy? Today I've seen poor Philip, even while drunk, happier
than he's been in years. If that's been achieved by Mae's crush
on him, all well and good. I can't feel sorry.'

He turns the bottle of water in his hands. 'But can't you
see, Starr? This is different. Those other times she was just
betraying me. Now she's contemplating betraying both of us.
That's not good for her. She'll lose sight of herself in all that.
I don't want that for her.'

I told you Billy was a very wise man. But perhaps he's just
too nice for this world. I heave this great big sigh. Here he
is, dragging me in, making me care about this situation, getting
me involved. I want to leave them all to it. I have these other
things on my mind just now. 'What do you want me to do,
Billy?'

'Speak to her. Tell her to mind her manners.'

'Why don't *you* do that?'

'She'll take no notice of me. Custom and practice. She
knows I won't leave her whatever she does. Mae has always
lived her life with me and Olga and George on her own terms.'
Oddly, Billy doesn't sound as wretched as he should. I suppose
he's speaking from experience. I admire him so much more
than I pity him.

He's the caring sort. He's certainly making me care, isn't
he? When I think of it, he – alongside Madame Patrice and
the man called Louis – seem to be pulling me back into this
world where I can feel Siri nearby, rather than remember her
slumped against a tree in South London, blood running down
her face.

I can feel her. Nearby.

SIXTEEN
Virgo

Nearly two hours later first Philip – hollow-eyed and just a bit shamefaced – comes downstairs, followed by Mae – showered, made-up, hair blown flat and glossy, new sun dress, hiding her eyes behind dark glasses. George is riding piggy back, one hand clutching her dress strap.

Mae peers behind me, as though Billy might be lurking there.

'Billy's having a shower down here,' I say, nodding towards the inner courtyard. 'Olga has defeated the three-headed monster and is bathing herself, on her own. Because, she tells me, at seven years old, you're supposed to do that.'

Billy emerges from the inner courtyard with a towel round his waist, rubbing his wet hair with another one. He has very good legs. How have I never noticed that?

Philip glances wearily around the kitchen then back at me.

I rescue him. 'No need to cook. Billy and I thought we would go down to the café on La Place de la Marine,' I say, although it was my suggestion. 'They say it sells good pizzas and pasta.' I thought it would be nice to eat with all of them in the place where I sat with Louis earlier in the day.

'No *pastis*, though!' says Mae from behind her glasses.

'Mae! For Christ's sake!' Billy explodes. I realize that he has nothing to fear from Philip, whose default position – part of his charm – of mild good humour would never withstand Mae's black wit.

Later we walk along the quayside and end up sitting out on the water on the café's pontoon, the wind furling its canopy like a sail, and lifting my newly washed hair which is reverting to its curly self. George hangs over the rail watching the ducks attracted by our presence and hungry for titbits. Olga hangs on to the back of his tee shirt. I eat the best seafood pasta of my life: creamy hand-made pasta, loaded with just enough *fruits de mer*.

We're served by the young woman who served Louis and me this afternoon. Her brown skin, dishwater-blonde, afro-style hair and elegant grey dungarees look endearingly familiar. She surveys the company and then looks back at me, her eyes unreadable. *'Jour Madame,'* she says. *'Encore ici?'*

Billy looks at me quite sharply but Philip, still rather pale about the gills and picking at his food, fails to notice. Mae calls the children over to eat. Eat! She devours her own pasta with relish. There is not much conversation. Everyone is very subdued.

My glance wanders down the river to a platform near the bridge, where boys are diving into the water, scrambling back up the bank and diving again. Billy follows my gaze and then his glance rakes along the other side of the river, where the more present-day elegance of the houses there are reflected in water lit by the slanting evening sun. 'Bit like Venice when you think of it,' he said. 'But without those wonderful smells.'

'Don't be stupid,' says Mae briskly. 'It's nothing like Venice.' She pulls her pashmina more tightly around her. 'We should have gone inside. I'm freezing.'

'The alcohol is still cooling your system, Mae,' said Billy, with more severity than usual. 'Just eat up and shut up.' She gives him a look that could kill and digs in to her pasta.

It isn't the most successful evening we've ever had together but I'm enjoying it because it's filled with shades of the afternoon – Madame Patrice, the canal and walking and talking with the man called Louis. My relish for this food and my relish for life are returning and sadly it's nothing to do with Philip and his anxious care. I know that Siri is near and I can feel my sense of the future returning.

Later, by the time I get upstairs, Philip is asleep and snoring. So I go up to my eyrie and lie on the daybed where I often spend my nights now. I lie there for a while, but – restless still – I get up and go to my work table and develop some charts for Billy and Mae. I put their charts together. Taurus and Capricorn. They are so very compatible – like a yolk and an egg. Things will tumble together for them again and again.

I get up and poke around among my stuff in the room. But still I can't settle. So I climb up the narrow wooden staircase to the roof and lie down on the lilo that lives up there. I can smell Mae's sun lotion. The night is warm, the sky is dark.

I take a very deep breath, pleased to be here alone with the sky.

Then I can hear footsteps coming up the wooden staircase and I feel a prickle of distaste. Philip will spoil this, spoil it, I know he will!

But it's not Philip. It's Olga. Silently she comes and lies alongside me.

I take another very deep breath.

Olga takes her own deep, noisy breath. 'What are we doing, Auntie Stella?'

'We're looking for Virgo. See! Those nine stars? One, two, three, four, five, six, seven, eight, and see that one on the end. Nine.'

Her chuckle warms the air between us. 'I see it! Like a little handbag in the sky. It's really pretty.'

'So it is.'

'What does it mean, the little handbag?'

'It means a lot of things to a lot of people.'

'What does it mean to you?'

'It means a person I once knew.'

'Which person?'

I hesitate. 'A girl called Siri.'

She lies very still, absorbing that. 'And is it her handbag, with her special things in it?'

'I hope so.'

Then her small warm hand raises itself and points at another constellation. 'And what is that one? That big pointy one?'

'Ursa Major. But we call it the Great Bear.'

She chuckles. 'I can see him! I can see his toes and his long tail. Who does he make you think of?'

I wait a moment. In the years since Siri was taken I have avoided thinking of him, avoided thinking that if I had gone after him with news of her, if I had broken his family and made him mine, Siri would still be here. Now I'm thinking about him and that night in the Deer House. 'I haven't thought of him for a long time,' I say carefully. 'It's a man called Ludovic.'

'Is he nice?' she said. 'Is he as nice as my daddy?'

'I think he might be. But I don't know him very well.'

Then minutes pass and there's silence beside me. My eye returns to Virgo and I project my mind, my heart, to that small handbag in the sky. Siri is near. It's funny about Siri being Virgo. Our signs are very incompatible but she's part of me and I am part of her. Another thing that puts the whole theory in flight, you might say.

Olga is mumbling something.

'What's that, Olga?'

'I learned it at school. It's your poem, Auntie Starr.'

> *'Star light, star bright,*
> *The first star I see tonight,*
> *I wish I may, I wish I might,*
> *Have the wish I wish tonight,*

'What do you wish for, Auntie Starr?'

I pull her close. 'I wish you a happy and long life, Olga.'

Minutes – perhaps as much as an hour – have passed by. Olga is fast asleep. I haul myself to my feet and pick her up. She's lighter than she looks. I make my way down the wooden staircase with her half over my shoulders and half in my arms. Then, in the room she shares with George, I heave her on to the top bunk and cover her with a thin sheet.

That's how Siri was when I last saw her. Under a thin sheet, the top tucked under her chin, her hair combed on the pillow, her skin cold as ice. Now I touch Olga's skin and kiss her on her warm cheek. I feel again the tenderness, the joy I felt for my living, breathing Siri. Then I go up to my eyrie and sleep soundly and dream of the red-haired boy who has all these wild people dancing joyously around him, ribbons swirling.

He looks older.

SEVENTEEN
An Enchanting Place for Exile

As he and his mate rowed the boat carrying Modeste and Tib up the river away from the city, the older sailor, whose name was Peter, talked rapidly to his passengers about how to make the frail craft work for them. 'You put your weight *so*, sire,' he said to Modeste, 'then pull back hard, then pause. Let the water do some of the work. The flow of the river towards the sea will pull you back a little, but you will make progress if you row steadily, steadily.'

He nodded at Tib. 'And you, young master, you know how I taught you to use the sail when you were young? Test the wind then raise the sail. Not yet. The wind will serve you better upstream.' He paused. 'In this sweep the offshore breezes could drive you out to sea and there, young master, you will be lost.'

Tib could hear the echo of his mother's voice in Peter's tones. 'Did my mother tell you to do this, Peter? To help us on our way?'

The sailor shook his head and stopped, resting on his oars. 'She was there, young sir, but it was your father who gave the instructions to row you upstream to safety. But your mother, young sir, asked me to give you these.' He rooted inside his jerkin and handed over a pouch. Tib rooted around inside and pulled out two chains with carved fish – one in amber and one in silver – dangling from them.

Peter was watching him closely. 'They're for you and the doctor, her ladyship said.'

Peter signalled the other seaman and started rowing again.

Tib took the amber fish and put it on over his head. Modeste, still flinching with pain as the boat surged forward, simply clutched his amulet in his hand.

So Helée, who had seemed to love the Emperor and worship the old Emperors to the exclusion of his own son, had today risked reprimand for not executing the two of them for heresy.

In fact he had risked death himself for helping them. And his mother Serina had given them amulets symbolizing the Nazarene to protect them on their journey.

When they were one hour upriver and away from the offshore breezes Peter steered the boat to a landing place and jumped ashore. He wished the travellers well and watched as they restarted their journey. Tib took his place on the rowing bar alongside Modeste, who was still weak and aching from his beatings. Until Modeste healed, Tib knew he would be of equal strength with his teacher. He rather liked that.

Tib's own injuries – more lightly acquired perhaps – had healed completely during the night. When Serina saw this she had nodded. 'Your gifts serve you well, my beautiful son.' Her husband was watching, so she could not touch Tib or comfort him in any other way. She'd looked silently across at the scarred and bandaged Modeste who, it seemed, would have to heal in a more natural way.

Now the two seamen watched as the man and boy rowed valiantly against the down-flow of the river, and shouted encouragement and instructions until they were out of sight. Then they turned to walk back to Good Fortune, glad that the onerous task was at an end. Marching on, Peter turned to the younger sailor and said, 'I knew that lad since he was a stripling. Born and bred in Gaul. There was no harm in him. I hope he thrives. It's a hard path he's chosen.'

In the boat Modeste rowed valiantly for some time but then he gave in, finally dropping his head over his oar. Awkwardly, Tib steered the boat to the shore, tied it up, and helped Modeste ashore into the long grass under the shade of a wild fig tree bent and twisted with age. Modeste slid down with his back to the tree, nodded and closed his eyes. Tib went back to the boat and hauled ashore the bags his mother had given the seamen to put aboard.

When he opened one bag, instead of the food and wine he'd expected, there were some of the things that had been in Modeste's boxes – the scrolls, the maps, the instruments. The boxes themselves were there in the bags. So Serina had made sure they had everything from the eyrie to hand. There was no food.

Seeing Tib's disappointment, Modeste smiled wanly. 'Your

mother is the wisest of women, Tib. She knows that food for the mind and the spirit is what will sustain us.' He closed his eyes.

Tib took a very deep breath. Then, invoking the spirit of the Nazarene in the way Modeste had taught him, he leaned across and made the sign on Modeste's sweating forehead. He prized the amber fish from Modeste's hand and hung it around his teacher's neck. He took both of Modeste's hands in his so the two of them made the circle. Then he sat there in silence, allowing himself to hear the song of the birds in the trees and feel the soft wind give life to the hot air around him. He could hear the hum of bees about their work.

When he unclasped his hands he opened his eyes and he saw an old woman, her grey hair braided around her head. She handed him a bag made of tightly woven rushes. Inside were two flat crusty breads and a thin-necked earthenware jug plugged with a wooden stopper. She blinked at them, one to the other, said something and left.

'She tells us she is from a nearby hamlet called Cessaro.' Modeste, wide awake now, grinned at Tib. 'Have faith, my son. Ask and it shall be given unto you!' They ate and drank with a will and when they'd finished Modeste stood up. He put his hand to his side and across his back and frowned.

'What is it?' said Tib.

'Gone, gone! The bruises are there but the pain is gone! Your touch heals, Tib.' Full of energy Modeste kneeled down to examine his maps and documents, then wrapped them up again in the oiled bag. 'Come on, boy. We'll get on and find somewhere for the night. The portents are good! Good!'

The boat eased itself into the shallows and Modeste pushed against the bank with his oar to get close in as Tib jumped ashore, then held the boat steady as Modeste followed him. They pulled down the main mast, hauled the boat on to flatter, drier ground, took out their bundles and secured them in the groin of a tree.

Modeste looked around. 'What a wonderful place, Tib. So green. Lush. Luxuriant. See those tall trees? See how every-thing flourishes here? This is the place for us.'

So, with a great heave, they upturned their boat. 'Shelter

for the night at least,' said Tib. He looked around at the sunlit grove, the long grasses, and the wild olive trees. 'Or more. This could be a fine place to live,' he said, rubbing his hands. 'Now we begin, Modeste. Now we begin!'

EIGHTEEN
The Monk's Cell

The drunken dramas of yesterday seem to have changed the atmosphere at the Maison d'Estella. I feel easier, more relaxed inside myself. But the normally laid-back Mae seems suddenly rather nervous of me, making explosive statements and laughing too loud, saying how I was always, *always* her favourite person. But now and then she puts a hand on Philip's shoulder. One time she literally pats him and he looks embarrassed.

The children are still in bed when the four of us breakfast together at the big kitchen table and so we eat looking out on to the courtyard. Philip insists on making Billy a full English breakfast with superior French ingredients. (Food is certainly his message system of choice.) The rest of us refuse. And Mae taps him on the arm, saying that he wasn't looking after her figure, was he?

At last Billy makes a comment. 'For Christ's sake, Mae, stop embarrassing yourself, will you?'

Her chair scrapes back and she stamps away. In a second we hear her shouting the odds at Olga. 'For Christ's sake, Olga, will you get out of bed? You're sleeping the sleep of the dead.'

I feel sorry for her.

'Well!' says Philip, clapping his hands together heartily. 'I'm looking forward to Carcassonne! Those dreaming towers of medieval chivalry.'

Billy grins. 'Rather the dreaming towers of medieval rape, pillage and slaughter,' he says, wiping up the last of his egg with the last of his baguette. 'I don't think you've done your homework, old lad!' Billy's certainly been doing *his* homework. He catches my glance. 'You coming, Starr? To Carcassonne?'

I'm already shaking my head. 'Not me. I've work to do.'

Philip gathers up Mae and Billy's plates and stacks them

neatly in the dishwasher. 'Our Stella always has work to do, doesn't she?' he says. 'Or – my God – she's gotta sleep! Or she's gotta look at the stars. Our Stella's not on the same planet as us more ordinary guys, Bill.' These are bitter words and his tone is uneasy. I feel sorry for him. It really sounds as though he's giving up on me. You can't blame him really.

I walk with them all down to the car park and watch them climb into the car, kitted out with everything they might need for a whole day away. Philip has packed a superb picnic. As she settles into the car Olga turns and gives me this deep look through her round glasses. I know she's thinking of Virgo and Ursa Major. And me, I am thinking of Siri.

I wave them off and turn towards the Café Plazza, finally allowing myself to look forward to seeing Madame Patrice. Neither she nor her bicycle is in place when I arrive, so I order my coffee and settle down to wait. I'm still waiting half an hour later but Madame Patrice does not arrive. I fight hard against the familiar, poisonous panic that floods through my body and makes the world black around me. I'm better now at dealing with this. I have to do it to survive. Not give in. Not end it all.

Find Madame Patrice, I tell myself, *find her*. Find out where she is. Go to the *Presse* and get a map of the town. She said she lived on *rue de la Poissonnerie*. I run down to the shop, bumping into people in my haste. Buy the map, open it up and look. That's when, standing there in the street, I laugh out loud. Two women raise their eyebrows and carefully walk around me. There it is on the map. *Her* street. It's only a dozen steps away from where I was sitting yesterday – it seems so long ago – with the man called Louis, on la Place de la Marine.

As I make my way to that end of the town, I find it more dilapidated even than the rue Haute of the Maison d'Estella. I remember what Madame Patrice said: '*the poor gather there, of whom I am one. Bad things are said of them but they are wonderful people.*' I pass a rather grand restored house and other even grander doors, portals to big houses, now battered and broken. Some are patched with plywood. Others are daubed in graffiti. On one door there is a white handprint on the faded green paint.

I wander into a side street only to be stopped by two boys playing football, immaculate in pristine Nike strips. Madame

Patrice said of the people here *'they look after their children, you know. That's a good sign.'* As I pass the boys they stand aside politely, football in hand. And they smile knowingly when I pass them on the way back, having been thwarted by a dead end. I push right to the back of my mind the thought of those two other footballing boys, locked up now in a cold British prison in some town in the north of England.

At last I find her. *Mme Patrice Léance* written in neat script beside one of the bell pushes. The names on the other bells are scribbled out. The doorway is painted a gingery moth-eaten brown, the last glossy layer on top of as many as twelve earlier layers of paint. I push open the door and see Madame Patrice's *bicyclette* in the dank passageway. I ring her bell three times. No answer. Again. Again. No answer.

I stand back into the road then go to peer into her window through a jungle of plants. Between the customary protective bars, I can make out a neat table with a flowered cloth; a crystal jug; high bookshelves; a daybed in the corner. I take a breath and concentrate, willing Madame Patrice to come to me, to tell me where she is. Then I hear the high-pitched bark of a dog and the clanking of elaborate iron window furniture. I look upwards and in a high window see the head of the man called Louis above a high-buttoned white shirt. 'Starr?' he says.

'I'm looking for Madame Patrice,' I call up. 'I thought I'd see her in the café but she's not there. She's not anywhere.'

He stares down at me. 'Come up,' he says finally. 'Climb up as far as you can.'

I'm gasping by the time I've climbed the fourth flight, holding my breath against the latrine smell that seems embedded in the walls of this place. Louis is standing by an open door at the very top, the little dog Misou in his arms. He hasn't bothered to fasten the cuffs of his shirt and they're dropping from his muscular forearms, loose, like flags.

I peer behind him. 'Is she here, Madame Patrice?' I can't explain to him why I'm demented by losing sight of this woman I've only met twice. 'Where is she?'

He stands back to let me into the room. 'She's well enough.' He pauses. 'She had to make a little visit to . . . the hospital.'

I move into the room. 'What happened?'

He frowns for a moment. 'She fell off her bicycle.'

He shakes his head. We both smile, liking the woman, not wanting her to hurt herself.

I glance around and the room whirls round me like a roundabout on fast forward for a second, then settles down. I've never been in a room like it, although I feel that I've images and paintings of rooms like this. It's small, no more than twelve feet square. Every surface is painted white. In one corner stands a bed, more like a soldier's cot; beside that a square cupboard. That's it; no other storage for clothes or anything else. Under the high narrow window is a large table made of thick planks placed on a trestle. On the table is a state-of-the-art laptop, a small printer, a pile of printed paper, a pile of blank paper and three folders bulging with documents. The chair pulled up to the table is the only one in the room. The wall to the side of the desk is covered with maps, some of them very old, flagged up with post-it notes. Stuck on to the wall alongside the maps are images of old rowing and sailing vessels.

On the opposite wall is a white ivory crucifix. In a niche beside it a statue of the Virgin Mary. Below that is some kind of low kneeler. I'm suddenly embarrassed at the earthly thoughts I've been having about this man.

'You're a priest?' Despite my good intention it comes out like an accusation.

He gestures for me to sit on the desk chair. He crouches down on the kneeler, his knees nearly to his chin. 'I am as I told you, Starr. I am a scholar.'

I absorb that, close my eyes and concentrate. *Do it, Starr. Do it, Mummy.* See what this place can tell me. *See* it properly.

Misou yelps. I open my eyes.

Louis is grinning, his blue eyes sparkling. 'Steady! You should be careful with that powerful stuff when Misou is around. It makes him prickle.

I close my eyes again. I can see a pair of hands with tapering fingers, light coming outwards through them. The hands open and a small bird flies upwards and perches on the window frame above the desk. It is plain brown with a reddish tail and a white breast. A nightingale.

I open my eyes and there is no nightingale. 'You're some kind of a guardian,' I say to Louis, suddenly sure. 'You are the boy's guardian.'

Misou has now crawled on to his shoulder and has coiled round his neck like a collar. Louis puts a hand up to stroke him. He stays silent.

'Madame Patrice? She's not really in hospital, is she?'

'She's gone,' he said. 'Passed on, you would say. She's been gone for a week.'

'But I saw her. I've seen her twice.'

'You did, didn't you? But that's what you do, isn't it? You see them, these people who are not properly gone.'

'But I haven't been able to do that. Not for . . . a long time. Three years now.'

'But it's beginning to happen again? You made it happen?' I stare at him. 'Yes. It's beginning again.'

'So . . .?'

I know now that he knows about Siri without me telling him.

'And Madame Patrice is still around?'

'She's taking care of you.'

'What do you mean, taking care of me?'

'Wait,' he says. He stares at me for a while, then blinks, as though he is forcing himself awake. 'Where are your visitors today?'

'They've gone to Carcassonne.'

He stares at me. 'Would you do something for Madame?'

'Anything.'

'Will you take care of Misou? We're not supposed to attach ourselves . . .'

We? Supposed? I don't comment aloud on this. I just say, 'I'll take care of him for her. Just for now. I'll take him for a walk by the canal.' I pause. 'I don't know what they'll think of me, taking Misou to the house.'

In the end it's all very businesslike. Louis finds a plastic bag, fills it with dog bowls and packets of food and hands me Misou's lead. Then before I can protest I'm out of the door and on the pavement. I look upwards to see the flash of a white shirtsleeve as the narrow window is closed again.

Misou tugs on his lead and I follow.

As I walk away I know I'd have liked to stay, to sit there in Louis's cell-like room and talk. I'd have liked to ask him about his scholarship and what it was he believed in. Ask him about the boy, and Madame Patrice. I could have told him properly about Siri. How the lovely midwife told me Siri

had been here before, that she had an old soul. How nice and
down to earth Philip was when we first met him. I would have
told him how being without Siri had been a kind of death in
life but how here in this place I could feel her around me. I
would have asked him about limbo, the interim place for the
un-baptised. Louis is probably an expert on limbo. I definitely
should have asked him about limbo.

'Starr!'

I look back to see him leaning out of the high window.

'Come back,' he says. 'Come back, will you?'

When I get up the narrowing staircases to the high room
the door is open. Louis is leaning against the opposite wall,
as though to make the greatest distance between us. His pale
blue eyes scorch into mine. Heat rises from my neck right up
to the roots of my hair. In one part of my mind I realize my
face must be lobster red. Very unattractive. How long is it
since I've cared what I looked like?

He relaxes then, and goes to sit on the bed. Misou settles
down on the table beside the laptop and closes his eyes.

'Sit with me, Starr,' says Louis quietly. I'm glued to the
spot, just inside the door. He comes and takes my arm and
unglues me. After that it's all very simple. He pulls me down
to sit by him. His hand goes to my hot face and I cool down.
Then I kiss him cleanly on the lips, then on the flesh of his
cheek and his brow. Then I kiss him again and Philip is in
my mind. How wonderful he was with Siri. But we never,
never kissed like this. Then I forget all about Philip. And Siri.

Now he's grabbing my shoulders and great heat comes from
him. His sweat tastes of honey. With my lips still on his I peel
off my shirt and his lips move on to my throat, down my body.
He groans and over his head I catch sight of his crucifix. Now
I wonder whether it's guilt, not passion that makes him groan.

His lips are hard on mine again and there is no objectivity,
no observation. I am pulsing with life in a world only alive
because of his lips on mine, his skin on my skin. Now we
crash in an untidy heap on the narrow creaking bed and smile
into each other's eyes as we sort ourselves out and begin again.
Slowly, slowly we become one creature without beginning or
end shuddering with life: one body and one mind, a universe
unto ourselves.

After that we drop into a zone of forgetfulness that some

might call sleep. When I snap into wakefulness he is propped up on one elbow staring down at me. I must look a real mess but I feel like the princess in the forest. One kiss and, after three years of sleepwalking, I am now awake.

I look into the face that is now so dear to me. But he is shaking his head. 'That shouldn't have happened.'

I glance across at the crucifix. 'Not the kind of thing you should do?'

He pauses. 'That's one explanation, but it's even more complicated than that.'

'I've always thought they were strange rules to impose on human beings.'

He smiles. 'They say they're rules made by man, not by God. But all people need codes of one kind or another to live by. That's what makes us sophisticated, civilized.'

He runs one light finger down the side of my face and my body starts tingling again. I sit bolt upright. 'I have to go. They'll be waiting for me.' I don't know why I say that. They're in Carcassonne after all.

'They?' he asks. I am pulling on my shirt. 'Bathroom across the landing,' he says.

Five minutes later I am back, washed and clean with my hair held tight on the top of my head by the tortoiseshell barrette I bought in the Thursday market. He's pulled on his shorts and the bed is smooth. Misou is prowling, ready to go.

Louis looks at me, his eyes clear and untroubled. The last hour might not have happened. Or it might . . .

This time when Misou and I walk back along the rue de la Poissonnerie we don't look back. Later, we are just crossing the road when a bus passes labelled *Grau d'Agde*. Sitting just behind the driver is the boy. I stare at him and he touches his brow and treats me to a mock military salute, just like Mae did yesterday.

He is everywhere, this boy.

As we pass the Café Plazza, I have to hang on to Misou because he's leaping high, pulling and jumping left and right between the tables, looking for Madame Patrice. I know just how he feels.

NINETEEN
Walking with Misou

Back at the house I lay out Misou's things in the inner courtyard and set him up with a big bowl of water. I am full of energy. I have another shower, wash my hair, tidy the courtyard, make a potato salad and a large *salade niçoise*, put the food in the cool shade of the inner courtyard, and lay the table for six.

I'm sitting here at the table with Misou when the others get back from Carcassonne. I glance at Billy – first through the door with an exhausted George on his shoulders – and say, 'Well, Billy, how was Carcassonne?'

He grins. 'Very picture-book, but those tiny streets still flow with the echo of blood,' he says. I think again that Mae's very lucky to have Billy, even if she doesn't know it. But he's lucky in her. She's an odd kind of life force.

Olga follows her father through the big door and shouts with delight. 'A puppy! Auntie Starr has a puppy!' She kneels down and tries to stroke Misou. He looks up at her, his head on one side, and she is lost in joy. I explain briefly that Misou is a grown dog but rather small. Then Mae comes in wearing a low-cut sundress that makes the most of her generous curves, followed by Philip, who takes one look at the set table and Misou and throws up his hands. 'What now, Stella? What have you gone and done now?' He sounds oddly disappointed that I've made such an effort.

'I've made supper, Phil,' I say. 'To save you the bother.'

I stand up and start to bring the food in from the shade of the inner courtyard, putting out plates, two jugs of lemonade and a bottle of local rosé jammed into a full ice bucket. Philip looks from me to *his* kitchen, back to the table. At a stroke I've taken his world from under him. Honestly, I hope you don't think I've done this vengefully because of all his messing about with Mae. It's just because of all this energy I'm feeling. I'm no longer the madwoman

who needs to be calmed down, fed fine foods, protected
from the world.

The courtyard stills to a tableau. Olga is stroking Misou,
talking to him, asking his name and where he's from. Billy is
sitting with the wakening George on his knee. Mae is lighting
a cigarette, her eyes bright with anticipation of dramas to
come.

In the end Philip catches my arm as I come in with a bowl
of fresh fruit and a jug of crème fraiche. 'Where's it from,
Stella? Whose dog is this? What are you going to do with a
dog?'

'His name is Misou. And I'm taking care of him for
someone.'

'Someone? *Someone?* You don't know anyone.'

'*Misou!*' says Olga in a strange purring growl. '*Misou,
Misou, Misou.*' She must think she's talking in dog language.

'Who?' he says. 'You don't know anyone in this city.'

Full of life now, I really resent the contempt in his tone.
'How on earth d'you think *you* know who *I* know in this town?
Have you spent any time with me here? Let's be honest, you've
spent your time running away from me. That is, apart from
putting food out for me, like you would with a favourite cat.'

'That's not fair, Stella,' Mae bursts in. 'Phil's only trying
to—'

'None of your business!' I flash back.

She screws out her cigarette on to a plate. 'Look, Stella,
how long do you want us all – Phil, me – to go on pussyfooting
around you? We know the thing that happened to Siri is the
worst thing that could happen to anyone. And we – especially
Phil – have held your hand through that. Don't you think other
folks have felt pain for themselves and for you? But it can't
go on. You've got the poor lad so that he has to get blind
drunk to enjoy himself . . .'

'Stop!' I hold up my hand as though to ward off a blow.
But she's right. I feel like falling through the floor. Phil is
shaking his head in protest.

Billy coughs. 'Starr's right,' he says. 'Mae, leave it! Mind
your own business.'

She turns on him like a viper. 'You! You slug, you! Why
do you never stick up for me? Oh no! Stella's the little starry-
eyed girl, isn't she? The interesting case: *A Study In Grief* . . .'

Now Billy stands up, puts George carefully on the ground. He walks to the glass door that leads to the salon where, yesterday, Olga played with her Gameboy.

He turns to her. 'A word, Mae,' he says evenly, then turns away from her and walks through the door. In a single moment Billy has evolved from the easy-going, mild, over-motherly spouse to the quiet man who'd been top of his year at medical school and, further back, the boy who captained his county team at rugby. Billy's bringing out his own personal big guns: a thing he rarely needs to do.

Mae mutters, lights another cigarette, and marches after him as though to berate him, to chastise him. Somehow we all know it will be the other way round.

Olga looks up from Misou whom she's now hauled on to her knee. 'Has Mummy been naughty or is it Daddy?' There was a thread of anxiety in her voice.

'They're just having a little chat,' I say. 'Nothing to worry about. Look, why don't you take George into the little room to wash his hands? And wash yours too. You can't eat with Misou's hairs on you, can you?'

Philip watches Olga, Misou in her arms, shut the door behind herself and her brother. He turns to me. 'She's right. Things have really changed with us, haven't they, Estella?' he says soberly.

'Are you sorry?'

'What do you mean?'

'Did you really like it, the way it was?'

He looks at me, frowning. 'Like it was?'

'I don't mean like it was, when you and me and Siri were together. That was all good, wasn't it? But what about since?' I say. 'You know, you wheeling me around like an invalid. Apologizing for my eccentricity. Feeding me ever more wonderful food to make up for me being so desolate. Making excuses to people for the grief, the madness and my obsession with the stars. Poor you. It's been hard, hasn't it?'

'I thought . . . gradually . . .' He's perplexed.

I just have to give in. 'Look, dearest of dear Philip. I'm truly sorry you've had all this on your plate. Me. You didn't sign up for all this that time at the all-nighter, did you? And you were wonderful – wonderful with Siri, who was not even yours.' Despite my good intentions I can't stop my voice breaking. 'She loved you.' For a second I can't go on. The lump in my throat is too big.

He moves towards me but I wave my hand in the air to keep him away. I swallow, trying to retrieve the energy of the afternoon. 'My dear boy. I have to be honest. Those ten years that the three of us had together were the best, the very best in my life. I'll never have that again. Well not in this world anyway. So I really thank you for that gift. But, really, there's no *us* without Siri, is there? So there's no *us* at all. I think it's over with us. I make you miserable and you don't deserve that.'

He looks wretched. 'What am I supposed to do, Estella? What am I supposed to say? What do you want me to do?'

'You should do exactly what you think is right for you.' I close my eyes tightly to squeeze back the tears and take a very, very deep breath. 'For now what I want you to do is to change your ticket and go back to England with Mae and Billy tomorrow. I want you to leave me here. I have things to work out and I know I can work them out here.' I don't know why I say that. But when the words come out of my mouth they sound right.

He looks around the courtyard like it's a crater of the moon. 'You're staying here? In this town? You don't know anyone!'

'That's where you're wrong. I do know people here.' Of course that's an exaggeration. I know one woman who may or may not be dead, one boy who may or may not be a vision, and one monkish scholar who I know is real because I've made love with him. Even so, his role in this world is a mystery to me.

Oh, and one very live small dog.

Just on cue, Misou barks from the little bathroom. Olga crashes through the door, face gleaming, dragging George by the hand. 'I'm so hungry, Auntie Stella, I could eat a scabby horse.'

'Ya-argh! Olga. What a thing to say!'

'That's what my Durham Granda says.'

I look up at Philip. 'Will you do that for me, Phil? What I ask?'

Before I can answer Mae and Billy come through the salon door, Mae looking entirely demure as though nothing has happened. Billy looks across and winks at me. Then we take our places around the table and eat our meal together in a kind of benevolent truce. It's a bit – just a bit – like the old times when I first got together with Philip and I took him north to meet Mae and her new doctor boyfriend whom she was flagging up to us like a trophy. It was clear even then that Billy absolutely adored her and felt that *he* was the one with a very special trophy. I remember now that on that night I had a twinge of envy, regretting the compromise I'd made in teaming up with Philip because, at that time in my life, it had seemed the best thing to do.

But tonight in the courtyard of the Maison d'Estella everyone is mildly witty and polite. Mae is paying due respect to Billy, and Philip is being absolutely charming to me. Olga is watching us all with her beady eye and George is seeing how many times he can nudge Misou with his foot before he barks.

At the end of the evening Mae – now the picture of virtue – shepherds the children to bed. Billy, Philip and I clear the table. When we get back into the courtyard the black stone walls are still humming with the heat of the day. The swifts are doing their mad aerial dance – darting this way and that and depriving the seagulls of their usual perching places at this evening hour. I light candles and put them in the centre of the table and Billy comes out with brandy glasses and a bottle of Armagnac.

Mae reappears in a long silk kaftan, her hair brushed down and her face scrubbed and shiny. In this light she looks eighteen. I remember how much she meant to me when I was young. I sit at the head of the table with Misou sitting on my feet like a muff. Philip gives his half-cough, half-laugh. 'Well, then!' he says. 'Here we are!'

Billy lifts his glass. 'I'll drink to that,' he says.

Philip nods and sips his brandy. 'I just . . . Well, Bill. The thing is, if I can grab a seat on your plane, I'll be travelling back with you tomorrow.'

Mae looks nervous. 'Phil, love, you don't think . . .'

I come to his rescue. 'Absolutely nothing to do with you, love. The thing is Philip needs to get back; he's wasted enough time over me. He needs to go. And I need to stay for a while. We're both happy with that.'

'Stay? On your own?' Mae's voice pitches up the shriek, charged with disbelief. '*On your own?*'

Misou jumps off my feet and barks.

Even Billy's staring at me. 'I hope this isn't about the shenanigans with these two idiots, Starr,' he says quietly.

I shake my head. 'Not a bit. Sorry to disappoint you, but it's nothing to do with Mae or you. In fact it's nothing to do even with Philip. Except I'm trying to be fairer to Philip than I've been for a while.' I pause, trying to be honest without giving anything away. 'It's just that I have so many things to work out. And I feel so much better here.' I look Billy straight in the eye. 'I can feel Siri here.'

Mae groans. 'I knew it! Better? She's getting worse!'

I shake my head. 'No, love. It means I'm getting better.'

Now we all just concentrate on our brandy glasses. Philip holds his so he can see the candle flame through it. 'Well,' he says quietly. 'Perhaps Estella will be better here for now. I don't really know but I understand now it's nothing to do with me. But if she thinks . . . well, she'd better get on with it.' He gulps off the whole of his brandy. 'Of course my mother will be devastated.'

'Your *mother*!' shrieks Mae.

For some reason this makes us all laugh and Billy half fills Philip's glass with more brandy.

I spend the next twenty-four hours in a dream, watching the Maison d'Estella empty of the bodies, the properties and the objects associated with Mae and her family. And Philip. I watch him go off with them: Philip, my beloved companion of the last ten years; Siri's beloved Pip.

He kisses me on both cheeks as he says his goodbye. It's as though we've just met. Mae looks uncharacteristically helpless but kisses me and clutches me very tight. Billy gives me a very big hug and whispers in my ear. 'You're on the right track, Starr. Set your course fair, old girl. And keep in touch.'

Now they've gone to the airport, and I walk around the house clearing up, black-bagging things they've left behind. For some reason I hang on to a big black tee shirt of Billy's that's still on the washing line and some black jersey pantaloons that Mae bought at the Thursday market and discarded as being 'too French'.

The house clear and clean, I walk Misou down to the harbour, along to the Place de la Marine and back up the rue de la Poissonnerie. I stand and look at the house, but there's no sign of either Madame Patrice or Louis. My mind fills with thoughts of yesterday when we kissed and made love in the narrow room. Misou jumps up at Madame Patrice's window but I pull him away. I stamp back up to the Maison d'Estella, disappointed but not cast down.

I work all the rest of the afternoon, doing charts and calculations, drafting emails and redrafting columns for the next three weeks, ready to file as soon as I can get into the library.

Drumming itself through me like a song you've heard too many times is the need to be *ready, prepared*. I know in my heart that all around me some kind of story is evolving which has Siri at its centre. I can feel this pulse in the air, like a storm gathering. It's like a cosmic version of what happens when I write my columns. I write the stories to fill the column inches and to make money – in the first place to keep me and Siri, and more recently to survive, so that I can see her again. These stories, written for such arbitrary reasons, have hit home with many people across the world, as though I dip into some big soup of memory that we all share and by a kind of magic say something unique to each of them.

Having done my 'send' in the library I have a shower using the last of Mae's shower gel and expensive shampoo. I brush my hair until it's so dry that it expands to twice the volume and crackles in the air. On an impulse, instead of putting on my pyjamas, I put on Billy's big black tee shirt that smells of that day's sun, and pull on Mae's black pantaloons. They are very comfortable.

And at the end of this day, as always, I cast Siri's chart, as though she's here beside me. Tonight, the conclusions are very interesting. What emerges from those calculations is a very complicated period for her: a worrying movement backwards and forwards. Unbelievably, it says that studies beckon. And there is singing: such a lot of singing. And one special person is being drawn to your side, Siri. That person keeps coming again and again.

St Etienne's bell tolls eleven o'clock and suddenly the air is torn apart with cracks and rumbles and explosions. I run outside into the dark alley and follow a crowd down to the quayside to see a brilliant display of the fireworks so beloved of the people here. A poster tells me that this weekend we're celebrating Pentecost when, it says, the followers of Jesus were given the gift of tongues.

Down at the quay people are still in their daytime processional costume – Druids, monks, medieval knights and ladies, sans-culotte revolutionaries, ill-fated aristos, Napoleonic heroes – men, women, young, old. In front of me are white-faced Druids dripping with red and white ribbons. All – all – are looking up in wonder at the dazzling display of artificial stars and planets that make the real thing fade into nothingness.

Then the noise and light reaches a brilliant crescendo, which is greeted with a storm of shouts and applause that dissolve into silence. And now people are throwing flowers, stems and petals into the air and they float down in the darkness like snow. Then the air is filled with huge claps of thunder – this time the real thing. One of the Druids in front of me turns round and I scream at the sight of his whitened face with the jagged, bloody scar painted right down one side. I look round for help and two men in friars' habits turn towards me. My heart leaps as I recognize Louis and the boy. I know them, but neither of them shows a blink of recognition at the sight of me.

Now all the faces turn to look at me, their bodies shimmering, their eyes shining, their mouths opening and closing without any sound. My body is burning and shaking and I can see the flashing lights again.

Misou yelps and yelps.

Something is pulling me across the black stones of the quayside towards the water. I scream. And scream.

PART TWO

TWENTY
The Feast of Pentecost

As time went by Tib and Modeste settled into their camp and began to explore the branches of the river, visiting hamlets and villages and offering their cures in return for bread and wine and vegetables from the gardens of people they met. But always they returned to their encampment near the village of Cessero where they now had a hut and a garden planted with the help of the Cesseroneans. At their camp they now had a beehive filled with bees which seemed to possess the air with their humming.

In these villagers – a reserved and quiet people – the man and the boy eventually found a gracious welcome and source of refreshment. Led by Léance, the husband of the first woman they met, they brought food for the strangers and sat at their feet listening to Tib's stories of the Nazarene who preached love and toleration, and listened to Modeste as he read the letters of Paul which were a guide to a good life. They revered Modeste's wisdom and his medicine, but were more moved by the boy, whom they saw as one of their own: a boy who radiated grace and goodness, who could cure a sick man of his demons with a touch. They relished the boy's beauty and his high intelligence and his insight into the human heart. They knew from experience that his touch could raise any human spirit to its highest. He offered instant cures to people he met in the road, and they revived just as the sun revives flowers and plants blighted by a storm.

It's crazy.

The fireworks have stopped, the storm has abated and here I am standing in bulrushes just by this rough landing stage. Misou is round my neck, the water is up to my knees. Billy's black tee shirt and Mae's black pantaloons are soaking. I lean down towards the water and meet the gaze of a mad woman with a halo of afro hair. Even crazier, my hair is full of flowers.

My mind pricks with a memory of another time, long ago I think, when I saw my reflection in a river and there was a man beside me whose name I can't remember.

I pull marigolds, daphne, clover, even small sticks of jasmine blossom, from my hair. If my mother could see me now! And there is this bird that must think I'm a bush because it perches on my shoulder and sings *Or ee ole, Or ee ole*, its whistling jarring in my ear.

Misou creeps from my neck down into my sleeve. The bird on my shoulder does not budge.

A dream. It has to be a dream. Or am I crazy?

Or both, because here before me are Louis and the boy, still in their friars' clothing, a kind of long tunic caught up with a rope belt, and a long pointed hood.

The sunlight glints off the boy's red-gold hair and he smiles. He smiles at me.

'*Mummy.*' I can hear Siri's voice in my ear. '*Mummy . . .*'

The bird on my shoulder stirs and flies away.

I feel faint. Louis catches me. 'Madam, how are you?' he says. It *is* Louis. But he sounds different. This has to be the dream effect.

'Louis!' I say.

'Not here,' he says. 'In this place I am Modeste.' He turns to his companion. 'And this is Tibery, known to all as Tib.'

The boy beams at me and it's like catching the sun in the palm of your hand. 'I dreamed of you many times, madam! I saw you and you needed me but we always passed each other by.'

I look into his eyes. 'Then we were dreaming of each other, Tib. Because I dreamed of you. I dream of you now.' I like the sound of his name on my tongue but I don't know whether he will understand me.

Louis reads my thoughts. His voice is in my ear. 'Is it not the feast of Pentecost?' he whispers. 'All people understand each other. The bird alights on our shoulders with the gift of tongues in its beak.'

What are we doing? Are we dreaming each other? Are we in each other's dreams? I clutch my brow. It's all too hard.

'Don't worry, lady,' says Tib. 'It will be all right. You will be with us. We'll take care of you.'

'So who am I?' I say, meaning *who am I in this dream?*

Louis picks a stick of jasmine from my hair. 'You're Florence, the lady of flowers,' he says, his blue eyes sparkling. He kisses my cheek and it's like the fireworks all over again. Tib chuckles and I look at him and know he's read my thoughts. I start to shake and shudder; my mind is shot with all the colours, all the lights again. I want to be sick.

Then the boy grips my hand and all the bright confusion goes away: the hurtful colours, the blinding lights. Now I can see a thousand images of Siri right there in front of me, like a pack of cards being flipped. She is born, she is three, she is five, seven, nine, thirteen successively. But she goes on further – seventeen, nineteen, twenty-nine . . .

He squeezes my hand again and even this stops. I feel wonderful. 'What does it mean, Louis?' I say.

'It is *Modeste*,' he says calmly. 'You must call me Modeste.'

'What does it mean, *Modeste*?'

'Louis?' The boy Tib looks up at him, frowning.

'My name is Modeste. That is who I am, here and now. And it means we need you here, now,' says Louis. No, he says his name is Modeste! 'We have reached out for you, Tib and I. Tib felt your need for Siri and he reached for you. And we need you because . . . well, you'll see why we need you.' He puts a hand on my shoulder. 'Come, we have shelter for you here.'

I look round. 'Where are we?'

The boy answers. 'We are here on the great river some distance from the town of Good Fortune, where my father is Governor of the city.' He squeezes my hand. 'We must get some clothes for you, or the good Cesseroneans will take you for a madwoman, as I did when I first saw you.' Misou peeps out of my sleeve and barks and Tib quickly withdraws his hand. 'Modeste! The lady has a rat! How strange is that?'

I clutch Misou closer. 'This is Misou and he's no rat. He's a dog. I am minding him for my friend.'

This dream is getting stranger. Here am I, standing like Dorothy on some yellow brick road of my own making, clutching a little dog in my arms and talking rationally to two people in another time, another place.

Tib smiles. 'Just accept it all, Florence! Come on! We have work to do!'

*   *   *

I'm not kidding you. When I wake up in the morning I'm in the same dream. Honestly. Here I am lying on some kind of palliasse on a slatted platform in the corner of this little hut that's not much more than a lean-to against a bank. There are two other palliasses, both now empty. I feel my arms and legs and am relieved that I am still wearing Billy's tee shirt and Mae's pantaloons.

I scratch my neck and my left thigh. I've definitely been bitten. I put my hand up to my head and my hair is matted and itchy. I swing my legs over the edge of the platform and see clothes have been left out for me. They're just like those Louis – no, Modeste – and Tib were wearing yesterday at the Pentecostal procession: long tunic, rope belt, pointed hood joined to a round collar. I pull them to my face to smell them, expecting them to be rank, but they smell of new-mown grass and honeysuckle. Not terrible at all.

Modeste sticks his head through the rush curtain that serves as a door. That same smile, that same shaft of hair pushed to one side, those same pale blue eyes. That same dimple on the left cheek. 'Starr! Awake now! I fear ablutions are merely the river.'

'Ablutions! Crikey!'

'That done,' he went on, 'I have a comb for that hair.'

I put my hand up to the tangled mess of my hair. 'Crikey!' I say. I'm not very original in my surprise.

'As you say.' His grin broadens. 'Crikey!'

So, after my . . . er . . . *ablutions* I find myself sitting on the ground between his knees while he picks the twigs and flowers out of my hair and begins to work his way through it with a comb carved out of a strip of wood.

Tib and Misou (who is sitting on Tib's feet) watch the procedure with interest. Tib hands me a small wooden paddle with sticky ointment on it. 'Rub it all over your skin,' he says. 'For the bites.'

I take it gratefully and rub it on. It's very soothing,

Now Modeste can start to comb my hair straight back and smooth it into a cue, which he ties with a strip of black cloth.

Tib puts his head on one side. 'You are quite beautiful, Florence,' he says thoughtfully. 'But not as beautiful as my mother.'

Modeste drops the hood over my head. 'But to our good people here you will be just another pilgrim.'

Their work table is two wide planks, like the deck of a ship, set across two tree trunks. This reminds me of something, like cobwebs hanging in the back of my mind that I can't quite reach, I concentrate very hard and remember it is like the one in Louis' room in the rue de la Poissonnerie.

On this table are boxes and horns containing powders and leaves. There's a stack of squares of oiled cloth and twisted vine stem fasteners. At the far end of the table, held down by stones, are the documents and maps. Familiar from . . . *somewhere*. I know – they're from the wall in Louis's room, his monk's cell.

All around us birds warble and twitter and sing song-sets like the chirruping of time. From the back of my mind – with some difficulty – I pluck the memory of the nightingales and the other river, long and straight, dappled in sunlight and lined with trees like soldiers on guard. Here perching above us in the wild olive tree are dozens of small birds, like elongated kingfishers, bouncing slightly on the finest, most fragile reaches of the branches.

Tib catches my look. 'They eat bees, their most favourite dish.' He flings out a hand to encompass the glade around the olive tree. 'We have to watch them so that they don't lay siege to our hives. But there are so many flowers, so many bees. There is balance.'

'You have beehives?'

'On the flat land beyond the garden. One of them was built for us by Léance, a man of Cessero. And another built by me on the instruction of Léance. The bees are a great resource. They are full of energy. They are a sign of the kindness here for us and our cause.'

As if on cue an old woman moves through the trees, a rush basket in her hands. Misou barks and the woman frowns down at him. Modeste stands up quickly to go to greet her and I too scramble to my feet.

The old woman bows very deeply to Tib, less deeply to Modeste, glances curiously at me and hands over the basket. 'I see you have a new follower, messire Modeste,' she says.

He nods. 'We have here a traveller, madam, a wanderer. He likes our message and our ways.'

'Is he from Good Fortune? Or Massalia?'

'He's from further away than we can think, madam, from across the sea at the far end of the Empire.'

She surveys me from head to toe. I bend at the knee so she won't see my bare, soft feet and my painted toenails.

'He'll have needed good boots for such long walk. But it's a blessing that our precious boy has another person to care for him. Soft-handed if I see things right.' She bows in my direction and I bow back. 'Take care of the boy,' she says.

'I will,' I say, deepening my voice. 'That is my purpose.' And as I say the words I know that is true. I've come from a world that's now drifting around in cobwebs in my head into a world that I hardly know in this strange dream. But I know there's a purpose to it. Siri is part of that purpose, and so is Tib. I glance at the boy and he nods his head slightly.

Misou yelps.

The woman frowns at him and looks up at Modeste, who is putting her gifts of bread and wine on the table. 'That is a very strange creature, messire,' she says.

'He too is from far away.' Modeste smiles slightly and bows to the woman. 'Will you thank the people of Cessero, Madame Léance?' he says. 'For their charity?'

She smiles slightly. 'We always look after our own, sire,' she says. 'And we always will.'

And then she vanishes back through the trees.

'And now, Starr,' says Modeste, 'you must be hungry. I think we should eat.'

TWENTY-ONE
The Old Soul

Have you ever heard of a dream extending to days? I've been in this dream long enough to know the routine here in this camp. (I can only call it a camp. It's not a house and we live mostly out of doors.) We eat fruit and fish that Modeste catches in the river. Sometimes the villagers leave their own fish as well as bread, funny kind of junket cheeses and this rough wine that's so thick and strong it needs diluting with clear stream water if you want to avoid an extreme headache. We always take the unsullied water from above the village. We cook the fish on a fire of vine twigs that Tib brings back from his herb foraging.

Tib does all of the gathering of herbs. Modeste tells me that once Tib knew what to gather, the boy insisted on doing all of the gathering himself. It seems that Modeste's methods were not particular enough for him. Tib's very particular – I would say obsessive – about which plants, where, which part of the plant to use, how to cure it and how keep it.

Sometimes Tib calls Modeste the Corinthian, in affectionate tones. 'Is that where you come from, Modeste? Corinth?' I ask, curious about his life here.

He smiles. 'Aye, you might say that, by way of the Imperial court. And they sent me here, to care for the boy. Tales of his genius had reached them even from these far distances.' Then he tells me this weird tale of favour, healing and banishment.

'His own father?' I say. 'Tortured you?'

Modeste shrugs. 'It's an edict straight down from the Emperor. Anyone following the way of the Nazarene is to be punished, even killed. There've been special games dedicated to the destruction of these gentle heretics. Tib's father risked – even risks now – his own life allowing us to live. The Emperor Diocletian is an impatient man. He wants us all to confirm, to pay tribute to the God Emperors and the old gods.

In refusing to conform we risk our lives. Many of us have suffered cruel deaths, in the great arenas, in private, in public.'

Now then, I've got some idea of the Caesars and all that. There was Nero fiddling while Rome burned. And I've seen Ben Hur galloping along on a reissued DVD. But I've never heard of this one. *Diocletian.*

I stop asking too many questions. I have to take in this dream step by step.

I see that Modeste and Tib have their rituals. Modeste reads his scrolls and pores over his maps. Tib recites old stories and prayers. They sit silent for long periods, eyes closed, looking inwards. They eat bread and drink wine in a ritualistic fashion. I don't question it or join in with them. I just observe. It's just my dream, after all. But it's their life.

One day Modeste and I are walking up into the village to deliver wooden dishes of ointment to two women who have suppurating sores on their cheeks. I feel confident enough today to ask Modeste about Tib in a broader way. Not about his gift of healing nor even about their faith, which I know is some sort of Christianity – a risky thing before it was the done thing to follow the way of the Nazarene, as they call him. I have seen the people who come to the camp for help and healing, some from many miles away. These people join in Tib and Modeste's simple ceremonies, as do many Cesseroneans who move into the camp like shadows to take part.

I now realize that I experienced Tib's healing gift myself, when he cured me of the strange fit I had when I first arrived at the camp. I'd experienced it before, in my waking life, in Agde, the town at the mouth of the river, the town *they* call Good Fortune. Even in my waking life, before we met here in this place, before I knew his name, Tib conjured up good thoughts of Siri for me in the streets of Agde.

But now, walking into Cessero, I try to get Modeste to talk about Tib's more particular oddities: the patterns and lines, the precision of the recipes for the medicines, the tendency to look away, when you know he's concentrating on you. 'He wasn't like that when I saw him in Good Fortune.' (I nearly said *when I was awake . . .)* 'He seemed light-hearted there; I remember when he jumped into the river and raced the boat. How merry he was.'

'That was his playtime. In this place now we're moving to

different, terrible times, different selves,' says Modeste briefly. 'There in Good Fortune he was experiencing the last of his childhood. He has hard times ahead.'

'Did he know this?' I ask. 'Did he know he was there, playing?'

He shakes his head. 'I can't say. Perhaps not. But I think it all adds up into a life lived.'

'But you knew?' I persist.

'It has always been my job to look over him.'

I can't pursue this because now we're walking into the straggle of houses that comprise the village of Cessero and people are coming to the doors of their dwellings to watch us make our progress. A stranger is theatre here. Some men raise a hand in greeting, some nod. One or two bow gracefully, an action at odds with their rough clothes obviously worn for years, patched and added to. They are barefoot and wear a kind of smock and britches, unlike the tunics and cloaks worn by both Tib and Modeste.

We come to two grander buildings with archways wide enough for wagons and large window hoists adapted from ships' gear. Warehouses, says Modeste. It seems that Cessero owes its modest prosperity to trade in wine and woollen cloth from further inland, shipped down on small boats to Good Fortune, and also to passing trade from the great road nearby that crosses over a great bridge and goes all the way to Rome.

'Did you travel here on that road? All the way from Rome?' I tease my mind to imagine horses, pack-donkeys, chariots, closed wooden carts. Pictures from textbooks. 'It must have taken a long time.'

He shakes his head. 'It is a good road, but that would take far too long. The sea is the best route, even with its great risks. By foot and horse from Rome to the coast, swift sailing ship hugging the coast for safety, landfall here. So much quicker than the road.'

Even so, I think this must have taken weeks. Time and distance are different here, that's for sure.

Now we're at the house of the two women. They are sitting with their faces to the sun, as Tib has taught them. They stand up and bow to Modeste but look at me with great disappointment. 'The boy's not here, messire?'

Modeste shakes his head. 'Tibery is praying and cooking

his cures. But he sends you more ointment.' He hands over the wooden boxes. 'Is there improvement?' They hold up their faces for inspection. New raw sores are surrounded by the receding tides of the old sores. 'Yes. It looks better. Rub this on each morning, drink clear water and eat young figs. Then your faces will have the bloom of a young maiden!'

'You say so, messire!' The older woman smiles faintly and nods. She says, 'Will you bless me, messire?'

Modeste puts a hand on each shoulder, says something, then makes a mark on her forehead. The younger woman stands while he does the same. Then all three of them take each other's hands and make a circle and close their eyes for a few moments. Then that's it. They all smile and nod and say their farewells. 'Give our love to the boy!' says the older woman. 'And our blessing, messire.'

As we walk back along by the river it strikes me that Modeste lives up to his name. All these cures and methods are from *his* knowledge and his long experience, yet all are now credited to the boy. And Modeste doesn't seem troubled by this one bit. As we walk, he tells me more about the village. 'It is named after a great emperor – Caesar – Cessero. See?'

'Which Emperor?' I don't know why I ask. After all, I only know Nero. And Julius, of course.

'The Emperor Tiberius. The Cesseroneans have a story that tells how he came here once, in the olden time. The old ones say six generations ago.'

'Tiberius? That's like—'

'Tibery! I know. Tiberius had been a great general. Tib's father has a shrine to him in his house. He gave his son that name in tribute.' He pauses. 'But the humble people here in the village see the boy's name as a great portent.'

Then I stumble on the stone-strewn pathway and he takes my arm. In the back of my dreaming cobweb mind I remember another time where I tripped by a broad, straighter river than this. I hug Modeste's arm into my side, clinging to this evidence of the then, and of the now. And it comes to me how much happier I am in the now, here in my dream.

When we get back to the camp it's empty. Tib's medications and medicaments are stored away in their boxes in the hut and he's nowhere to be seen. 'Where is he?' I ask.

Modeste gives his characteristic shrug. 'Sometimes Tib

takes off, walking from village to village, giving his advice, laying on his healing hands. To be honest the people like it best when he's on his own. My job's nearly done here. But, healer though he is, he's too young to leave on his own.'

'Yes. How old is he? Ten? Eleven? He needs to be taken care of.'

Modeste smiles, his dimple deepening in his left cheek. 'Master Tibery has an old soul, older than yours or mine, believe me. It's he who takes care of us, Florence, you may be sure of that.' He looks around. 'Now, what shall we do while we await his return?'

TWENTY-TWO
Pestle and Mortar

While we wait for Tib we sit at Modeste's end of the plank bench and he lays out his fine vellum maps to show me how he got here from Rome. 'We shipped out from Ostia then changed ship at Masallia. Then round the coast to Good Fortune. Always within sight of the coast – venture further and you may be lost to storms or pirates.'

He frowns. 'In the end these arrangements about Tibery were made in a great hurry. I was just on the point of embarking for Corinth, to visit the church there and see my brothers and their children.' There is tension in his voice. 'But I was called, then, to this task.'

'And you, Modeste? Do you have children?'

'Alas, no. My scholarly vocation does not allow for children.'

I frown at this, offended on his behalf. 'Is that forbidden then?'

He shakes his head. 'No one demands this of me. But since I became a free citizen I've lived this itinerant life, curing and teaching. My gifts have been offered to other people's children – and now to Tib! He's no son of mine but he's my fate. He is the son of my heart,' he says simply.

I reach up then to kiss him on the cheek as he takes a smaller map out of a slender leather tube and lays it on the larger one. He squeezes my hand then flattens the map with his hand, trying to smooth the curl out of it. In the end he finds stones to hold it down. It's very old and faded but has pathways drawn on it in a fresh hand. 'And what's this?' I say.

'This is where we are. See? Here is the estuary of the great river and the lagoons running down the coast that make the harbour safe. And across here is Setus, a greater city than Good Fortune. And here is Nemausus, the place of many

monuments to the Emperors that has the great games ring.
The place is a thing of beauty and awe. I've heard of many
good men of faith killed here for sport,' he adds soberly. His
finger moves across. 'And here is Good Fortune and here . . .'
His finger moves up and left. 'Marked by me, is Cessero. This
is the great bridge I told you about. See the way the land rises
just here? This is where the village is.' His finger moves along
the river, following his drawn line. 'And here is our camp.'

It seems a simple enough map to me. I saw it on Louis'
wall in the rue de la Poissonnerie. I point on the map to the
river – clearly the River Herault. 'And this is the river you
rowed with Tib? From Good Fortune?'

'It is so,' he says. 'And here by Cessero is the road built
for the Empire. Like all roads, it leads to Rome. I've checked
this map in many different times. I've walked these pathways
in many different shoes.'

'But,' I say, 'why *do* you search this map? Why *have* you
walked *these* pathways? What is this fascination?'

He looks up at me and then looks beyond me towards the
river. 'Once, Florence, hundreds of years ago now, three women
and two men landed here, after a journey more than twice as
long and twice as dangerous as mine.' He pauses and seems
to concentrate very hard for a second. 'What do you know of
the story of Jesus the Nazarene, the great rabbi and prophet?'

'He was crucified, died and after three days he rose up
again.' I chanted the words from the Easter services at school.
It was ordinary as cheese, like the sun rising in the morning.
It was ordinary, undramatic, its meaning thinned with
over-use.

'Well. There are documents in the possession of my family
in Corinth that tell other stories, originally written by people
who were actually there.'

'Other stories?'

He shrugs. 'They don't *all* tell the *same* stories. When we
write things down we tend to add, to decorate, to make up.
It's the way of things. Some are stories of people who claim
the rabbi actually *survived* crucifixion. Then others say the
Nazarene was nurtured in his tomb for a single day by his
uncle and his wife and his mother and emerged miraculously
fit and well. And there are stories of how the verifiers went
and found the empty tomb and became very afraid. And others

tell of how some people saw the rabbi days later, fine and well with no marks on him. For them it showed he had gone to heaven and returned. The prophesy had been fulfilled and here was a miracle that would take an emerging religion on to its next great stage. This rabbi, this great teacher rising from the dead and then returning to Heaven, fulfilled the prophesy.'

Of course I have a vague notion of all this. I've read accounts in some of the more esoteric magazines. I don't believe them or disbelieve them. What do we really know, anyway, about what really happened two thousand years ago? 'Right. I get it,' I say now. 'But what has all that to do with Cessero?'

'There are other stories. One story is that the teacher actually did die and the soldiers were coming to take the body elsewhere to be burned so that this place did not become a place of pilgrimage. So, this story says, the rabbi's friends and family took away the body and brought it by a perilous journey here to Gaul. They thought it would be safe here, not destroyed by the vengeful Romans in the Judea uprising. Or got rid of by jealous people of his own race who feared his breaking of their rules and his advocacy of love and tolerance.' Modeste put the flat of his hand on the map and drew it across the whole area from Cessero to Marseilles – *Masallia* on this map.

'After a perilous journey across the great middle sea they sailed on to this place. It seems such a simple thing, doesn't it? Such a great thing that ordinary, brave women and men should do such extraordinary things to save their own great idea, that their story should survive the ravages of their age?'

'And you believe this?'

'I've been taught to believe in the resurrection; that is a matter of belief. But five travellers *did* come here. I have notes, maps and letters that account for such a journey.'

'Who were they?' I remember something from a rather soapy film. 'The Magdalene?'

'The woman from Magdala? Some stories say this.' He strokes the surface of the vellum.

I look around at the river, the woodland and the rising ridge where Cessero lay. 'So these stories are important, Modeste? Even in these times?'

He nods. 'Our fragile church has gone through many changes since those first days. And now in these days there are new waves of vengeance from the Emperor, who wishes us extinguished like light from a candle. Even so, we become stronger and our people willingly sacrifice themselves for our beliefs.' He pauses. 'But I feel we need the best truth from these stories, Starr – Florence. The best truth. Our church fears what we may find.'

I'm still puzzled. 'So you are following the stories and hoping to find . . . nothing?'

'There will be something. The stories are too strong for that. But I hope not the bones of a man who survived cruci-fixion. That would break us apart.' He pauses. 'That's why I'm here, if you like, to prove the stories wrong.'

I look at him, loving the silver strands in his black hair, the broad planes of his cheeks. 'I thought you were here to nurture Tib, to help him survive?'

He blinks hard and looks at me, frowning. 'Why am I telling you all this? I've sworn not to speak of it to a living soul.'

I put up a finger to smooth the frown from his brow. 'I don't count, though, do I, Modeste? I'm in a dream. I'm dreaming you, and you're dreaming me.'

'It's not quite as simple as that, Florence. Starr is dreaming, but *you*, Florence, are here. Just as Tib is here. *He* is not my dream.'

I struggle to get all this, to understand. 'If Florence were really here, Modeste, she'd be a person with a real past. But I was never here until you found me on the riverbank. I'm Alice through the Looking Glass!'

He shakes his head. 'It's beyond ordinary explanation, Florence. Just leave it. Let it lie.'

I cannot let him off that hook. 'Anyway,' I say, 'you're really here on *two* missions, aren't you? One to disprove that story. One to take care of Tib. Is that not so?'

He hesitates, then decides to trust me. 'I have this . . . patroness, a friend. A woman who is a brave, deep thinker and a secret friend of our church. She recognizes the dilemmas of uncovering this truth. It's she who saw Tibery as a reason for me to come here. She told me to try these stories till they break. Or prove them. This has been my task through time. This is how I met you in another place.' He frowns. 'I can't quite remember now, when that was.'

'Don't you remember making love to me in your little room?' I am disappointed. 'You don't remember that?'

His brow clears and he smiles. 'I would never forget. Such things are beyond time.'

I'm reassured. 'So, what about this patroness woman?'

'My patroness risks death or assassination in contemplating these ideas and discussing them with me. More, she bravely risks exclusion from our church, if my findings here do not accord with their traditions. This is why my search has become more than one life's study, Florence.'

'And Tib?'

'He was the very best excuse. My patroness thought that if his talents lived up to their reputation he would be a benefit to the Empire and also a good advocate for our church from inside the court. There was no doubt that his father, being a loyal servant of the Emperor, would want him to become a loyal citizen of Rome.'

'A spy? A sacrificial lamb?'

He shrugs. 'One way to put it. But see how it has turned out? Now the Empire, and his father, they both threaten him. Amazingly the boy has embraced our beliefs and practices. His very innocence is a great resource. And now, through his gifts, his great spirit, he has become a vessel for our church, for what we call The Way.'

'You believe all this, Modeste? Every bit of it? The church? The teaching of Paul of Tarsus? The divinity of the Nazarene?'

He looks at me and he is both Louis and Modeste. 'My search has been very long. I think there is more.'

I push him. 'More?' The air between us is shimmering with energy. It's like the other day – yesterday? – just after we made love.

Just then a movement in the shrubbery beyond the edge of the garden breaks our bond and I see the gleam of Tib's head. Alongside that head is another one, with a familiar halo of dark curls. I leap to my feet and race to the boundary. Tib walks jauntily down the path to meet me.

'Where is she?' I say, angry at his nonchalance.

'Who?' he says.

'Siri! I saw her.' I take his face in my hands. 'Tib! Look at me! I saw her. She was alongside you. She was holding your hand!'

Those bright blue eyes, too large for life, stare into mine.

'So, Florence, you saw her,' he said distinctly, pulling his face away. '*You* saw her!'

I fall to my knees and he steps round me. I'm crying and laughing at the same time. Modeste is beside me, pulling me to my feet and wiping the tears from my eyes. 'Come now, Florence. Tib needs you. I need you. There's time for that other thing. Lots of time.'

After sunset Modeste cooks the fish while Tib writes on his slender rolls of vellum, listing his finds in order and then adding them to his store. We eat the slightly burned fish with some bread and cheese washed down by water from above the bridge. I can feel Modeste's eyes watching me closely as we eat.

At last Tib retires to his palliasse to sleep his serene and well-deserved sleep. That's when Modeste takes my hand and leads me to the little grove, the hidden garden where I go to look at the stars and where now Modeste and I make love. I think that's what we'll do now: make love properly to dry my recent tears and allow my heart to warm with proper memories of Siri. I wait for him to turn and take me in his arms. But he doesn't do this. He lies by my side, takes my hand and continues the conversation of the afternoon.

'I've told you of my experience, Florence. And my belief.' He pauses. 'But I feel it's even more important than all that. My greatest and most profound belief is that great souls are invested again and again in great people, generation upon generation. See up there? See your beloved stars? I believe we all live in many times, in many places. This is the adventure of our essential spirit, what we call our souls. I've experienced this as a living dream, just as you do now. I've experienced it and sometimes I remember it. Sometimes not. Mostly I do and that makes me unusual.'

I struggle to get to grips with this.

He goes on. 'Even more, I think all times exist together. Or twist around each other like spinning tops occasionally bumping into each other. I don't know how this can happen – although men will discover that one day. I do not know why it happens but I believe it is something about our improvement. We cannot think yet at a high enough level to understand the proper *how* and *why*. That would be like the bees in the beehive understanding Tibery, who tends them every day.'

He lies there, silent for a moment. It must be tiring, framing up such thoughts. But he goes on. 'Given that as Tibery is to the bees so to us there is a being, an entity, an energy greater than the self-serving pagan gods and the creeping tide of rule-bound public virtue that seeks to confine the human spirit. Such confinements happen even in my own church.'

I tell you, I'm really struggling with this. 'So . . .?' I say, both helpful and helpless.

He coughs. 'Well, what I do think is that there are great souls, suffering, significant souls which are somehow rein-vested in new people, to keep our world in balance, to help it survive. These souls live in one guise in one time and another guise in another time. They may be great leaders or much simpler souls who do good things. Each of them, however, all take us forward in some way.' He's speaking very fast. 'As I said, it's even harder to understand that periods of time are not like beads in a row. They are more like beads in a jar being shaken and crashing into each other all the time. Or sand being pounded in a mortar, or heated at high temperatures to change form. And out of this process new thoughts emerge – unthinkable before – clear as glass.' He pauses, out of breath now.

'You're right, Modeste.' I squeeze his hand. 'It *is* hard to understand.' I reach for an idea. 'And the Nazarene is one of these great souls?'

'Perhaps the greatest. Or perhaps belief in his virtue and his resurrection was the pestle that has transformed forever the nature of time and place. I'm still trying hard myself, and failing to grasp it all.' He reaches for me and now I'm where I want to be: in his arms with his hard body close to mine. 'But one thing is not hard to understand, dearest Starr, dearest Florence. It is the simplest thing in the world to love you in whatever time, whatever place we meet.'

Later, still awake, I stare at the stars and think of Siri, and how I've seen her now, laughing, hand in hand with Tib. That boy has finally shown me not just that he can make things happen but that he's wise beyond his years about the human soul and its yearning.

Then my mind moves on to the complicated things Modeste was trying to explain to me. Spiritual refreshment? Now, I've heard of reincarnation but that's a mere echo of what he was telling me about. His bigger idea takes on the notion of time and space. I can't help myself thinking of the Time Lords. But the Time Lords are a fiction of *my* time. Smiling a little at the notion of Modeste as a Time Lord, I finally drop off to sleep.

Funny, isn't it, that you can sleep within a dream?

TWENTY-THREE
The Search

The next day, Tib is away with the sunrise, his rush bag over his shoulder. I'm sitting at the big table under the trees with sleep still in my eyes. Already the day is hot, close. The sky above the dense tangle of trees is a true, bright blue, full of pulsating light. I peer with my night-fogged eyes towards the bushes, looking in vain for Siri who danced there last night with Tib. Now the bushes part and here is Modeste, up from the river, his skin gleaming and his hair slick and wet. He has this shine about him. Sometimes I see it and sometimes I don't. Today I do.

He nods at me, goes into the hut and emerges with the small leather tube that holds his precious map. He places it carefully on the table then sits beside me to pull on the soft leather leggings that go under his sandal straps. He always wears them when he goes on his lone wanderings. Then he brings another set – Tib's I should think – and puts them on my knee. 'Put these on,' he says. 'The undergrowth has teeth.'

'But you always go on your own.' I'm puzzled.

'But now you're here,' he says. 'And you know my quest.'

While I tie on my leggings he lays out the map and looks at it closely again. 'See here? I've been here. And here, in this time and others, I've searched so long.' His own pathways are marked on the path in dots of ochre paint. 'I've been to each place suggested by my reading and my other maps. And other places hinted to me by the good Cesseroneans who have long history in their heads. And always I am brought back here, to this ridge by Cessero. There is something here, I'm sure of it . . .' There is strain, worry in his voice. I have to say I feel perverse delight deep inside to hear the always so calm and assured Modeste sound uncertain, almost boyish.

So we set out, side by side, following the pathways Modeste has marked and along other ways where there is no path at all. At one point we're parallel to what Modeste calls 'the great road', well paved with shining basalt blocks. We turn away at the point where the way leads over a wonderful bridge carrying the road over the rushing river below.

We tramp through the village of Cessero and the people watch and bow as before, but today Modeste isn't carrying his doctor's pack so they leave him in peace. After a while we begin to climb upwards through trees and undergrowth, towards a ridge of land that looks down on Cessero. Finally we come to a stand of five ancient lime trees just under the ridge. They're growing at an odd angle. Some parts of them reach to the sky but near their roots other trunks have been forced to twist upwards to find the sky again.

Modeste places a hand on the nearest tree. 'I think these trees are a pointer, a clue. Perhaps the land collapsed inward here. An eruption? There have been many around here.' He looks around. 'The Cesseroneans don't come here often. They look on this place with awe. One old man, whom I tended as he died, said there's a temple somewhere here dedicated to Emperor Tiberius, who travelled here in retreat from his worldly cares.' He smiles faintly. 'But then the old woman who brings us bread tells me it is the grove of Cernunnos, their old god of fertility and animals. Also known as the Horned One.'

I begin to realize that he's searched for this place within my waking life as well as here in this dream. I shiver and he smiles. 'These are innocent beliefs, Florence, made real by the way these people live their lives. Even those who pray with us in true belief bring flowers and woven gifts to this grove in the spring to bless the planting. They leave their offerings at the edge of the clearing. It's their custom.'

He leads me to a space between and behind two of the trees which have grown so closely together. He pulls away some branches. Now before us is a gaping hole about three feet square. On the ground is an iron scoop and a rush lantern, obviously his. He takes flint from his pack and lights the lantern and holds it into the hole. 'Look!'

At the far end of the hole I can make out a wall with a tessellated frieze at the bottom. The wall is muddy but I can make out ochre and a dirty blue, which might once have been purple. He holds the torch closer. 'Look!' he repeats. There above the frieze, in paint as black as liquorice, someone has drawn a fish. And someone else has drawn one in green above it, swimming in the opposite direction. This is Pisces, my pagan sign, but also the sign by which these believers know each other.

The hair on the back of my neck prickles. He puts a hand across my shoulders. 'The Cesseroneans have it right, don't they, Florence? This is a holy place. A proper place to protect something precious.'

'So you think the women brought . . . brought . . . here?'

I can feel him shrug. 'I don't know what was placed here. But something was.' He's excited. 'It could be something about the Magdalene and the Maries who landed. Or it could be something much older. I have this news of a better map in a letter from Setus. We're near the end, Florence. I feel it.'

'It could put the cat among the pigeons of course!' Irreverent, I know, but they are the words that come out of my mouth.

'Just so.' His body stands rigid beside me.

'So, do we dig, to find out more?' After all, he's a scholar as well as a priest. A searcher after the truth.

He relaxes and squeezes my shoulder. 'Sufficient today, Florence, that I've shared all this with you. You have helped me think about this, made me think it might be worthwhile to come back and dig further.'

I breathe out, relieved by his procrastination. He throws the torch down, then scoops the earth back into the hole so that it covers the wall again and spreads the branches and shrubs to disguise the disturbance. As we trudge back in the direction of the camp I can feel Modeste relaxing, putting from his mind the heavy responsibility of what to do about the explosive contents of the shrine. I take his hand and we walk slowly back along by the green glittering river. The sunlight flickers over our faces through the overhanging branches and small animals skitter across the path before us. The air is thick and warm and above us in the trees the birds sing as though they are in paradise.

Later, having welcomed Tib home from his foraging with hugs and questions about his haul, we eat supper together. Then he, bleary eyed, retires to bed. Modeste and I sit for a while then make our way to our hideaway where we lie side by side looking up at the stars. He asks me how – in my way – I see

Pisces, the sign of the fishes. I try to explain but I keep seeing the crude painting on the wall of the cave and my voice fades at the triviality of it all. Then he brings an end to the talk by kissing me and I have to adjust my view.

This is the very best of the dream. No doubt about that.

TWENTY-FOUR
Intruders

Misou is barking loudly, weaving between the trees, jumping up and down, vanishing and reappearing into our hideaway. Embarrassed at the thought that Tib might follow the little dog, Modeste and I spring apart and leap to our feet, brushing off the sticks and leaves still adhering to our habits.

A shadow emerges through a curtain of dark, bearing a torch. Now we can make out a man – no, two men; one younger, one older and grizzled. They have the rocking walk of sailors, or squaddies. The older one lifts his torch and peers at Modeste. 'Messire Doctor. I see it is you.' He swings the lantern towards me. 'But this is not the boy, the Governor's son. Where is he? Who might this one be?'

'Welcome, Peter,' says Modeste briefly. 'We have here another follower. The Governor's son is in the encampment. You should follow me.'

Modeste's tone demands compliance. He leads the way and I bring up the rear, walking behind the younger sailor down the narrow path back to the camp. Outside the hut Modeste calls Tib's name. We can hear rustling and muttering. We've obviously woken him up from his customary deep sleep. He comes out of the hut rubbing his eyes.

The old sailor stands before Tib and bows very deeply. The younger one follows suit. 'Messire,' says the old one. 'My master, and also your mother send you greetings.'

Tib doesn't ask about his parents, as most children might have done. He stares at the old man, a flicker of something in his eyes. Fear? Curiosity? It's hard to tell. Modeste moves forward, so that his broad shoulder is slightly in front of Tib. He says brusquely, 'It's a long way merely to bring a message, Peter.'

The old man nods. 'We are but forerunners, messire. We bring news that the Governor's wife, mother to the young master, is nearby. She's on the river even now on the Governor's barge, taking her rest till the morning, when we will guide her to your . . .' He looks round at the simple camp, which looks nothing in the shadows of night. 'The place where you're living.' He pauses, obviously aware of some drama to come. 'She will greet you here and then you are to return with her to Good Fortune to speak to the Governor.'

Tib looks up at Modeste and across to the seaman. 'My father?'

'Peter,' says Modeste sternly, 'you're aware that it would be unsafe for the boy to return to his father's house? You and I know the boy would not be safe.' Modeste knows this man; he is obviously no stranger.

The old man shrugs. 'I just obey my master's orders, messire. I heard rumours of your sojourn in Cessero so I knew where to come. My mistress will talk with you and the boy. She says there will be assurances.' He sounds anxious, unwilling to do a bad thing. A good man – Aquarius, I would guess. But in these times would you know precisely when a person was born? Is the calendar fixed? I wish I'd taken more notice in school.

Tib steps out in front of the man called Peter. 'We handled the sail well, Peter. Is that not so, Modeste?' His tone is friendly.

Modeste nods. 'I cannot deny this. You taught him well, Peter.'

The man nods, smiling slightly. 'That's good to hear, messires.' He turns to go.

'Where do you go, Peter?' says Tib, quite sharply. Not for the first time I think that for all Tib's light voice and small stature, he has the presence of a man.

'Back to our boat, messire. Then downstream. We'll report back to the Governor's wife, then, catching the downstream current, fast home.'

'You must stay here.' Tib indicates the hut. 'I will sleep with Modeste and you and your mate can share my bunk.' He pauses. 'And tomorrow that gripe you have in your belly will be gone.'

The seaman puts a hand over his stomach. 'But messire . . .'

'Do it, seaman!' says Modeste, grinning. 'When Tib speaks we all jump.'

So that's how I end up spending the night in very close quarters with three men and a boy. I have to say I've had better sleeping experiences, even inside this dream. The new combination of grunts, farts, and snorts is just too much, so within an hour I take Misou out to the clearing and lie there with him on my chest to keep me from freezing.

I'm stiff as a board at daylight, when Modeste comes in search of me. He rubs my chilly hands and face to bring them back to life and tells me that the seamen have returned to their boat to guide Lady Serina's barge nearer our landing.

Misou jumps down, shakes his body as though he's just been doused with water, then skips off to greet Tib.

'So Tib is summoned?' I am finally able to talk. 'He really has to go to his father?'

'We're both summoned. The fact that Lady Serina has come for us means we must go. We cannot flee, for our honour.'

'Surely it could be very dangerous? You said his father . . .'

Now Modeste is picking twigs off my habit. 'I just don't know, Florence. I know the Lady Serina wishes us both well. But her husband Helée? He's a difficult man. He's a weak man who presents himself as strong. And he worships the Emperor and the Empire above all. Even his family. That makes him dangerous.'

When we get back to the camp Tib is at the big table already sorting herbs. He beams steadily at me. 'My mother Serina comes today, Florence! She will love you and you will surely love her. We will greet her and go to my father. Modeste and I have prayed and I know this journey will be a good thing. We will all go. You as well. My mother will love you.'

I smile back at him. He's irresistible. As Modeste said to the seaman yesterday, when Tib speaks, we all jump.

TWENTY-FIVE
The Governor's Wife

The lady coming towards me could only be Tib's mother. Not much older than me, she has a broad, curvaceous figure under the folds of her embroidered linen tunic. Her yellow silk shawl is floor length, pinned over one shoulder with a copper brooch in the shape of a daisy with glittering petals of amber. The lady's hair, bright as a penny, is crimped and drawn back in a sculptural fashion, making her blue eyes wider and her sandy brows more marked. Unlike Modeste, or most of these Gauls, she is not at all dark.

Somewhere behind us Misou is barking wildly. The oldest seaman has him by the scruff of his neck.

This meeting is all quite formal. Modeste bows deeply and she nods, half smiling. Tib bows a little less deeply and she puts a hand on his shoulder. He looks at her quickly and then away. 'Mother . . . Lady Serina,' he says.

Lady Serina turns Tib's face so he's looking directly at her. 'Dearest Tib,' she says. 'You are nut-brown as a sailor. And how you have grown.' Tib pulls his face from her hand, but still he looks pleased.

I think she must have missed him sorely, though not, I think, as much as I've missed my Siri. No one could experience that much missing.

Lady Serina turns to Modeste. 'So, Doctor,' she says, 'you have taken good care of my son?'

Modeste nods and bows again. 'And will continue to do so, gracious lady.' He pauses. 'However I'm concerned about his being summoned to Good Fortune. Dare I ask – is it certain that the Governor will welcome Tib home? Or does he listen to Rome and wish the boy harm?'

She draws in a big breath and sighs a very deep sigh. 'A pity you should have to think so, Modeste. The truth is, the Governor *is* listening to Rome – or Nicomedia, where the court now sits. News of the work you and Tibery do here has

sailed on ships around the Interior Sea as far as Nicomedia;
it has travelled the roads of the Empire. Much of the talk is
about Tib's gift with those people tormented in their heads.
These tales of miraculous cures have drawn the attention of
the Emperor.' She lowers her voice. 'One might wish that were
not so.'

Modeste glances across at the seamen and the imperial
soldiers that attend the Governor's wife. 'One might indeed
wish that were not so, madam. But the boy has a true gift. Of
that there is no doubt.' She nods at him and the two of them
move away from us, towards the garden and the beehives,
where they're out of earshot. He is talking, making a point
with her, and she is frowning.

Then they stroll back and I hear him say, 'There cannot be
one thing without the other, Serina. The true healing comes
through him, not from him. You know that.'

His use of her name tells me there is more about these two
than mistress and servant: even though he is a Roman citizen,
Modeste – as he has told me – is the son of a man who had
been a slave to the Romans.

Lady Serina goes up to Tib and takes him by the shoulders.
'This is a great honour, Tibery. The Empress herself wishes
you to attend her at court. It seems the son of her daughter,
a great favourite with the Emperor – though alas merely
adopted – is sorely afflicted with a terrible *maladie*. The boy
has fits. He scratches himself. He tears his clothes. He must
be watched day and night. Knives are kept from him lest he
harms himself or someone else. There are such benighted
children in the world, so this might not seem extraordinary.
But for some reason the child has caught the Emperor's fancy.'
She glances at Modeste. 'Some say the child is closer to him
than a grandson.' Her voice falls silent.

The silence that follows fills with the morning call of the
nightingale.

She goes on. 'This is the thing, dear Tibery. The Empress
commands your presence at Nicomedia and there you will cure
this boy for the Emperor's sake. I come here at your father's
command. I am his agent. His emissary.' Her tone is grave.

Tib's face lights up in a grin. 'Of course. I can help the
poor boy, just as I help the people here in Gaul. These *mala-
dies* strike fisherman and princes alike . . .'

Modeste interrupts him. 'There is a condition, Tib. Hear the condition first!'

Serina's full lips tighten. 'You – both of you – will travel under the Emperor's protection. You will be perfectly safe. However, for your own safety, in your curing you may only invoke the extraordinary powers of the old gods, and the god emperors. There must be no other blessing, no mention of the Nazarene, no sign of the fish.'

I see that she's well informed of Tib's ways of working. It's not only travellers who have told her of her son's powers. Modeste has obviously acquainted her with these events. I see now that he is her agent. *Her* emissary here.

Tib is scowling now. 'Mother, this is not possible. I heal because I believe. It's only through my belief that the wonders occur.' He glances at Modeste. 'Oh! I know we make our own cures and they are natural wonders in themselves. But it's only through the spirit of the Nazarene that the impossible occurs.' His tone is firm, mature. I recall Modeste calling him an old soul.

Modeste and Serina exchange glances. Then Modeste shrugs. 'I think we have little choice in this matter, Tib.' He shows the boy the letter-scroll that Lady Serina has given him. 'This is a letter signed by the Empress herself, begging you – most politely – to come. Her beloved grandson is in danger and you are her last hope.' He pauses. 'It seems quite simple and straightforward. But it bears the Imperial seal. To refuse would be to declare yourself a traitor.'

The soldiers at the edge of the path shuffle their feet, short swords clicking against their metalled sheaths. Misou, still clutched by the scruff of his neck by the sailor, squeals again.

Modeste goes on. 'And there is another message here for me, from your father. He is very plain and direct, as is his custom. He tells me that unless you obey the Empress he will be forced to put you to death. He himself is threatened with death should you not go.'

Lady Serina tightens her grip on Tib's shoulder and whispers in his ear. 'Listen to me, dearest Tib. There are many here and right across the Empire, even in the heart of Rome, who look to the Nazarene, as do you and Modeste. These are people at all levels, not just rebels and heretics who insist that the Emperor martyrs them for their faith. But there are many good people who are biding their time, which will come, believe me.'

Of course. I know she's talking about herself.

The three of them stand staring at each other in silence. Then the tension is broken by Misou who wriggles out of the sailor's grasp, leaps to the ground and makes for Lady Serina. I scoop him up just in time and hold him struggling to my chest. I can feel Serina's bright blue eyes on me; see a glimmer of a smile around her mouth. 'So . . . who have we here, Modeste?'

'This is a new follower, Madam. A traveller who lives with us and helps our mission.'

Her lips twitch. 'And why, may I ask, have you a woman with you, Modeste? And in such a strange garb?'

He smiles. 'Madam, this is our friend Florence. We found her by the riverside, very wet and – well – a bit beside herself.'

He's right there. Maybe *outside herself* would have been a better way to put it. He could hardly say I swam into this time through the feast of Pentecost.

'Tib cured Florence of her sad condition,' he goes on smoothly. 'And now she helps us and we help her.'

'Florence is a great person,' butts in Tib. 'We found her raving by the river and now she's well. She takes care of us and we take care of her.' He echoes Modeste's words. He smiles at his mother. 'I told her she was beautiful, Mother. Nearly as beautiful as you.' This is a lot for Tib to say at once. He is a boy of few words.

Serina looks me up and down, then nods. 'I see. Well, I have clothes on the barge that are more suitable for your friend Florence.'

Misou yelps.

The Lady Serina holds my gaze. 'Woman of Gaul! Will you go to Nicomedia with these two recalcitrants? Will you continue to care for them on this journey?'

Woman of Gaul? Is that what I am? I glance across at them. Tib looks young again, quite anxious. Modeste watches me calmly. I think he knows my answer. Where else would I go?

I meet her gaze again. There is something about this woman. Something about her look. Something familiar. I scrabble in vain at the cobwebs in my mind. Misou, struggling in my arms, leaps into hers. She holds him tight and laughs out loud. 'What's this?'

'It's a dog,' says Tib, who frequently has a tendency to be over literal.

Misou is wriggling with joy, trying to lick the lady's plump cheek.

Modeste says quietly, 'Misou recognizes you, my lady. He recognizes you as his friend.'

The cobwebs in my head clear. I look again at this tall, plump, well-fed woman and am reminded of Misou's mistress, a much slighter, smaller and older woman, who sat and talked with me in a café. Somewhere . . .

Misou is quiet now, his head on her bosom. She is stroking him and peering into his eyes. 'It is good to have a friend,' she says.

'He's called Misou,' announces Tib. 'You should keep him.' He turns those eyes on me. 'She should keep him, shouldn't she, Florence?'

I'm used to Misou now. He's my friend. My fellow traveller in this dream wilderness. But I look at him in the arms of this Roman matron and I know he's found his true friend again. He's back with Madame Patrice.

The cobwebs lift, and then fall back again. I glance across at Modeste and he nods slightly, his eyes warning me not to comment. This clearly is his *reinvestment of the spirit*. Whether Serina came before Patrice, or the other way round, is not clear. I'm sure Modeste would say that's not the way to think of it. Time, he would say, is not merely a long measuring stick.

I nod my head and he smiles slightly.

'I will take care of Misou, Florence. You can be sure of that.' There's this familiar thread, this tone in her voice. Then the cobwebs fall back in place and now I just can't bring to mind the name of the woman in the café.

Then, stroking Misou's silky head, she turns back to Tib. 'So, will you do this, Tibery? For your father if nothing else?'

Tib looks at Modeste, who raises his eyebrows and keeps his face blank. Then Tib turns to his mother, his gaze just over her shoulder. 'So I will go. I will go for you and my father; I will go in the name of the Nazarene, and they may make of it what they wish.'

'But Tib, the risk!' I know the alarm in her voice. I myself should have felt alarmed when I sent Siri merrily away with her friend to play football. But I didn't. My heart clenches.

'Be calm, lady.' Modeste's voice has a warning in it. Again I see that their relationship is clearly equal, not one of mistress and servant. 'We will go. We must go. And Florence and I will keep good watch over him. And, as you know . . .' He pauses. And lowers his voice to a whisper. 'We have friends and comrades in Nicomedia. They are discreet but strong in their faith.'

So, she *is* one of them! I see this now.

She lets out a long sigh and relaxes. Misou escapes her tight grasp and climbs up on to her shoulder, just as he used to with . . . *Madame Patrice*, was that her name? 'We must go at once,' she says. 'Your father is waiting.'

Tib shakes his head stubbornly. 'Modeste and I must make stores of medicine for the people here. We must leave instructions and messages. We must assure them of our return.'

Modeste nods slowly. 'If we work quickly and tell the good people of Cessero our dilemma they will be our agents and pass on messages. There is quite a network now.' He takes Serina's hand. 'Return to your barge, lady. We will join you before dusk. If your rowers are as good as their reputation we will be docking at Good Fortune before nightfall. The Governor will have no complaint.'

Lady Serina turns away, then turns back to Modeste. 'Walk with me to the river, Modeste.'

Tib, already back at the table with his head over his herbs, does not look up when his mother says her farewells. 'Hurry!' he says to Modeste. 'There is so little time.'

Later, all our tasks completed, we follow the seamen through the thickets and brambles to the ornate barge and climb aboard by means of a cunning series of ladders. The rowers stand respectfully, their oars held like staffs. The old seaman gives a signal and the sailors pull in the ladders. The rowers move down below, set time, and we are away.

Modeste and Tib move forward and stand by the seaman Peter as he gives the sign to cast away and one of the rowers uses his single great oar to push the boat from the bank. Down below, unseen, the oarsmen easily, carefully, steer to the centre of this great river and start to row and the heavy, ornate barge drives through the river like a swift arrow. Then, eerily, a rhythmic song floats through the porthole gaps that allow the oars to move, keeping time with the splash of the oars. You can't see the rowers but you can hear their growling song as they work.

Lady Serina makes her way to the prow to greet us. She's obviously relieved. Perhaps she really did think we would all run away. Then again perhaps that was the sensible thing to do. She nods to them and turns and nods towards me. 'Come with me, Florence. My slaves will find you something less disgraceful to wear.'

So here am I standing in the small salon next to the prow of the boat being dressed like a Barbie doll by two elegant girl-children who laugh and giggle as they go about their task and occasionally stand back to admire their handiwork. They hold up a shadowy grey oval mirror glass in a copper frame. I have to admit it's an improvement. They put my hair up in quite tight braids and bleached bone pins and dress me in a simple floor-length tunic in green linen with an embroidered border. Then they set this wide fringed russet scarf around my shoulders and make me sit down while they buckle on supple green leather sandals.

When I go forward again the only comment is from Tib. 'Your hair! They've spoiled your hair! Where are your curls?'

His mother, standing behind him, her hands on his shoulders, tells him not to be silly. 'They haven't cut them off, have they?'

'They've spoiled it,' he says sadly. 'I like Florence best when she is wild. It's not the same.'

This sad, even sulky tone is unusual for Tib. Perhaps he, like us all, is worried about what is to come. I glance at Modeste whose great quest has now been thwarted. I look at the Lady Serina standing there, swaying slightly with the movement of the barge. Misou is coiled around her neck and her hands are on the shoulders of her son, the fringe on her shawl lifting in the breeze created by the forward thrust of the barge. Does she know about Modeste's quest? Is she his mysterious patroness?

The barge turns a wide sweep of the river and we can see now the port of Good Fortune. My eye searches in vain for the familiar mass of the black stone cathedral but all I see are a cluster of streets and houses and a busy wharf tumbling with ships. One of the rowers mounts the prow of our barge, puts a long horn to his lips and blows a high piercing signal. As we watch, other rowers cut the water frantically, making several boats pull away, clearing the way to a yellow and green painted landing stage under a wooden arch topped by a carving of an eagle.

Modeste puts a hand on my shoulder. 'Here we go, Florence!' he says, his lips close to my ear.

TWENTY-SIX
Empire

The journey from Good Fortune, then to Massalia was simple compared to the longer, much more perilous journey to the coast near the city of Nicomedia where the Imperial Court sits. We endured chilling storms at sea and three times I had to be tied to the mast to keep me from falling overboard.

But as we travelled south and then east, the air became hotter, the sky an unrelenting blue. I have to say the heat was good.

But it's not all been good. We were seized as soon as we landed. And here I am, flat on my face, arms spread, on a marble floor as big as a tennis court. The marble's not as cold as you'd think; rather it's kind of warm and soapy. Being so much further east, Nicomedia is much hotter than Good Fortune – the air, the bright plastered walls and the stones beneath your feet have the ambient warmth of storage heaters switched up high.

During those long days heaving up and down at sea I had time to think about this Imperial capital. I imagined buildings of grey stone like Durham Cathedral or the Houses of Parliament; I envisaged that sandy stone you generally associate with ancient ruins. But this place is all coloured marble, bright painted walls and gold flourishes on fluted stone pediments that flaunt statues in solid gold. On the floor beneath my flattened body horses are writhing in battle and heroes are vanquishing enemies. The image is so fine it could be a painting, but in fact it's made up of millions of tiny shards of coloured stone.

You might say art appreciation is slightly inappropriate for a woman in my position and you might be right. The truth is I've been examining all of this with such concentration to take my mind off the much more dangerous matter in hand.

Alongside me – equally prone – is Modeste. Our fingertips

are touching. In front of us I can see the soles of Tib's sandals
as he too lies like a starfish on this gorgeous floor. Because
he's the most important person of the three of us, he lies ahead
of us.

My neck aches. I turn my face to the other side to see the
silver and gold leather of banquette couches and the heavy-
duty studded leather soldiers' tabards – so many soldiers!
Modeste says this Emperor is more of a soldier than an
Emperor, keeping the whole of the world under his pagan heel.

Then I see jewelled sandal straps, the brown horny feet and
the sweeping hem of the long cloaks of courtiers in a cluster
alongside the plain leather sandals, the brown legs and the
shorter gear of lesser mortals. The air smells of burning sandalwood oil and lemon balm, cut through with the foetid canteen
stench of the great city.

It seems like hours ago, just when I was pushed on to my
knees, that I caught a glimpse of a woman, who, by her
clothes, must be the Empress. She was sitting on a great
throne, one of two. Beside her was an elegant, muscular black
man fluttering a great fan, creating some movement in this
dense, scent-laden air, saturated as it is with the breath of
supplicants.

I can hear the chirruping sound and the occasional shriek
of birds in cages. The only other distinct sound is the murmur
of voices of the men clustering around the Imperial thrones
as they mutter into the ears of the august couple, elaborating
on the earnest pleas of the people like ourselves who have
come here for an audience. It is these interlocutors, not the
Emperor, who transmit the judgements he mutters in their ears.

Twisting further and lifting my head a bit I catch a glimpse
of the Emperor's face. It's more rough-hewn than I expected
– chunky and strained, with heavy shadows under his eyes: a
soldier's face with the folded straight lip line of a leader.

Then at last amongst the murmurs I hear the name *Tibery*.
My heart beats loudly in my ears. Tib gets to his feet. Modeste
tries to get up too, but he's kept down by a narrow-faced
flunkey who taps his shoulder sharply with what looks like a
golden wand stuck with jewels as big as jelly babies. The
gems are genuine; they glow brightly in the light from the
torches that flicker on the walls.

Even without seeing Modeste's face I can feel his

frustration. He doesn't want to leave Tib standing there alone. Then we hear Tib's clear young voice piercing the throb of sound, as he answers the questions put to him. 'That is so, my lady.'

I hope he's looking straight at the Empress with those wide blue eyes of his. I hope he's not looking over her shoulder, as is sometimes his habit.

He goes on. 'I am well known in Gaul, my lady, for curing the sick and those troubled and afflicted in mind.'

Now there is more muttering between the Empress and the interlocutors. One of them speaks and Tib answers. 'Yes, my lady. It truly is my power to help the afflicted, to calm them down and make them kinder to themselves and those around them.' His voice is steady, composed.

I am proud of him.

Now the Emperor's interlocutor asks him a question.

'No, my lord, I do not invoke the power of Jupiter or any of the God Emperors in affecting my cures.' He pauses and I know Modeste's warnings are ringing in his ears. But Tib is incapable of dissembling. He goes on. 'I feel, my lord Emperor, that there is something in me that . . . sort of . . . straightens out the creases inside a person. As well as this I have some simple potions and tinctures that sustain the cure, make it last longer than my presence. So, you see, my lord, it really is quite a simple thing. There is no need to call on the gods or the God Emperors. It is a simple cure.'

More murmuring and the rustling of a parchment, then the Empress puts up a hand. I hear the clatter of heavy bracelets. And I hear her clear voice. 'You are very young, master Tibery, to be a healer of such reputation. I hear you healed your own father – a great servant of our empire – of his blindness?'

'That is so, my lady. I have a great mind and a great gift. This is undeniable. I have the knowledge of someone twice my height and twice my age. It is proven. My mother tells me this has been so since I was in my cradle. She tells me I cured my nursemaid of a dreadful pox by laying my small hand on her face.'

'And you think that this gift of yours will cure our poor benighted grandson of his mad affliction?' The clear round tones of her voice echo in my mind somewhere and a shiver goes down my spine.

Now Tib says, 'I am sure of it, gracious lady.'

Beside me I hear Modeste draw in a loud breath, worried, I know, at the direct boldness of Tib's claim. I know there have been times in their wanderings when a cure has not been affected, even though the afflicted one may be calmer, less agitated.

Then at last Tib moves backwards in our direction and Mr Goldwand taps both Modeste and me on the shoulder and leads us out of the chamber with Tib at his side. We trail him through anterooms, past fountains and pools, through a great atrium where one whole side is a great cage with two lions prowling amongst greenery. Tib is intrigued by what are to him very strange creatures, but Mr Goldwand sweeps us along like a housewife clearing her kitchen of rubbish. We're hurried up a staircase and through some wide double doors. Now we are in a high chamber with window grilles inset above eye level. There are paintings on the wall, of great landscapes dotted around with strange animals, only some of which I recognize.

The room is scattered with couches and long tables decorated in gold leaf. On one of these is a clock that works with water. Mr Goldwand lifts it and puts it down again. 'Wait here!' he says.

We watch the water clock until the double doors open again and the Empress sweeps in, dressed in a long silk tunic and an embroidered velvet over-gown. She has a gauze veil over her head and across her face. Beside her is a soldier, a great giant of a man whose skin shines like ebony. In his arms is a waif of a child of about six or seven with a pale face and rough hair and bite and scratch marks on his arm from wrist to elbow. Occasionally he clamps his mouth to his forearm to muffle the screams and sobs.

Ignoring the noise the Empress speaks quietly to Modeste. I can tell somehow that they know each other. Then she turns to Tib. He bows to her, a very low bow. I have never seen him bow so low to anyone before. *Render unto Caesar the things which are Caesar's*. Those words from the Bible flash though my mind.

The Empress looks down at Tib and says gravely, 'Thank you for making such a great journey to come to our aid, Master Tibery. Your gifts and your spirit are greatly needed here.'

No glance in my direction. I might not be here.

The Empress nods to the soldier. He sets the boy down but still he clings to the soldier's beefy thigh, his eyes wide with fear, one wrist clamped in his mouth.

Tib goes and stands before the child and then glances back at the Empress. 'Is there some small place, lady, where I can sit with the boy? This place is too high, too wide. A person cannot find their size in a place like this.'

She nods at the stout serving woman who stands close behind her. The woman opens the narrow door to what looks like a closet or dressing room. Tib puts out a hand towards the boy, palm up. And he waits. Finally the child unclamps his hand from his mouth and puts it, shining with spit and beaded with blood, into Tib's hand. The serving woman directs the two boys into the room and closes the door behind them.

Then the Empress glides across the marble floor to a window grille set in the wall. Modeste and I follow her. Through the grille we see a small room lined with great wooden chests. A tall mirror of polished silver set with shadowy glass stands at one end, and a long sleeping couch at the other. I wonder to myself whether her husband, or some other person, watches the Empress robe or disrobe through this same grille.

Now we watch Tib as he puts an arm round the shoulder of the trembling child and whispers in his ear. With his other hand he strokes the boy's tear-stained face. This goes on for an endless twenty minutes. But finally the boy is perfectly calm, his hands quietly on his knees. Tib makes a sign on his brow. There is a flicker between the Empress and Modeste. He nods and she smiles very faintly.

Then Tib takes the child's hand and leads him out of the small room and up to his great soldier-nurse who nods gravely at Tib then sweeps the child up, up on to his shoulder. The child hugs his broad head and smiles.

The Empress and her serving woman clap their hands. 'A cure indeed!' she says. 'Thank you, Master Tibery and thank you, Doctor Modeste.' She graces him with a title.

Now I'm feeling far too invisible. I long for the Empress to look at me, directly into my eyes as she does into theirs.

Tib takes out two horn containers from the satchel that Modeste has been carrying and hands them to the big soldier, looking into his eyes. 'Add a pinch of this to hot water for the boy to drink at sunset and sunrise. Be kind to him. Stay calm in yourself. I will return tomorrow to see him.' The great man bows to Tib, then turns to bow more deeply to the Empress and, the boy clinging happily to his head, he leaves the room.

The Empress turns to Modeste. 'You will stay here in rooms tonight, Doctor?'

He shakes his head. 'You are gracious, my lady. But we have lodging nearby with good friends.' He pauses. 'Friends who might be known to you.'

She stares at him and nods slowly. 'I see this. You must go to your friends.' It's hard to see her eyes under her veil but clearly there's a familiarity between them.

Then my knees sag and I realize just how exhausted I am with all this strangeness and uncertainty. This is turning out to be a very hard dream. Modeste reaches out to catch me, his arm tight round my shoulder. I can feel him nodding over my head to the Empress. I want to be away from here, on my own with Modeste and Tib. More than that, at this moment I want to be out, out of this dream while I know it for what it is.

The Empress turns to follow the boy, lifting her veil back over her head as she goes. On her way through the door she throws a backwards, smiling glance in my direction. My brain freezes and I clutch Modeste tightly to stop me falling over again.

As the stout serving woman leads us down steps, my brain is racing. We follow her through rooms and anterooms, past fountains and bright pagan sanctuaries smoky with votive candles, carefully placed to illuminate statues and painted portraits. As we near the colonnade that will take us outside, I tug Modeste's arm. 'Who was that woman? Who was that really?'

'The Empress. You know who it was.'

'But you know her. You know her more than that.'

His voice loses its humour. 'Wait, Florence! Hold your tongue,' he says sharply, glancing around.

The serving woman hands us over now to Mr Goldwand who sniffs in general displeasure before stalking on under the colonnade, indicating that we should follow him.

When we are outside, clear of the great gates, away from all these dangerous strangers, Modeste taps Tib on the shoulder.

'You did well there, Tib. Even in one encounter you made great progress with that benighted child.'

Tib smiles up at him then glances sideways. 'With the blessing of our great teacher, and of our own God-given medicines, the boy will be calmer, less fearful. He'll not hate his very own flesh. He'll seem calmer to others and they will not fear him. He may even now be able to cure himself. It's in the hands of our Lord.'

Modeste draws in a deep breath. He seems less sure of himself. It might seem simple to Tibery but none of this is straightforward for him. At present he is bent on our survival, which involves pleasing the Empress, who, it seems, is his friend. He puts an arm around Tib's shoulder. 'We need to be discreet, Tib, if we are to continue our work. The Emperor is about to move again against our church . . .'

So *that* was what they were whispering about.

'One slip could mean death for us. Be discreet!'

Tib twists out of his grasp. 'We must not deny our faith, Modeste! You taught me this.' He says this severely as though, of the two of them, he were the adult.

'But discretion is essential my dear lad, here in the shadow of the Imperial Palace Martyrdom may seem sweet to some but we'll be of no use to anyone with our heads separated from our shoulders. We've worked too hard to get to this moment. Come!' He charges on ahead, stamping his displeasure into the glittering black stones that line the road. *He* is every inch the adult now, and we are the children trailing behind.

He leads the way without pause to a row of narrow shop fronts and knocks on a door. The door is opened by a dark, thickset man in a knee-length felt tunic with bound leggings underneath. When he sees Modeste he reaches out to hug him, a broad toothless smile splitting his face. He steps outside the house and shuts the door. 'Come! Come,' he says and leads the way through a series of narrower alleyways and lets himself into a house with steps up to the roof, where we find another doorway on a superstructure on top of the roof. Inside are three wooden sleeping bunks and two stools. A small shelf holds a stoneware jug and a lump of bread. Underneath it is a wooden bucket of clear water.

'Latrine on the corner of the roof, lets down into the stream below,' the man says briefly. 'You should sleep now. And tomorrow I'll bring you food and we'll talk. There's a meeting at dawn.' Then he vanishes into the darkness. At this moment I'm relieved, pleased when he goes. I've seen enough strange things today to last a lifetime.

What I really want to do is sit and think about that brief backward glance that the Empress cast in my direction. I tell you here and now that what I saw in that glance was my Siri absolutely to the life – not in the face nor the person just that particular, peculiar *look*. But I'm too tired now, even to think about this. Not now. All I can do is fall on to the couch and let the muttering chat between my companions lull me gratefully into a dreamless sleep.

Later. I'll think about all that later.

TWENTY-SEVEN
Remembering Forwards

I t's dark when I wake up. My thighs and the small of my back ache, and my mouth feels full of dry sandpaper. I lean over to rake around in my sack, take out my monk's habit and pull it over the now dusty court clothes given to me by the Lady Serina all those weeks ago just as we left Good Fortune.

This hut on the roof of the shop is deserted. No Modeste. No Tib. I dip my hands into the wooden bucket and splash water on my face, drag my fingers through my hair and re-tie the cue. Then I take a deep breath and make my way down into the house. I follow the sound of murmuring voices through the ground floor rooms into a broad space that smells of horses and chickens. Three doors lead off it. From behind the narrowest door I can hear the prayers and invocations familiar to me now from Modeste and Tib's morning rituals.

Suddenly I'm pushed from behind with a force that flings the door open. The people inside look around, startled. A circle of people are standing around a table with three smoking candles at its centre. In the circle are Modeste and Tib, the man from last night and a woman who must be his wife. At the end of the table are two grander ladies in long hooded cloaks: the Empress and her servant woman. The Empress catches me with her glance and I feel again that iron clutch at my heart.

Someone is holding me by the neck of my habit and I'm nearly choking. His deep voice is in my ear. 'I found her listening at the door, my lady.' It's the tall man from the palace: the one who cooled the Empress with the fan no doubt keeping watch for her.

Modeste comes forward, removes the man's hands from my neck, and smooths down my habit. Even here, in this situation, my body thrills to this touch. He puts one arm around me and brings me into the circle of light. 'You recall our friend

Florence, my lady? She was with us at the palace. She's not one of us but she's no threat. She travelled with us from Gaul.'

'Does she not follow the Way?' The Empress's voice is quite sharp.

Modeste hesitates. 'She's a learner, my lady. A student. She wishes to understand us.'

I move further into the light so I can see this woman properly and she can see me. Again I have to tell you, no kidding, that when I look into her eyes I see Siri. There you are! I'm as mad as that boy who bites his arms. I'm mad and this is a mad dream. I look into the eyes of this fifty-year-old woman and I see Siri, my little girl.

She stares at me, frowning. 'Your name is—'

Tib interjects. 'Her name is Florence. She came to us with flowers in her hair.'

I keep my eyes on hers. 'But . . . in another world,' I say slowly and clearly forcing myself to remember in the fog of the dream. 'In another life, my lady, my name is Estella, sometimes called Starr. And in that life I had a daughter called Siri . . .'

A flicker of light catches those grave eyes. 'That is a pretty name. *Siri.* How did you come by such a name?'

Hard, this. 'It was given to her by the midwife who delivered her.' I pause. 'She looked into my baby's eyes and said she had a *very* old soul, as though she'd been here before. I called my daughter after this woman.'

The Empress stares at me, hard, for a very long moment. Then she blinks and turns back to Modeste. 'You and the boy must be very careful, Modeste. Whether or not you cure my grandson you will still be in danger. Already I've been told I myself must sacrifice to the old gods to appease them for calling for your help. And sacrifice more to ensure that it appears the old gods have affected a cure.' She pauses. 'I hear that you and the boy will also be called on to make offerings to the old gods.'

'Never!' says Modeste.

'Never!' echoes Tib.

She sighs and turns to me.

'Never ever!' My turn to echo.

This is interesting. I've never joined in the prayers of those two in our camp, and they've never asked me to. I've watched with respect as they went about their worship. I've watched them at their work in Cessero and the wider countryside of Gaul. I've watched them at prayer in travelling wagons and on the deck of the ships on the endless journey here. I've seen them heal sailors and beggars. I've done all this and never been tempted to join in their worship. But now they're in danger and I must stand up for their beliefs.

It's even more complicated, of course. I know that Modeste himself has a secret, even from his devoted and beloved Tib. His great faith in this growing church of theirs, in their brave cause, in their One God is compromised by his intellectual problem with the fundamental tenet of their faith: a man-made God who died and rose again to be taken up into Heaven. In this lower room only *I* know this, only *I* know of his search for the bones – or even the person – of the Nazarene brought to Gaul in the aftermath of those events more than two hundred years ago. Even Tib doesn't know that.

I've learned so much from Modeste. And now, having glimpsed Madame Patrice in Tib's mother, and seen Siri in the eyes of Diocletian's Empress, I have a lot more time for Modeste's idea of the reinvestment of great spirits. His theory now makes more sense to me, but it leads him down the road of yet another heresy against his own young church: that their Nazarene did not rise again but died like any mortal man, his bones protected by a journey to Gaul and secret burial there.

So where does that leave me, in this dream? I'm in the company of an Empress who is a member of a proscribed church where having one's head chopped off for one's faith is the best death among the most grizzly fates. Weird. *Alice Through the Looking Glass* has nothing on this. *Off with his head! Off with her head!*

Now the room is filled with bustle as the Empress and her maid take their leave. As she passes me she puts a hand on my arm and kisses my cheek with soft lips. 'God's blessings on you, stranger. You have a good soul.'

I put my hand up to my cheek. Tib catches my eye and stares straight at me. He nods his head. 'I told you,' he says quietly.

TWENTY-EIGHT
The Fish Mark

I t takes Tib and Modeste five days and five nights to establish the cure for the Emperor's grandson. As well as Tib attending and soothing the boy by the laying on of hands, the process involves Tib and Modeste consulting at night in our lodgings and praying with others in the lower room. We all talk a good deal with the boy's soldier nursemaid, who loves the boy and never leaves his side. Modeste explains to him about the calming herbs and the need for fresh fruit and clean water every day without fail. He shows him how to pound fresh chicken liver into a paste with herbs to make it palatable on bread.

The Empress and her maid come and watch through the grille as Tib and Modeste go about their work. She is gracious with me, but guarded. I know she has felt our connection but grand as she is, is unsure of what it means. Here is this woman, the greatest in her land, beloved of the Emperor, who must be the envy of the women of her time. Modeste tells me she's more than this; she is a fine scholar and seeker of the truth. I realize now that she's Modeste's sponsor at court, and even perhaps the inspiration for his quest for the truth about the fate of the Nazarene. I wonder if she, like Modeste, hangs on to this core of scepticism that could threaten their fragile young church.

As well as these strictures, on two sunny afternoons we take the boy outside the city walls for walks in the countryside with the soldier nursemaid carrying the boy on his shoulders. We point out the birds and show him flowers and Tib manufactures a simple press for him to use to preserve the flowers and begin to make a collection. The boy begins to find his own flowers and hold them up in delight. Modeste forages with the soldier for herbs and teaches him how to use them for the boy.

On the second afternoon the boy lets me hold his hand and

leads me to a shrub to show me the flowers he has found. I remember doing this with Siri and it makes me smile, glad to think of the half-remembered pleasure.

On the fifth day the Empress sends a chariot for us and we take the boy to the coast. Modeste and I sit side by side on the shore and watch as the soldier and Tib entice the boy into the water. They play this game of ducking into the sea and coming up like porpoises. The boy laughs at the merry game and stands quite still as Tib makes the fish mark on his forehead.

Beside me Modeste stirs. 'Time, I think, that we travel back to Gaul to continue our work. The boy is cured. See? The bite marks have healed completely.'

On the shore they all strip off to their bare skin before rubbing themselves with dry cloths and putting on the fresh clothes we have brought. Later the boy sits on my knee as the soldier guides the chariot past farms and along narrow track-ways back into the city. Men leaning on tools and boys up trees watch our progress through the streets. Some of them bow very low indeed.

On that last night Modeste and Tib go out alone and when they return to the lower room they have the boy with them. Modeste says they had to put a potion into the soldier's drink to get the boy away. 'He visits Lethe for a long while. We will get the boy back before he knows a thing.'

The boy is here to be blessed by the larger local community of believers. Modeste has his doubts about this. He recognizes the risk and thinks it's unnecessary. But Tib insists it must be done. 'Otherwise, dear Modeste, the cure will not be fixed. The boy will tumble backwards into his old ways.'

There are strangers in the room. Modeste assures me that no one here knows the identity of the child in their midst. But I am uneasy. They must know from his fine tunic that he's no ordinary boy.

The little ceremony has become familiar to me. A man reads from a scroll, which is a copy of those in Modeste's posses-sion – a letter of Paul of Tarsus to the citizens of Corinth. Then Modeste talks about the greatness of Paul: 'The letter urges us to keep the faith and not quarrel amongst ourselves,' he says firmly.

Then Tib blesses the wine and bread and takes it around to

everyone in the circle. They all take turns in doing this. Tonight it is Tib's turn. When he reaches the boy he turns to the company and says something about him. The boy is watching the proceedings with wide eyes. He's calm now. He has lost his wild look and the deep bite marks on his arms are entirely gone. I know this is more than just ordinary healing.

Now Tib puts a hand on the boy's shoulder and looks him deep in the eyes before making the fish mark on his forehead. Then, one by one, each person in the circle does the same. That is except me. I shake my head. I look round and protest that I'm a simple stargazer, no expert in these things.

The Empress is waiting in a closed chariot in a nearby alleyway. Her sturdy servant woman is holding the head of the horse. Tib holds a flaring torch and Modeste lifts the boy into the chariot and he climbs on to her knee. He puts an arm around her neck and sits there, still and content. She lifts her veil and peers at Tib. 'Thank you, Master Tibery. You have restored to us our child shorn of his affliction. I honour you.'

Tib and Modeste bow very deeply and I follow suit. Modeste speaks clearly in the darkness. 'You keep the faith, my lady. You know the Way. That is enough.'

She bows her head to him and turns those eyes – Siri's eyes – on me. 'And you, Florence. Do you keep the faith?'

I look into those eyes for a few seconds, willing her to know who I really am. Who she really is. 'I am a stranger in these places, my lady. A mere stargazer out of my time. But I love and honour the work of Doctor Modeste and Master Tibery. I honour it, and I keep its secrets.'

Her veil lifts in the air as she shakes her head. 'There is something particular about you, madam. Something I can't quite put my finger on. Something that renders my mind into a fog.' She pauses. 'I sense we must have met before, Florence. But that can't be so.' Then she blinks and adjusts her veil. I can see her shaking the feeling off and I am deeply sad. Bereft. All around us is the rustle of the night, the rush of the stream that serves the latrines.

The Empress hugs the boy to her. 'The boy's absence must not be noted. We must return at speed.'

'Lady,' I say, to keep her here for just a few moments. 'The boy's parents? Where are they?'

'Modeste will tell you that the Emperor has adopted the

boy, who is my daughter's son. His stepfather, my son-in-law, is away campaigning in the East. I've sent his mother, my daughter, on a mission for me to Rome. She was disturbed by his condition and is carrying another child. I can't have her mixed up in all this. Too dangerous for her.' She sinks back on the cushions and hugs the boy to her. The servant woman climbs aboard, flicks the horse with a small whip and drives the chariot forward, skilful as any man.

We stand and watch the chariot as it rocks down the narrow alleyway. Modeste claps his hands and rubs them together. 'A job well done, friends. Now we can return to Good Fortune and Cessero. God's own country. We've work to do there.'

Tib nods his head, his red hair glittering in the light of his torch. 'Our bees will be buzzing around for us,' he says. He sounds young and boyish again: not like the grave healer he's been these last few days. I'll be glad too, to return. On the long journey and the short stay here I have not been properly alone with Modeste and I miss him. I so need the refreshment of our private times. This refreshment is both physical – the sheer joy of our bodies entwined – and mental, the puzzling challenge of our conversations. They help me keep balance in this time and this place. They sustain the reality of this dream, almost like charging a battery.

We climb up to our roof eyrie for one last time where I sleep in one corner on a low couch and they sleep in another corner together on a kind of long shelf. And because I know I have to wake to travel in the morning I find it hard to get to sleep. I remember the rocking boat and the endless journey. Returning will be no simple thing. Then when I do sleep I dream of Siri: a dream within a dream you might say. Dangerous. In my dream Siri is dead, laid out on this long soapy marble slab decorated with writhing horses. She is dressed in an embroidered tunic – a miniature of that worn by the Empress under her flowing cloak. Someone is hovering over her body with a golden stick, using it to point to her head, her chest, her shoulders. I hear phrases like *sustained bruising* and *blows to the chest and the side of the head*. The tunic is stained with blood. But as well as this Siri is standing beside me, pale and shaking but here still whole and unbruised, pulling at my sleeve like she did when she was a very little girl. 'Come *on*, Mummy!'

I wake up sweating and terrified. Then I force myself to breathe very deeply ten, twenty times. Now I conjure up the face of the woman in the chariot, the face of a woman in her prime. And I'm certain that within that great soul is the living soul of Siri, whose life with me was so, so short. Here surely is the life after and the life before death – Modeste's *reinvested spirit*.

Then like a lightning bolt, here among these brave people who are risking all for their faith, I'm visited by the blasphemous thought that the truth is not about some man-made ritualized magic about a man who died and rose again in three days. The truth is this DNA of the spirit that reinvests itself, generation after generation.

Now I'm aching for some private time with Modeste, to try to put these wild thoughts into a coherent cosmic whole. Of course, the legacy of Paul of Tarsus has made him a true believer in the great spirit force for good of the man he calls the Nazarene. But over and above all this, Modeste has seen the world and time in a pattern that can incorporate those beliefs into an even larger whole.

At this point my meandering thoughts are shattered by the deep bark of men's voices. My ears are assaulted by the hammer of footsteps up the stone steps. I leap to my feet to see that the palliasse on which Modeste and Tib sleep is empty. I pull my habit up to my chest and draw right back into the corner.

The door bursts open and a man in a metal ringed tunic fills the open doorway. At his shoulder is the other man from the palace, the man with the rod of gold: the one who kept us in order on that first day in the palace. Mr Goldwand. 'That is the woman,' he says, gasping, his voice puny with excitement. 'Florence is her name. Take her!'

I need Modeste. I need Tib. Where are they? I put my chin up and look him in the eye. 'Are you a spy?' I say. He brings up his stick – this one a wooden one, tipped with a golden fox head – and strikes me hard in the shoulder. The violence of the blow makes me drop to my knees. 'I am the servant of the Emperor,' he snarls. 'My mission is to protect him from heretical bitches like you and your dog friends.

'But I'm not . . .'

He was already turning away. 'Bring her down,' he says to

the guard. 'The only way to stop this vermin spreading their filth around this city is to clear them out.'

Down below in the courtyard, trussed like turkeys, are the lodge keeper, Modeste and Tib. They must have been disturbed and come down before I heard the footsteps pounding on the stairs. The others must have got away. Modeste's cheek is blighted by a black and blue bruise the shape of a fox head. Tib, also trussed up, meets my gaze tranquilly enough. There is no fear in his eyes. But my heart is full of fear for him, and for all of us.

'Florence!' says Modeste. 'Don't—' Another blow across the cheek with the fox stick stops him saying anything further.

Goldwand directs a soldier to tie my arms behind my back and to hobble my legs with a length of rope. That done, the soldier throws me over his shoulder like a sack of coal and my calls for Modeste are muffled by the soldier's metallic tunic. He throws me into a wooden wheeled barrow and then covers me with some kind of canvas. I can smell the sea. This canvas has been a sail at one time. Are they going to throw me into the sea?

The barrow jerks and then moves forward. The man could be pushing or pulling it. I don't know what's happening to me. I've lost my Modeste and my young Tib. I don't know what will happen to them. Or me. *Tib. Modeste.* My brain freezes with fear as I am bumped along.

With all my heart and all my soul I wish that this dream would end. It's all too hard. I wish I could see my stars on their eternal path through the heavens. I wish I was back on the roof of the Maison d'Estella, staring up at Virgo and Ursa Major. My heart was broken then, but things were so much simpler. I find myself wishing . . .

Star light, star bright,
The first star I see tonight.
I wish I may, I wish I might,
Have the wish I wish tonight.

TWENTY-NINE
The Fox

I crouch here in the smallest of spaces. I think I've been in this poky, stinking space for two days and two nights. There's this window slit high in the wall and in daytime it fills the room with grim grey light; at night the room is pitch black. I've made marks in the hard earth floor with my heel: one for each night. I realized straight away that keeping track of time would be a useful thing to do. I read this once in an autobiography of a man who had been taken hostage and survived. Find a means of keeping track of time.

I have to use the corner of the room as a latrine and I survive on water thrust through a hole in the door every few hours. For two nights I've not even seen the night sky. Not one star. At first the darkness by night and the dimness by day engulf me. And this forces me inwards, makes me contemplate this dream I'm inhabiting or which is inhabiting me – I don't know which.

Every hour or so, as my mind drifts, I deliberately bring Modeste's face before me. And then I call up Tib's honest, wise stare. I've been bringing them into my mind the day I saw them both in Agde, the town that in these times they call *Good Fortune*. I think of them on the canal boat – Modeste with his book and the boy swimming in the water, racing the boat. I remind myself of Modeste in the guise of Louis, the twenty-first-century scholar with a mission leaning out of his window, his shirt cuffs flying like white flags.

I remember lying on the roof of my house with Olga by my side, looking up at the night sky for Virgo and invoking that wish. I remember Madame Patrice in the café with Misou, her little dog. How glad I was that she, unlike Philip (*was that his name?*) had seen the redheaded boy. And I conjure up the vision of Tib's mother Serina who – in her deep soul – is also Madame Patrice and also loves Misou. And in these two dark days in this stinking cell how many times have I conjured up that backward glance of the Empress, which contains so much of my Siri in its bright gaze?

This is all very hard but I feel I'm making this painful effort so I can remember a safer future, to give myself some distance from this stinking room where I am forced to use the corner as a latrine.

In the middle of the third night the door creaks open and standing there is the Goldwand, Fox Man in his grand cloak. A soldier moves in front of him, sticks his flaring torch into a metal holder, hauls me to my feet and stands behind me, his hands on my upper arms.

The Fox looks around the space, his small nose wrinkling. I'd estimate that he shares Hitler's star sign. Aries tipping over into Taurus. A dangerous combination.

'Ah! Madam Florence,' he says, smiling. 'I thought you'd be entranced to know that we have broken the boy. I have to say that he was a hard nut to crack. Did not waver, even when he witnessed the terrible sufferings of his teacher. As I say, he was a hard nut to crack, with that blank gaze of his.' The man's eyes glitter in the flickering light of the torch. 'But in the end . . .'

I turn my face from him. I want to put my hands over my ears to shut out this evil talk but that is impossible. The soldier is holding tightly to my upper arms. Tears run down my face. I am sobbing.

The Fox sniffs and goes on. 'The key to my success is this nail board I had especially made for vermin. It has a very good mechanism that stretches the soul out of a person. In the end the boy was begging – begging – me to allow him to rise from the bed of nails and pay sacrifice to our proper gods rather than that degenerate Nazarene.'

'No! No!' I shake my head and my tears fly around the room, glittering in the torchlight. 'I don't believe you. Tib is a brave soul, a true believer. He would not betray his faith. Never!'

The Fox giggles out loud at this. 'You will see, madam. It will be proved for your own eyes.' His eyes narrow slightly. 'Your lover the doctor has a much more intractable soul. He resisted our finest persuasions. Our best! Our finest!' He pauses. 'Even her gracious majesty the Empress could not prevail upon him. She asked him to join her in her holy sacrifices to our gods but he refused her.'

His mention of the Empress sets warning bells away in me. She must be in danger too. Someone must have betrayed her as well as us. 'I don't believe you!' The words burst from me. Then I stop. Part of me wishes I could tell him I am really from another place and although I don't believe in his pagan Roman gods, neither do I quite believe in the divinity of the Nazarene for whom Modeste and Tib – and now the Empress – risk their lives. *I am neutral!* I want to shout at him. *I am neutral about these things.*

My back is aching and my arms are sore in the clasp of the soldier. It would be so easy to placate the Fox with a half-confession that although I don't believe in the Roman gods that I've read about in primary school text books, I also don't believe in what Tib and the people in the lower room believed. I believe in the stars and the universe of the sky and the universe of inner personality. And now I half-believe in Modeste's notion of reinvestment of the spirit because I've seen evidence of it with my own eyes. *So I have my own crazy church in my head and don't want any of yours, thank you very much.*

He pokes me in the ribs with his fox stick, a flare of anger in his eyes. 'Pay attention, woman. I want you to tell me of these two reprobates and their deviant ways.' He lifts his stick and brings it down on my shoulder. The pain is overwhelming. I squeeze my eyes to stop shameful tears falling.

My eyes move to the wall, then raise to a narrow interior grille, like the one where I stood by the Empress and her woman, and watched Tib work on his cure of the little boy. I know she's there now. And there's someone at her side. A man: a bulky shape.

'I will tell you about them, sir.' The words force themselves through my lips.

'A-aoh!' There is pleasure in that exhalation, satisfaction at a task nearing its end.

I take a deep breath. 'I have never seen either of those two – neither man nor boy – do a bad thing.' I raise my voice, so that my words may be heard through the grille. 'The last thing I saw them do, here in the Imperial Palace, was to take the poor crippled soul of a boy and straighten it out. They stopped him destroying himself. They saved his life.'

The stick comes down hard, sideways this time, on my legs. I stagger. The soldier behind me keeps me upright.

I go on. 'And before that I saw them cure many people of their physical ailments. But mostly I saw them dissolve the madness in many poor souls and restore them to laughter.'

Thwack! On my face. I don't know if I can stand this. I look up at the grille and force my bruised mouth to form my words. 'I wish to see the Empress. *She* saw Modeste and Tib help the grandson of the Emperor. I want to look her in the eyes.'

Thwack! I hear a cry of protest somewhere outside my swimming head. The soldier behind me moves uneasily. I can smell his sweat, even in this stinking space.

The Fox man growls, 'Slaves like you may never look on the great and holy.' There is spit in one corner of his mouth.

Thwack! This time the fox stick hits me across the face. Blood in my eyes; swimming darkness. In the mist I hear a bell ringing. A neat, clear sound, like the one you ring in hotels when you want service. Then total blank darkness. I have a vision of the night sky but there are no stars. It is all a deep blue-black. It's a terrible thing, a night sky with no stars.

My fingers creep to my shoulder to press it hard: to make it ache more. My head is splitting. I breathe in very slowly to thin out the pain. Slowly, slowly a reaction ripples through me from my head to my heels. Then I realize that I'm breathing in clear sweet air that's not rank and foetid as it has been for days. I open my eyes to see the white sunlight of early morning flooding past wide open shutters through long window spaces.

I close my eyes. When I open them again it's pitch black beyond the windows and the space in here is lit by lamps. Now I can feel gentle hands stroking ointment on my bruised shoulder. I twist sideways and I see the broad face of the Empress's serving woman, I turn the other way and see the Empress herself sitting on a high-backed chair beside the couch on which I lie. Her troubled eyes meet mine; underneath and above them her skin is dark, shadowy. She looks older. 'Lie still, Florence,' she says quietly.

'Where am I?'

'I came to get you. Lie still. Sarah will help you with your pain.'

I close my eyes and just lie there under those soothing hands, taking in the scent of lavender and some kind of resin. The hands stroke away not just the pain but the humiliation of being at the mercy of the Fox. Someone – it must be the woman called Sarah – has washed me top to toe. I can smell lavender and bergamot; I can feel clean linen against my skin. I am changed. Mine is not the stinking body left on its own in a filthy cell for days on end; not the body punished by the Fox Man for his own delight.

At last Sarah lifts me to a sitting position and drops a silk tunic over my head. She makes me stand and smooths the silk down my waist and on to my thighs. She sits me down again and lifts my legs back on to the couch, then she leaves.

The Empress sighs. 'Now, Florence,' she says hesitantly.

'Why has this happened, lady?' I burst in. 'Why have you let this happen? We tended your grandson. He is well now!'

She looks at me steadily and I try to stop Siri being there in her eyes. I try to make this woman into the stranger she really is to me. I'm angry with *her.* But not in this or any world do I want to be angry with my Siri.

I storm on. 'And what about Modeste and Tib? The Fox Man did those terrible things to them. Did he really do that? Allow Tib to see the torture of Modeste? Did Tib fall to his persuasion? I can't . . .' A sob catches my throat. 'And Modeste . . .'

She leans across and puts a hand on my lips, to stop the words tumbling from my mouth. 'Enough! I've been tried enough with all this suffering.'

All right for her, I think sourly. 'You!' I say. 'That horrible man, the man with the fox rod . . .'

'He's but an instrument, Florence, recruited for his base character. He's but a willing instrument for his allotted task. A cunning, resourceful man who knows how to twist minds his way. But he does it at the command of others.'

My head is aching. 'Others? Who? The Emperor?'

She shakes her head. 'The Emperor's a soldier. He works only for the good of the Empire. But he's loyal to the old gods and his advisers fear this new sect whose beliefs, they believe, will flush away the world as we know it. And replace it with . . . who knows what?'

'But you joined Modeste and his friends in the lower room for the blessings! And Tib and Modeste rescued the Emperor's grandson from that terrible sickness. They're good, mild people, as are their friends, whatever sect they belong to.'

'Things are not so clear-cut, Florence,' she sighs. 'Look at this! One part of His Imperial Majesty is pleased at their success with the boy. Even grateful. He's not a terrible man. His grandson climbs to his knee and plays with his beard. But the Emperor is a soldier. He's responsible for the greatest empire the world has ever seen. Now he sees it as his mission to stop it collapsing from within, or being invaded from without. He relies on his soothsayers, who see this new sect as fouling the Empire with a new religion that only sees one God and despises the old gods of Rome. Now these Emperor's soothsayers have seen the future and he's approved a new edict to destroy them, to wipe out all people like Modeste and his friends.'

I sit up straighter so I can scowl at her. 'But us? Tib and Modeste? How were we betrayed?'

Her shoulders move in a shrug under her velvet cloak. 'It was the child. He dipped his finger in the Emperor's wine and made the sign of the fish on his grandfather's forehead. The sign that Tibery made on the boy's forehead in the sea.'

My heart sinks as I imagine the drama of this moment. 'Cat out of the bag,' I say.

She frowns, then smiles. 'Ah yes, such a quaint saying.'

'So they came to find us?'

'Yes. And I was called before the Emperor and his Oracles. I had to assure them I had nothing to do with the sect and they told me to persuade Tibery and Modeste to recant. I tried to do so but they would not. Modeste smiled his forgiving smile at me. Then, in my presence they were badly abused but still would not recant. I stood there and watched them, but I stayed silent, fearing that my turn would be next.'

My distaste, my revulsion, must show on my face.

'You look askance?' she says. 'Martyrdom is sought after these days by believers, determined to live in eternity on the right hand of God. It's almost fashionable.' She shakes her head. 'But I have to be practical. I have more work to do here. I'm sure of it. One more martyr will make no difference.'

'But we're no threat to the Empire, lady! We're just people who live in a place by the sea called Good Fortune. Tib and Modeste help people, the most ordinary of people.'

She draws her breath in another deep sigh. 'Don't you understand that the oracles and their advisers see this as a problem? The fact that you influence ordinary people to believe in the Nazarene through your good works? To them, that threatens the Empire from within.' She falls silent and seems to sink within herself. Even from my poor bruised body my heart goes out to her.

'And Modeste and Tib?' I whisper. 'Are they dead?'

She shakes her head. 'Young Tibery did not give into them. They became afraid of him because his body healed itself before their eyes when they rested from their savage labours. And the stalwart Modeste resisted the most awful assaults although he does not have Tibery's gift of healing and remains injured. And you yourself didn't concede.'

I shake my head. 'You saw me?'

'Yes. Through the grille. The Emperor saw too. He heard your cry and commanded it to stop.'

'Why? Why has he decided to give up on us? Wouldn't our deaths still have been a victory for him, and those people who whisper in his ears?'

She stands up, moves her stool forward and sits again, very close to the bed. I can smell musk and cinnamon. Her mouth is close to my ear. 'The tragedy, and my guilt, Florence, is that it's not you, or Modeste, or even Master Tibery over whom they wished to be victorious; it was me.' She pauses. 'They are all as subtle as foxes. In the end, I could stand it no longer. My friend Modeste, the boy, and then you. I could bear it no longer so I gave in.'

'So . . .?' I am still puzzled.

'So, this morning, in the great temple here I made sacrifices to the old gods. I made pleas and poured libations. It is nearly two years since I have done that and this has been troubling to the Emperor and his Oracles. Such a bad example, you see? A crack at the centre. Now he and his oracle are satisfied.'

'How terrible . . .'

She smiles faintly. 'It took some consideration, I may say. But I meditated on it and knew I must do this so that Tibery and Modeste can go on with their work with you by their side. In this way your courage would be balanced with my cowardice. I feel sullied, spoiled by my action. But there are other times, other days, to live true.'

Again I shake my head, which is tumbling now with all sorts of emotion. I feel proud of her. It's taken courage to do what she has done, in this nest of foxes. I want to cry, not for my Siri, but for this noble woman of her time who is above all a midwife for change.

She puts her hand over mine; I can feel her heavy gold rings. 'I will survive this time,' she says. 'And I can pray in private to the one true God. I need no oracles or priests.' She pauses. 'My daughter, the boy's mother, is a true follower of the Way. I sent her away for her own safety. It's for her also that I do this. And now the boy is healed and on his way to be with his mother, lest, in his innocence he . . . *lets the cat out of the bag* again. Is that how you said it?'

Now she leans across and kisses me on the cheek. Her kiss burns my flesh. It's as though she is the mother, not I. She picks up a bell sitting on a table and rings it. I hear the echo of the bell I heard through the blood in that stinking cell. Then she turns to me and frowns. 'Are you sure we haven't met before, Florence? I have this feeling . . .'

But then her serving woman comes bustling through the door, followed by the big soldier who was the boy's nursemaid. She greets him. 'Ah, Lupinus! Your new mission. The boy you cared for is lost to you but now you must play carer for these three friends.'

She turns to me and smiles. My heart turns over. 'Lupinus is named after the wolf. He keeps the jackals and foxes at bay. He'll take you and your friends to safety. All the way back to Good Fortune. The oracle doesn't know it but this is agreed with the Emperor.'

'All of us?' I say quickly.

'All of you. As I told you, the boy Tibery is on good form, untouched by the worst of the tortures. In the end his torturers feared him. I have to say, though, that my good friend Modeste is sore afflicted. But with Lupinus to guard him and you to love him and take care of him and Tibery to bless him he's in good hands.'

She stands up and pulls me to my feet, then takes the velvet cloak from her own back and wraps it around me, and I am standing there in clouds of cinnamon and sandalwood. From the table she takes fur lined canvas sandals and kneels to fasten them on my feet. Then she thrusts me in the direction of Lupinus. 'Take care of this woman,' she says. 'She's as a daughter to me.'

You can see how tangled up this is getting.

The giant called Lupinus picks me up and holds me in his arms as tenderly as he held her grandson. Then he strides away, away from her down the corridors and under colonnades. There are Imperial guards on all the corners, but they stare straight ahead, ignoring us.

At last we're out into the cold night alongside this long covered chariot set behind four thickset horses held still by a man in a long hood. Lupinus thrusts a coin in his hand and lifts me into the covered cart. Once inside, by the light of a tiny swinging lamp, I see the woollen carpet that lines the interior of the cart and the wolf skins on the floor.

On one side I see Modeste rolled in a thick blanket. His face is livid with purple weals. Beside him, sitting cross-legged like a gnome, is Tib. His flawless face splits into a grin. 'Florence!' he says. 'We've been waiting for you! Look! The Empress saved our pendants!' He holds his hand up and their pendants, the gift from his mother, dangle on their silver chains: two fishes glittering in the light of the little lamp.

Modeste's eyelids flicker and he mutters something but Tibery puts a hand over his eyes and quietens him. The voice of Lupinus comes from the darkness behind me. 'The lady must lie down, master. She's been sore tried by that devil. She needs to lie down and rest.' His voice is deep, like the creak of a ship's timbers.

Tib pulls back Modeste's blanket. 'She can lie here with my Modeste. They can keep each other warm.'

So I lie beside *his* Modeste and Lupinus throws a wolf skin over us both, saying, 'Have no fear, madam. I'll drive this beast myself. We'll have no more treachery.' I know him now as a great soul, if not an old one. In minutes the long cart is moving.

So here I am, lying beside *my* Modeste with Tib holding my hand, in a long cart driven by the great Lupinus. I feel sure I've seen the last of the Empress who has Siri in her eyes and I'm setting out again with my friends on my journey back to Good Fortune. Surely nothing worse can happen to us now.

THIRTY
Long Journey Home

I lose track of the days on the long journey home. Home? Home for me in these days has to be Good Fortune and Cessero. One part of me is sad. But as we travel – first by fancy cart, then by barge, then by large sailing boat – the sky seems to brighten with hope; sail tackle jangles and the breezes whistle with optimistic fervour.

On our journey, under Tib's healing hand, Modeste recovers from his savage injuries, even though he emerges a thinner, wirier man, more shadowed under the eyes than was his former self. Modeste's recovery makes Tib merry, allows him to become the child again. Each day he looks forward to the moment the sun sets and they set about their prayers and religious offices. Despite my misgivings I now feel obliged to join them. After all, I've joined them in their suffering which, even in my dream, has proved a harsh reality. For good and all I am one of them. So, alongside the captain of the boat and Lupinus, I join their circle, I say the words, although I do not allow Tib to make the sign on my forehead.

As Modeste recovers he and I stay late on deck and look at the stars together. But now there's no discussion about the cosmos or locating the cult of the Nazarene within a larger concept of the universe and the confluence of time. His tortures have locked Modeste solidly into this present time and place. His pain has somehow squeezed out the larger concepts and left him with the immediacy of his faith in the teacher Jesus of Nazareth, who was put to death almost within memory of these times. His faith is now one of conviction rather than reason: in this he is now at one with the child Tib.

As we move about the boat he touches and holds me freely, although we can't make proper love under the lugubrious eye of the captain or the sailor on watch. At long last we reach Marseilles – called Massalia in these times.

We give our thanks to the ship's captain. Lupinus, who has taken a turn rowing on this journey, holds him in a comrade's clasp before he leaves. So the four of us make our way off the ship and into the harbour. Tib dances around with the joy of being back in his Gaul, his home land. Then he goes off with Lupinus to find a ship to take us down the coast to Good Fortune. Modeste and I comb the harbour streets for a lodging house that has rooms with couches rather than a floor to sleep on. We find a lodge keeper, who – eyes gleaming at the glitter of the Empress's gold coin – offers us his own bedroom with new straw mattresses. The room turns out to be surprisingly tranquil compared with the chaos below. Great sheets of Egyptian linen cover two large beds and someone has lit two sandalwood oil burners which fill the air with blue smoke and mask the other lodging house smells.

I throw myself on one of the beds and take off the Empress's sandals, pushing my feet down the pure clean linen. Modeste pulls a chest across the door and reaches up to push open a shutter to let out the sandalwood smoke. Then he peels off his own leather leggings and comes to lie beside me. We roll inwards to each other on the great mattress and hug and hold each other, stroke bare cheeks and – quickly divesting ourselves of the rest of our clothes – we lie together skin to glorious skin, as close as any two people can be. Then we kiss, first on the mouth, then – in a laughter-filled race – on every part of each other's bodies. I make sure to kiss the fading scars that tell the story of Modeste's recent suffering. This seems to convulse him and suddenly we are making mad, ferocious love, first he above me and then I above him. This is a wild dance of love, made more intense by separation and by true fear of what may be ahead of us.

This is the best of the dream.

After a while we are forced to lie back with exhaustion. Then much more slowly, much more gently, we start again. Afterwards we fall into a doze only to be woken by a hammering on the door. In seconds we scramble into our clothes – excepting our footwear – and Modeste is pulling away the chest.

Tib falls into the room, followed by Lupinus, who has food in woven straw bundles. Tib glances at me, sitting demurely on the low window ledge, and says, 'Food! You would not believe, Modeste, the food on offer here. Strange stuff, from way beyond the furthest sea . . .'

Lupinus heaves the bundles on to the second bed. 'And bread. Take your supper here, Sirs, Madam. The boy and I have arranged the passage tomorrow to Good Fortune with a captain but now I go to check his credentials. I'm told there are pirates and scoundrels on and off this shore line.'

Modeste protests. 'Share our food, Lupinus! Don't leave us.'

Lupinus shakes his head. 'I'll dine with the men from the boats. That way I'll get a better sense of this captain who might just take us to Good Fortune without stealing our gold.'

THIRTY-ONE
Cessero

We hold hands, Tib, Modeste and I, savouring this magical moment. Before us a bracelet of islands floating like grey ghosts on their silver lagoons stand watery guard on the mouth of our great river. The flat sun of the evening melts into the trembling mother-of-pearl ripples of the estuary, and casts our landfall, Good Fortune, into shadow.

Soon the long harbour wall comes into view, with its jingling double line of boats sitting there with furled sails. Two other boats have, like ours, docked at dusk and that section of the harbour is busy. Two others are anchored at the other side of the river, waiting their turn to move to the quayside. We, of course, do not have to wait. Our oarsmen cut the water, heaving fast towards the Governor's landing. There is no greeting party. Tib looks upwards across the roofs of the houses to the ridge where his father's mansion stands – a grand building but even so not quite as grand as the colonnaded temple alongside it. 'There! There's my mother,' he cries.

She is a shadow against the night sky, but she is there. The flat sun picks out the gold on her headdress and the decorated torc on her neck. She's clearly been watching but has not been allowed to greet us. Our shame has gone before us.

'Messires!' It's the Governor's boatman, Peter, bowing low before Tib. 'We have a boat here for your return to Cessero! I am to row you all the way.'

Tib drags his gaze away from the figure silhouetted against the night sky. I suddenly remember how young he is. Eleven? Twelve years old? He is too young for this.

Modeste speaks. 'Such a pity that a child may not be greeted by his parents after this long and dangerous journey.'

The boatman bows less deeply in his direction. 'I have orders from the Governor, messire. The boy is to be transported directly onwards to Cessero.'

Modeste nods. 'Very well. The loss is theirs.'

The boatman glances curiously at Lupinus, then leads us all along the quayside to the upriver end of the harbour. We all look down at the small boat moored by flat rocks at the river's edge where the women do their washing. The seaman senses our disappointment. 'This is a fine boat, Master Tibery,' he says heartily. 'Much better than the last one. There are provisions aboard. Warm cloaks. We'll make good speed up the river.'

'We'll not need your strength, boatman,' says Modeste. 'We are strong ourselves now. And we have a comrade.'

The seaman looks up at Lupinus. 'This is a giant, messire.'

'And a giant in spirit,' says Modeste. He puts a hand on Tib's shoulder. 'Jump on board, Tib. We need to catch the light for Cessero. We are going home.'

Tib and I take the lighter oars and Lupinus has to temper his strength to match Modeste's lesser skill with the oar. He still has a limp from his ordeal but Tib's care and the weeks at sea have given him greater strength than before. So on our journey to Cessaro we make speed, rowing against the flow of the smooth green river, the rising water slapping against the painted sides of the boat. The banks are the same tangle of greenery, blackening in that familiar way as the light fades. The last rays of the sun turn the river silvery grey and above it the trees make a lacy black silhouette against the dark sky.

'Greeting, O great river!' shouts Tib. Then he corrects his pagan thought. 'The Lord's blessing on you!'

Behind me, I hear Modeste chuckle. 'Sometimes it's hard to cast off the old ways, Tib. They served us well, I think.'

Lupinus makes us stop rowing, puts up a sail and starts to catch an unseasonal late evening breeze that helps us zig zag on these broader reaches of water as the river turns. Tib leaps to the prow and takes the tiller, watching keenly as we swing round the sweeping bend. Modeste moves to the stern to sit beside me and put an arm round my shoulder. The light is really fading now. We need our flares to reach our destination.

Tib calls down from the prow of the boat. 'Do you remember, Modeste? Do you remember furling the sail of our little boat on that first night? When we knew not what was in store? When we hadn't yet met the wonderful people of Cessero?'

Modeste stirs and sits up straight beside me. 'Aye. We sought sanctuary and found a beautiful place and beautiful people.' He squeezes my shoulder. 'Nearly home, Florence,' he says. 'Nearly home.'

Lupinus steers us through one of the arches of the great bridge, a great reminder that the Romans rule here in Gaul.

In a very short while we arrive at the flat reach of ground near Cessero. Word has got around: there are torches at the landing place. Léance greets us with a gathering of men carrying torches and they lead us along to the village. Women and children are standing there, holding high their own smoky straw torches. They come forward to touch Modeste, to bow to Tib. A little girl takes my hand and kisses it. I am filled with lightness and the true feeling of homecoming.

When we get back to our camp everything is in good order, even though we heard the Governor's soldier order the destruction of the camp as we left. The garden is tidy, well turned over. The vines are bright green, the small dark grapes hiding underneath the leaves. Somewhere deep in my mind I hear the snort and jingle of horses.

I meet Léance's watching gaze. He shrugs. 'They came and wrecked it. It was a small thing to put it together again. The bees were not happy though. Three soldiers were stung. One died.' A slow smile crosses his broad face. 'We hid the doctor's boxes in ox-skins under the wine press. The soldiers were more interested in the wineskins on the next landing, ready for shipping down to Good Fortune.'

But for all Léance's smiles and assurances he fails to warn us of the visitor we find as we enter the hut. My heart flips. I should have thought more about the sound of horses. Inside the hut we find Helée, the Governor himself, standing there, one of his men at his shoulder. He must have ordered Léance not to tell.

Helée touches his own shoulder in a soldier's greeting to his son. Tib goes to stand before him and waits calmly to hear what his father has to say. The Governor looks him in the eye. 'You were fortunate indeed, my son, at the Emperor's forbearance in letting you go.'

I jump in. 'It was the Empress who commanded our release, Governor,' I say quickly. 'And then only after Tibery and Modeste had been sorely and unfairly injured.'

He turns his hooded, tired eyes towards me. 'I speak to my son, madam.'

'And Florence was beaten,' says Tib calmly. 'She was beaten very hard. Modeste was nearly killed.'

Helée surveys his son from head to foot. 'You have no mark on you.'

Tib grins. 'I'm blessed by God through Jesus of Nazareth, Father.'

'His swift recovery,' intervenes Modeste quickly, 'is because Master Tibery is perfect, uncorrupt, and his body heals without intervention. And this is why he is enabled to heal others. How, for instance, he was able to restore your own sight, your honour, through his faith and his innocence.'

Helée smites one great soldier's hand against another. 'Do you see? Do you see? Out of your own mouth, Corinthian, you are betrayed. It's you, isn't it, who led my son into these zealous ways, made him believe in himself as a healer. It's you who have led my son into the disfavour of our Emperor. It's you who has led him into danger.'

'You do not see clearly, dear father.' said Tib quietly. 'It's my fate to do this work of mine, messire. Modeste merely gave my fate a name.' He turns his face away from his father.

At last Helée puts a hand on his son, grasping him by the shoulder, forcing him to meet his gaze. 'I wish you to stop this proselytising, Tibery. I wish you to stop going among the people, doing your curing, preaching this Way of yours. Hasn't it led to you and your friends here suffering sorely? And it'll get worse, you can be sure of that. There are whispers from the Imperial Court that the oracle has advised once more the death of all followers of the Nazarene.' He puts one hand on Tib's face and strokes it. 'They will not be happy until all of these heretics are dead,' he murmurs softly, In the flaring light of the torch I see the deep look that passes between them. Helée flinches. Then he coughs, pulls his hand away and rests it on Tib's shoulder. 'I cannot protect you, son,' he says quietly. 'It's out of my hands.'

'My master in Heaven will protect me,' says Tib. 'If not, let His will be done.'

Helée's hand drops from his son's shoulder like a dead thing. Then he fastens his long cloak with a snake pin and pulls on leather gauntlets. 'I must get back to Good Fortune. I have adjudications tomorrow.'

Tib looks away from him. 'And my mother? How is she?'

Helée's mouth becomes thin, pinched. 'She makes sacrifices at the temple of Venus each day, for your safe return. I have told your mother she may only see you at the Governor's house in Good Fortune. And you may only approach the house if you forswear these blasphemous beliefs.'

'Will you give her my greeting?'

Helée sighs. 'I will give her your greeting.' Then, unexpectedly, he turns to slap Modeste on the shoulder. 'Whether or not, Corinthian, you're the author of this misbegotten business, you have suffered alongside my son. Now I order you to take the best care of this boy.'

Astonishingly, Modeste puts a gentle hand on Helée's armoured shoulder. For a split second they are equals. 'Unto death, messire, I will take care of this boy. He is your son, but he is as a son to me.'

Helée glances at me but obviously doesn't think me worth a word. Then he strides out, followed by his soldier at arms. We wait a few minutes and follow them. Lupinus is still there, leaning against the big olive tree, but the villagers have melted away. The presence of the Governor and his soldiers has given them the jitters.

The three of us go and sit near Lupinus and stare into the darkness. I glance up into the sky. The stars are just emerging, faint pinpricks on dark blue velvet. So perfect. So meaningful. So permanent. 'What now?' I say.

'Now we thank the one God for our safe delivery,' says Tib quietly. He stands up and we all do just that. Lupinus stands alongside us. I know the words and the gestures and I join in.

Afterwards I feel totally at peace. I think now that I believe; I believe in Tib and his extraordinary gifts. I love Modeste for his own gifts of the intellect, his physical body and courage. In these moments in this dream world I'm finally Florence, not Starr. I know the dangers and am committed to the here and now with these two marvellous beings, whatever the outcome.

THIRTY-TWO
On the Ridge

The next day was like the first day of term – great promise intermixed with pure fear. We're all excited. After the departure of the Governor and a good night's sleep we check our stocks of medicine and make a list of the shortfalls. Tibery seems to have swallowed his disappointment at not seeing his mother. I know he's hiding this under his chatter to Modeste about the women with sore faces and the boy from Cessero who walked for the first time after Tibery had blessed him. 'Do you think he walks still, Modeste?' he asks, with welcome traces of his childlike earnestness.

Lists made, Tibery packs his leather bag – a new one out of Africa, given to him by a grateful merchant of Nicomedia – then sets out with Lupinus to make house visits in Cessero and further afield.

Modeste and I – he still leaning on his stick – walk around our small domain. We note that the grapes are now plumped and bloomy under their leaves, and the ground has been cleaned and harrowed by the Cesseroneans, ready for new planting after being chewed up by soldiers' boots. We go down to the hives and say hello to the bees as Léance has taught us. The slow hum within their house tells us all is well for now, in bee-world.

Then Modeste sets out his planks on the trestles and builds again his large table under the shade of the ancient olive tree. He retrieves his boxes from the ox skins in which Léance has preserved them for these recent months. We find new documents in one of the boxes: a folded map and a letter on vellum. Léance must have put them in the box for our return.

'Wasn't Léance curious?' I ask 'Surely there's danger . . .'

Modeste laughs. 'Léance is a practical man who lives in the present and the future. He's more interested in filling his jars with oil and wine to send down the river to Good Fortune, than musty old papers that tell of things that happened here more than a hundred years ago. The old boy's fond of Tibery and sees him as a healer, so he watches out for us. But Léance is no more interested in the Nazarene than he is in the Emperors or Jupiter or Athene. His gods are much older than them. They come from older ways.'

Modeste picks up the map that's made of fine lambskin and folded like a concertina. He lays it on his table and weighs it down with black stones. The map is a kind of pictogram with trees and plants and a river with spouting fish. It has been cleverly drawn and somewhere in the fog of my mind it reminds me vaguely of the endpapers of the *Swallows and Amazon* books from my wideawake time.

The bright sun filtering through the old olive tree bathes the map in light. Modeste is excited. 'See, Florence! This is the river above Good Fortune! And here's the great bridge! And here's Cessero! See the olive trees and the oxen and the little houses? But look here!' His voice thickens with excitement. He points to two tiny figures in the left-hand corner, women in cloaks and hoods. His face, very close to the map, is alight, and stripped of the scars of recent torture.

I look closer. The map's not right. 'Look!' I say, catching his excitement. 'That's clearly an escarpment, just above the village. But . . .'

'Yes. No, now there is no escarpment. Just a rise in the land . . .' It's so wonderful to hear this life, this excitement in his voice.

'Perhaps a landfall, Florence?' he says. 'An earth movement? Not uncommon in these parts. See how close it is to where we've been digging? We're on the mark, Florence. On the mark.'

'We should go,' I say.

He's already refolding the map and putting it in his shoulder sack. Then he returns his boxes to their ox skins and tucks them behind the back wall of the hut. Then, from the back of the shed he hauls the iron scythe and two iron mattocks we use for the garden. Clearly this morning he means business.

I now have two choices of footwear, so I opt to wear the Empress's sandals for luck: walking in Siri's footsteps can do me no harm. We turn off the old river path and make our way upwards. We know the general direction but now and then Modeste stops to consult the map. He reads the land very well.

We walk fast and he finally throws away his stick, takes my hand and we walk faster. I have to break into a run to keep up with him. It's as though we are one body – just as we are when we make love. We are one thing, just as a tree with its branches is one thing; just as a turtle with its shell is one thing.

We pass people as we go: children peer at us from behind squat olive trees; a man with a pack of sheep wool on his back trudges on, head down; a young woman helps a very old woman down the slope, both faces in shadow under long hoods. They stop us to ask the whereabouts of the young master, as their son and brother is hearing voices and seeing stars falling to earth.

Then we come across a man with a towering pack of vine stems on his back. He's wearing a green felt doublet and wooden soled clogs that I've never seen here before. The man acknowledges us. 'Greetings, Doctor!'

'Greetings, friend! You have a veritable mountain on your back.'

'Vine stems for a bakeshop in Good Fortune, messire. There is a great oven there, famous for its bread, which has a very hungry stone mouth. The baker loves my vine stems. I take them down the river in my little boat and he pays me well.'

We walk on. When the man is out of earshot I ask Modeste, 'Is he real, that man? Is he here in this time?'

Modeste does not slacken his pace. 'Are you?' is all he says.

Now we're on the very rise of the land. Down below the luminous morning light shines on the scatter of low dwellings that make up the hamlet of Cessero. Some houses are fronted by clusters of olive trees as well as the odd row of vines. Here and there a field is under cultivation. Beside one hut stand a pair of tethered oxen, waiting for their working day to start. In the far distance we can even make out the spreading top of our own wild olive, older than any of the houses on this horizon. Weaving through the trees to the south of us the river glitters like beryl aquamarine.

Now we're standing on a kind of shelf spread entirely in dense underbrush and stunted fig trees, picked through with equally straggly bay trees. I pull a sprig of bay and crush it in my hand and remind myself of the fish pie my mother used to make. I always thought it strange that she took the leaves out after the fish pie was cooked. I start to tremble and blink and Modeste says quite sharply, 'Not now, Florence. Not now!'

My panic subsides and I watch as he peers again at the map and starts to hack away at the underbrush with the scythe, a thick iron blade set in a lump of wood. Then I pick up my mattock and work at his shoulder, scraping away the brush as he cuts it. I dig out the fig and bay trees that are in his way.

We finally reach a layer of stones tangled in the starving tree roots. 'Look!' he says exultantly. 'The stones. They show a mason's hand. Sharp clear edges.' He grabs his mattock and redoubles his efforts. I toil away, lifting the stones and piling them up to one side. Every stone is shaped with skill. Some are coloured marble, dark blue veined with red. By the time the noon heat stops our labours we have a small mountain of stone beside us and a marble-strewn space in front of us.

Modeste is sweating and strained: his enthusiasm has outstripped his energy. It's very hot. Even the birds have stopped singing. We sit down on a stone the size of a large suitcase to eat our bread and drink water from our stone jars. He closes his eyes and puts his chin on his chest for a moment. I wipe the crumbs from my mouth and lean back, offering my face rather than my back to its burning rays. My clutching fingers encounter something on the side of the stone. I get down on my knees to see better. 'Look, Modeste! Look here!' I hiss with excitement. Modeste leaps to his feet and comes to kneel beside me. His hand over mine, we trace the sign of the fish, an elegant design cut deep into the stone.

Now there's no birdsong, no movement in the undergrowth; even the leaves have stopped rustling. It's as though the world is taking a breath; as though the past, present and future is held in that breath. Then someone, somewhere flicks a switch and the birds sing and the natural world comes alive again.

'Messire! Messire!' Léance comes labouring up the slope shaking his stick in the air. He's shouting at the top of his voice. Modeste cups his ear and I strain to listen.

'Leave it, messire, madam! Leave it! No good can come of it!' Léance gasps as he reaches us. He stands beside us, looking down at the carved stone. He gulps for breath. 'No good can come of it!' he says, slowly pulling a hairy arm over his face to wipe off the sweat.

'No good can come of *what*?' demands Modeste. 'What?'

'Of *that*, messire.' Léance gestures towards the hole we are making through the stones.

'What?' repeats Modeste grimly. 'You must tell me. You must know what we're about. You saw the map. You followed us here. What is it here?' He takes hold of Léance's shoulders and pulls him down to sit beside him on the big stone. I sit in the dust at their feet.

'Now,' said Modeste more gently. 'What is it that we must *not* do here, old friend? And why? Take a drink of water and tell us.' He hands Léance his own flagon. 'Drink!' he says.

Léance drains the flask and starts to breathe more easily. He looks from Modeste to me then back again. 'Well, madam, messire, it's a story from my grandfather's grandfather. This man was not from Gaul; he was from another more faraway place and he was a stonemason.' He runs his fingers over the fish sign. 'I have his very tools in my house. He could have cut this with one of them,' he said in wonder.

Then words start to stream from him. 'I'll tell you. You may have heard of this. A great Emperor, a very sad man, once came to this place and liked it. He built a shrine, a small place but very beautiful. The floor had all the colours of the rainbow. It was entirely underground but it had a great chimney that opened on to the hill, letting the light flood down into the shrine.'

'You saw this place, Léance?' says Modeste.

Léance shakes his head sadly. 'No, messire. I know the story of its building, which was told by my grandfather's grandfather to his son and so on. I heard it from my own father.'

'Why was it built, this shrine?'

Léance hesitates. 'They say Tiberius, an emperor who was then a very old man, had a vision here and caused it to be built.'

'He lived here?' I ask.

Léance shakes his head. 'They say his ship landed in Good Fortune and he came up here with the Governor on a great hunt for a bear which was well known in these parts and twice the height of a man. He liked to hunt, just like the boy doctor's own father, messire. Anyway, when they cornered this great animal, the spear of the Emperor was raised for the kill and he saw something. Some say it was a great column of light. Some say it was a bolt of lightning. Some say it was the face of his brother who had been murdered by their own mother. Whatever it was, the bear got away. Whatever it was, Tiberius left gold, and orders for the secret shrine to be built on the very spot by stonemasons from his own land.'

He went on. 'Our own village, Cessero, was named for him. From Caesar, do you see? The village grew from the people who had worked on the shrine and were pledged by Tiberius to guard the secret. They gave up being masons and made themselves farmers, though all around you and down in Good Fortune you may see fine stonework that comes from those old skills.'

'So that was it? A shrine was built and a village grew? Because a great bear escaped.' I whisper. The great bear is in my mind. *Ursa Major.* I have this pain at the pit of my stomach.

Léance waves his hand to shut me up. His story is not finished. 'Then a message came from across the sea that the Emperor had died and not long after two women and two men came to the village. They were very sad. They knew of the shrine, knew the place and had this picture of the inside, drawn on fine calf skin. This picture could only have come from the great man's stonemason.'

'Did they bring something with them, these women?' says Modeste quickly.

Léance eyes him. 'They say – and remember, messire, this may all have grown in the telling, as flour and water transform to bread – they say that in their baggage they had a crude box made from ship's timbers and inside that a beautiful box in sandalwood.'

'And inside that?' says Modeste.

Léance shrugs. 'Who knows? No one has seen it. But in my family there have been many speculations about what was inside. It could have been jewels, or fine possessions. But the legend in my family is that the women carried it with too much reverence for mere gold.' He shrugs. 'It's a very old story. Could be mere fancy. Sorcerors' tales.'

'Well . . .' I try to express my wonder.

He flaps his hand at me again. 'There is more! In the time of the ancestor who came *after* the first mason, there is this great movement of earth on the ridge. That's not unusual here.

The ground here on this coast is even now still in the making. In those days the ridge was twenty feet higher. But this earth movement was so great that the top of the ridge toppled entirely. And in the space of an hour the whole land from here to the river was churned up. Good Cesseroneans died, including three members of my own family. The course of the river changed. And so, you see, the Emperor's wonderful shrine was eaten up by this great stirring up of earth.'

He took a good swig from the bottle and went on. 'Now, I must tell you that this grandfather was of the old religion, so much older than your old Roman fellow Jupiter and his hordes. *He* said the old earth's convulsion was a sign that the shrine must stay hidden and be safe. It also was a sign that the people of Cessero were released from their pledge to Tiberius. Now they could go from this place as they willed.'

That shrug again.

'Not many did that. Old habits bury deep in a man's bones. Anyway, they planted the whole ridge with olive and other trees so it would look no different from any other part of Cessero.'

There is a long pause and then Modeste takes Léance by the shoulder and pulls him to his feet. 'If you were so determined to keep the secret, old man, why did you pass on the map to me? Why did you not hide it? Burn it?'

Léance looks him in the eye. 'That time before, when you were walking in these parts, messire, we watched you on your wanderings around Good Fortune and around Cessero. We saw you find that older place near the river with Madam Florence here. I noted how you were squaring the land like a hawk and would not cease till you found the place. And then with you came the doctor boy with his miracles, whose name was Tibery, like the great man who built the shrine. Our wise man here said this was a sign.

'Then the Governor's soldiers came to get you, even the woman, and we were very sad. So while you were away I prayed to our great god Taranus that you would be safe. While you were away two men came from Setus and asked for you by name. I showed them your camp and said you would return. They lodged the map with me and I put it in your box. I tell you, messire, when that map was brought from Setus I knew it was a sign. So I sacrificed again to Taranus and promised that if you returned safely I'd let you have the map and allow you to complete your quest.'

Modeste nods slowly. 'I understand that, but what about today? Why do you come galloping up the hill to stop us?'

Léance smiles sheepishly. 'It's hard, messire, to squeeze hundreds of years of custom from a man's thoughts. Despite my promise to Taranus I still doubted that I'd done the right thing.'

'But now the cat is out of the bag,' I say. That phrase again.

Léance frowns a moment, then understands. 'I don't know this, madam. I think that would only be so if you returned the cat to the bag. My ancestors promised to keep the secrets.'

Modeste reaches out to hug Léance and the old man wriggles free of his grasp. 'Go back to your house, Léance,' says Modeste. 'I thank you for your story but you should not be here.'

'What will you do, messire?' asks Léance.

'I'll do what is right but that will mean no betrayal to you. Your secret will remain.'

Léance nods, satisfied, and turns and climbs down the hill, using his stick only occasionally for balance. On his way down he passes Tibery and Lupinus, who are on their way up.

Modeste looks at me. 'Now, Florence, we will begin!' he says.

THIRTY-THREE
Salt and Sandalwood

We dig on through the morning, the four of us taking turns. We use the dug out stones and columns to support the trench so that it does not fall in on us. We're aware of being watched, from all sides, but we keep digging.

Tib and Lupinus lend an energetic hand, not questioning the task. When they arrived Tib told us that the villagers had sought them out, told them to come to this place. He eyes Modeste thoughtfully. 'So this is what you've been searching for, Modeste? Ever since we came to Good Fortune?'

'So it is,' says Modeste calmly. 'Now I've found it, and now I must dig. So it's fortunate that we have four pairs of hands instead of two.'

'And what will we find? Great treasure?' Tib's excitement is childlike, untroubled.

Modeste sits down and drinks the water they'd brought for us. I tell him the tale that Léance had told us.

'So now,' says Modeste, 'we must dig, to find out why Tiberius – your namesake, remember – had them build such a beautiful shrine.'

I thought it was curious that there was no talk between them of the Nazarene. Tib runs his fingers lovingly over the crisply carved outline of the fish but says nothing.

The steady rhythm of digging with the mattock leaves me room for reflection. Modeste has taken on so many different guises to fulfil this task. He was searching for this shrine in my waketime; he's been searching for it in this dreamtime. And probably in other times about which I know nothing. He's driven to find the shrine and name its contents. He's the perpetual unsatisfied scholar, the doubter who looks for truth and needs proof. Perhaps in his first incarnation his name was Thomas.

Odd then that Tib, Modeste's own convert, needs no proof. His faith shines from him; it is his fingerprint. It's as genuine as it is unquestioning. In him there is no doubt. His faith joins his intelligence to inform his kindness to people, his proven ability to heal. Tib lives in his present, not other people's past. Perhaps this is the sign of a very old soul.

And it looks now as though Modeste's search is reaching its end. Why now? Perhaps this is because in this time, in this place, he came across the boy Tibery? Perhaps it's because I, in my savage mourning for Siri, am here travelling with him, jumping from my own waketime to this dreamtime? It looks like the time and the place for the discovery of the shrine *has* to be here and now. The Cesseroneans are the key. They recognize Tibery and allow Modeste into their secret, which has no written record but must rely on the truth pulsing from generations of storytelling. Believing in gods much older than Rome or Nazareth, their craftsmen's pride ultimately means that it was they, not the Romans or the followers of the Nazarene, who possessed the secret of the shrine. And it's Léance who, in the name of his craftsmen forefathers, was the one to let Modeste into this old secret.

The sun has climbed to its height and Modeste, Tib and I stop to wipe our brows and cry thirst. Lupinus keeps digging. Tib runs down to the river to refill our flagons. Lupinus suddenly grunts and we look down at the earth beside his mattock. He rubs it with the sole of his sandal and we can see a pattern. He has hit a tessellated floor.

Tib jumps into the hole and trickles some water beside Lupinus' moving foot. I rub with my foot, then get down on my knees and rub the ground hard with my gown. The floor is black and white with touches of green and red: some kind of corner design with green leaves and dark red roses.

'This gives us the direction,' Modeste says quietly. 'We follow the pattern.'

We work on with a greater will now, using our shoulder sacks to hurl soil up out of the hole. Finally the low slant of sunlight shows us a round arch and we dig on. Then we use our hands to claw away the soil. Lupinus jumps up out of the hole to kick away the pile on the top so it doesn't tumble back in. Tibery is standing back watching as my hand keeps bumping into Modeste's as we scrabble away at the soil.

My hand finally hits something that isn't soil. 'Modeste,' I say. He puts his hand over mine. It's a lump of greasy wood.

Lupinus jumps back into the hole. 'Stand away!' he says. 'Stand away!' he repeats.

We climb out of the hole and watch as he clears away the last of the soil from what now looks like a very large box and hauls it out from under the arch. The box is five feet long and two feet wide and is bound with what looks like heavily greased ship's ropes. From the way Lupinus grunts as he lifts it out of the hole it must be very heavy.

Now we can see it is made of what looks like blackened ship's timbers. And around us there is the faintest smell of the sea. Tib puts a hand on a rope and pulls it. It comes away, falls to pieces in his hands. Modeste peels another away, then another. I look up to see Lupinus pulling his hand down his face to get rid of his tears.

'Now what?' says Modeste, his voice trembling. 'What do we do?'

'We open it,' I say firmly. 'Open it, for goodness' sake.'

'Open it, Modeste,' says Tib. 'You've waited a long time.'

'Open it, messire,' Lupinus' deep voice whispers.

Modeste pulls away the last of the rotten rope and looks across at me. That look contains all our time together: the talk, the laughter, the work, the lovemaking. 'Help me, Florence,' he says.

I take one end and he takes the other and we both pull at the top. It doesn't budge. Tib and Lupinus come to help: now there are four hands on four corners. The lid creaks, and finally it moves. And falls to pieces in our hands. We look into the box and all we can see is pebbles. I sit back, disappointed. This seems very cruel. Have Léance and the Cesseroneans played a trick on us?

Then Tib leans forward and removes one pebble, then another. We all join in, scooping out the pebbles at random. My palm hits a carved wooden surface and we slow down, moving the last pebbles with great care. The object in its pebble bed is hard to make out in the shadowy depths of the hole.

'Wait!' Lupinus puts a hand on my shoulder and on Modeste's shoulder and we stand back. He leans down and plucks a heavily carved box from its pebble bed. It is the size of a walker's backpack and smells faintly of salt and sandal-wood. He walks backwards and places it on a piece of clear ground.

The afternoon sun is shining, the sky is Delft blue, and the land is still. There is no movement but still I can feel the watching eyes in the scrubland around us. We are seen. We stand around the box, paralyzed by fear, by delight.

At last Tib kneels down beside it, clicks two wooden levers and it opens. I kneel down beside him. Modeste kneels beside me. Lupinus towers over us all. Whatever is inside is covered by a small, perfectly preserved purple cloth embroidered in gold around the edge.

For a second the world slows to a halt about me. I see the midwife holding Siri, offering her to me that first time. The world starts up again and, when I lift the purple cloth from the casket, I'm the only one who is not surprised. Around me a chorus of groans greets the sight of a baby perhaps three or four months old. Perfectly preserved she's lying on cloth of gold, and wrapped in fine wool the colour of new cream. She has a topknot of black hair, an olive complexion and round smooth features. Beside her are miniature sandals, as beautifully wrought as the sandals given to me by the Empress. By her head is a little felt hat in red, the colour of Siri's hat in the attaché case at home: the hat Siri was wearing when we met Philip.

Behind me Lupinus sets up a continuous muttering. Modeste clutches my arm too tightly. Tib murmurs, 'Hello baby!' in a voice without fear. I hear my own voice echoing his. This is – or was once – a real child.

Each of us in turn touches that cold, exquisite face: we offer her a kind of greeting. 'Who are you, baby?' says Tib. 'Who are you?' Modeste touches the black hair, smoothes it across the fontanelle. Lupinus starts to hum a strange, gruff lullaby.

How long we have been here I don't know. But suddenly the sun has lost its daytime heat and I shiver. Someone, probably Léance, has lit a fire under the trees and left wine and bread. He's also left us torches – bundles of sticks tied with rag and dipped in beeswax. He intends us to work on into the night.

'We will eat,' announces Modeste, carefully drawing the cloth across the baby's face and closing the lid of the carved box. 'We should eat.' He nods at Lupinus, who stands up, lifts the casket, puts it safely under his arm and heads for the tree. Tib leaps to his feet and follows, and Modeste and I follow him, our hands joined.

We sit around the casket and eat, breaking the bread and drinking the wine in silence. The bread tastes of nuts and sunshine; the wine tastes of earth and roses. Finally Tib wipes his mouth with the back of his hand. 'Now, dear Modeste,' he says. 'What have we here?'

Beside me I can feel Modeste shake his head. I sense his disappointment. 'It's not clear to me at all. I've searched for it through many ages. My mission was to find it. I thought it might be . . .' His voice trails off. 'But I am not sure.' His gaze moves across to the hole in the hill, the tumbled stones and columns, the rash of pebbles, the detritus of our desperate digging. Now Tib stands up and holds out his hands, one to me, one to Modeste. We all stand up and now Lupinus is between Modeste and me holding our hands, completing the circle around the casket. They start to say their prayers, familiar to me now. Lupinus' deep tones join their lighter ones and I close my eyes. Behind my lids I see again the baby's round dark face. Her eyes blink open and widen in – what? Appeal? Recognition? They are very dark with violet just around the iris. I've seen those eyes before. Then the fragile eyelids close again and I open my own eyes to find the four of us standing there around the casket, staring at each other.

Now I know why I am in this dream. 'This baby should be left here,' I say firmly. 'No one knows who she is. She may be a child from your story. Or she could be something to do with the emperor who built the shrine. If we bring her out and talk about her she'll be the plaything of idiots.' I turn and look Modeste in the eyes. 'She is some mother's child and we should leave her in peace. Believe me, you and Tib may be the wisest of souls, but I know about this thing. She is some sad mother's child. We should leave her in peace and let her stay undisturbed. We should not hold onto her.'

Modeste sighs as he looks around our little circle. 'Florence is right. Perhaps she herself is here with us now just to show us this truth. We could force the baby into our legend and weave stories about her for our own virtuous ends. But we have raked her out of her last cradle and we should return her there. Any other way has no honour. I see now that my search is over.' Despite the authority of his words his tone is very sad.

'Poor baby,' says Tib. He looks at me and in his eyes I

see twin reflections of Siri with her cloud of black hair. 'Let her go.'

Let her go. Let this baby go. As I must let Siri go. I see now that my grief has clung to Siri, not allowed her to go. In my heart I forgave – or at least understood – those boys who killed her but I could not forgive her for dying, for going from me.

We all stare down at the sandalwood box. Then I kneel down and open it again. My nose twitches and I want to sneeze. The sandalwood smell has gone. It has been replaced by something more bitter – earthy and acrid at the same time.

I lift the purple cloth and gasp. The others mutter in surprise. The fresh pink bloom on the baby's cheek has turned grey. 'This is it . . .' I search for the right words in my head. 'This is it. Why we had to find her. It can't be right that a baby's body stays intact, remains uncorrupt . . .'

Modeste joins in. 'She was halted on her way, imprisoned still in her body. Her preservation in the shrine prevented . . .'

Now Tib: 'We can see now why you had to find her, Modeste. You had to free her to go on her journey.' He nods. 'So now we've freed this little one. Now her body will decay and she'll be free to go on. We have touched her and she is ready to go on.'

I pull the cloth back across the blackening face of the little girl and close the lid of the box. 'We have to put her back there into the hill.'

'We must make haste,' growls Lupinus. 'We're losing the light.' He leans down, picks up the sandalwood box and puts it on his shoulder. He takes one of the beeswax flares, lights it from the dying fire and marches up the hill. We take two flares each and follow him. Above the hole we give light with our torches as Lupinus jumps into the hole and makes a new cradle for the casket. He works quickly, making the cradle with fallen columns and flat stones. Then he places the casket at the centre of the cradle and fills it with the pebbles before lying more flat pieces of marble across the top. Then on top of this he carefully places the rotting planks that have been the little girl's cradle these hundreds of years.

Then Tib and I hold the flares while Modeste and Lupinus work frantically to refill the hole from the soil and detritus all round its edges. They are both grunting and sweating by the time they have finished and the hole is roughly filled.

'Look!' says Tib, pointing. 'Trees walking.'

A torchlit procession of men, women and children is mounting the hill. On their backs they are carrying woven baskets with trees and branches poking out in all directions.

Léance comes first, carrying two torches. He stands before us and bows deeply to each of us in turn. Then he looks towards the hole, where Lupinus and Modeste are still working frantically to finish the backfill. He bows again. 'Messires! We note that you decide to restore the mystery and are glad. Here are the men and women of Cessero come to help you to make good the ground with new trees of fig and olive. In this way no one will know the hill has been breached and the secret will remain with our ancestors.' He pauses and looks again at me and Tib, then back at Modeste. 'Are you happy, messire, with your discovery in the shrine?'

Modeste nods. 'We are content.' He pauses. 'Are you not curious, Léance?'

The old man shakes his head. 'Such things are the fancy of the men who flood across our land, messire, like water finding its own level. They stay for their own reasons and depart for their own reasons. They leech all our goodness away and plant their strange seed. But you, messire, and the boy doctor want nothing from us; you leech nothing away. At least you recognize that we live by older rules.' The light from his torch flickers across his face. 'Now, messires, we must work on. The making good must be done before the night is through.'

The digging that had taken many hours during the day is now made good in what seems to be minutes by the men and women of Cessero, helped rather limply by the four of us. Then we stand back and hold new torches, one in each hand, as they set about planting their olives and their figs. They work quietly, by feel. It's too dark to see the whole effect but I know it will be good.

Finally we put our bags and tools together ready to trudge back to the camp. But Léance will not hear of our returning there. 'Good friends, you should not – must not – return to your camp. Danger lurks there. They say there have been soldiers across the land, looking for you. Some may already be at your living place. Else they will be anchored on the river waiting for daylight. There's word of a new edict and your names on documents for arrest.'

So we end up this day – probably the most exciting of the whole of our lives – sleeping in one end of Léance's cowshed on palliasses of prickly grass. I go to sleep in a second, too tired to worry about tomorrow.

The next day Modeste shakes me awake before dawn. 'We're going back to the camp,' he says. 'If the soldiers come for us they must not find us here. The Cesseroneans risk their lives sheltering us. Come!'

THIRTY-FOUR
The Swarm

Léance was mistaken. When we got back to our camp there were no soldiers lurking in the undergrowth, no imperial barge on the river. All was peaceful in our hideaway. The bees, though, were angry, buzzing in clouds in the old olive tree and settling in heaving clumps on the roof of the shed.

In the days following our discovery of the shrine we settled into a kind of Heaven; a world in suspension. Day by day Tibery and Modeste offer their medicinal skills to all comers to the camp. The crowds of pilgrims swell; they come from far and wide. We hear tales of how long it has taken to walk here from Setus, from Massalia, from Biterre where the road is pretty decent, thanks to the Romans. They also tell tales of comrades killed there in the great Arena, sacrificing themselves and being sacrificed for their faith in the Way.

One of the women from Setus takes Modeste's arm and leads him to the other side of the great tree, talking swiftly in his ear. 'Who was that?' I ask him later that night when all is quiet in the camp.

'She's the one who sent me the map,' he says in my ear. We are lying spoon-like on his palliasse. Tib is down in Cessero, playing a bat and ball game with some of the travelling children.

Modeste goes on. 'It seems she got it from a man of Corinth who called there some years ago. When she heard of my searches and that I was also from Corinth she sent me the map.'

I'm suddenly afraid. 'What did you tell her, Modeste? Did you tell her about the shrine? About the baby?'

I can feel him shake his head. 'No,' he says. 'I told her the map made no sense to me. That its contours must refer to another place.'

I'm relieved by that. I want that baby left in peace. I feel as well that although Modeste found no answers for his intellectual quest in our discovery of the shrine, he too is at peace now; no longer striving.

And still people keep coming to the camp for help. As far as I can tell the cures offered by Tib and Modeste are mainly down to knowledge of herbs, reassurance and care, cleanliness and order. Always, though, they offer prayers. Tib's special caring is for the possessed, the convulsed, the disturbed. It's with them that I witness his personal magic. His very presence seems to calm these people, to drive the light of madness from their eyes. Many go away tranquil and clear eyed. It would be comforting to say that there's a rational explanation for what happens. But there isn't. Like the people of Cessero and the whole province now, I've come to accept Tib's gift as God-given.

As I say, since our discovery of the shrine and its contents, since the planting of the new forest of olive trees to protect it, Modeste has become quieter, less driven. He's more loving, more childlike, and somehow much less powerful. We touch each other lovingly even when Tib is around and sometimes we go off to our secret garden to make love. But the passion is fading. These are wonderful, quiet times infused with a kind of mournful grace.

The only blot on our landscape is our bees. They have finally buzzed off in a swarm and no matter how hard we look we cannot find them. I miss them. They have become part of my life, pointers in the day. And I feel now that they have something on their communal mind.

Then one day, Peter the seaman brings the Governor's barge up the river. Watchers on the banks run to Cessero with the news and Léance comes to tell us, his face worried. Then, with warnings and anxious shouts he herds the pilgrims still milling around our camp like distracted sheep, back to the village.

Modeste, Tib and I run with Lupinus to the landing place and wait for the boat to dock. It moves with its splashing raw grace in its familiar livery, brightly painted and immaculate. In minutes the oarsmen are standing to attention, their oars held vertically, like halberds. Then Tib shouts with delight and runs forward as he watches old Peter lead his mother Lady Serina down the double plank. She's clutching Misou to her

bosom. On dry land she puts the little dog down and he
scampers across to me to lick my hand with his soft, rasping
tongue. Then she turns and draws her son to her and embraces
him in an excess of emotion I've never seen before. Tib has
tears in his eyes. Over his head Lady Serina's eyes – the
window also to the soul of Madame Patrice – meet mine. They
are dark and full of sorrow. She speaks to me. 'My husband
is travelling in the north of the province pronouncing judgment
on the . . . people of the Way.' She turns her gaze to Modeste.
'I'm forbidden to come here, dearest friend, but time is so
short now.'

She pushes Tib from her and looks into his face. She has
only to bend slightly now to kiss his round brow. 'My, you
have grown, dear Tibery! And your face is thinner.' She pauses.
'Good Fortune is alive with news of you. Of your mission.
Of the mission of the good Modeste and Florence. Many of
the people travelling through Good Fortune, to and from
Massalia and Setus, sing your praises.' She looks across at
Lupinus. 'And who is this, Tibery?'

Tib smiles at her. 'And here is our friend Lupinus, Mother,
who came with us from Nicomedia and has proved a true
friend. Lupinus speaks little but he knows all. He makes us
feel safe and carries us along when we are tired. Lupinus, this
is my mother.'

Lupinus bows deeply to her. She bows her head in return
and then smiles up at him. Then it's Lupinus who leads the
way back to the camp and it's he who sweeps the papers to
one end of the big trestle table so we can sit there.

In minutes Léance's wife appears with a big jug of beer and
pours it into the round jars that serve us as cups. Léance hovers
under the olive tree. Tib sits close to his mother, his arm around
her waist; the urgency of the moment has wiped out their more
formal ways. It's as though we're all holding our breath. We
wait for Léance and his wife to leave and at last the table
becomes alive. Serina turns again to Modeste. 'So?'

He nods. 'We found it, my lady. We found it.'

She sits quietly as he describes the sandalwood box. He
says, 'This poor baby, whoever she was, had somehow not
been allowed to shed her earthly body. By broaching the hill,
and opening her grave box, we began that process. She'll be
free now.'

'We think now that this is why Modeste was driven to find her,' says Tib. 'To set her spirit free.'

'And this child, then? Who is she? Who was she?'

Modeste shrugs. 'That's merely to be imagined, madam,' he says. 'But the way she was buried tells us she was important. The purple cloth is a tribute to Tiberius, perhaps. The old story of those women who came to these parts tells me something else. As does the fish carving.' He hesitates.

'We think it might be the woman from Magdala, Mother. The Magdelene,' says Tib. 'Florence saw her in a vision. We've all talked about this. The baby is from the woman from Magdala and the Nazarene. I'm certain what Florence saw was true.' He speaks with authority. 'The baby was placed there for safety perhaps but was somehow imprisoned and we had to set her free. And in exchange she showed us that we must believe what we believe.'

'So . . .?' Serina looks at me with steady eyes. 'The community would value—'

'This baby must remain a secret,' says Modeste firmly. 'She must be left in peace. Else she'll be the plaything of charlatans and will remain in limbo forever. No child should suffer that fate.'

Lady Serina looks at us, one to the other. Her glance lingers on me again. Lupinus and I have been silent during the storytelling. Then she shrugs her shoulders as though throwing a weight from them. 'The child will be left in peace. There are more pressing matters today.' Her gaze fixes on her son. 'I am the bearer of bad news, Tib. The Emperor has signed yet another edict proscribing followers of the Nazarene. In every part of the Empire writings, scrolls, places of worship are being destroyed. That's what Helée is doing even now, in the north of the province.' She looks around our humble clearing and our lean-to hut. 'Followers of the Nazarene are not allowed to meet, anywhere. They cannot appeal to the courts; they can be freely tortured under this new law. Senators and soldiers who praise the Way are deprived of office and rank. Freedmen who follow the Way are to be enslaved again. This is all so very serious, Modeste. My husband the Governor is bidden to root out such people across this province.' Her despair ripples like acid through her voice.

'Poor Mother,' says Tibery. He pauses. 'And poor Father,' he adds.

'There's worse,' says Serina. 'People are being killed in numbers. They say the Emperor has no blood lust. But his advisor Galerius, an iniquitous man, is very thirsty for blood. He encourages judges to use their powers and execute these people of our faith. This means the sword for citizens of Rome but, even worse, burning alive for others.'

My blood freezes. *Others.* I am the only *other* here.

Serina's voice thickens with remorse, with sorrow. 'And even worse. Your father has received a document from court specifically condemning all three of you. The deed is done.'

Tib pulls away from her. 'But my father—'

'Can – and *will* – do nothing. He may be a hero in the field but he is a coward in the family. In the end accounting he loves his Emperor more than he loves his son.' Her voice is dry and hard and Tib clutches her waist more tightly. Misou jumps from my grasp to go and slink round her ankles in an attempt to comfort her.

Modeste, who has been listening quietly, comes to life. 'We must travel north! Get your bags together, Tib, Florence. Lupinus! We will go north.'

And this is when we hear the creak of leather and the jingle of metal and the whinnying of a horse. I turn around to see foot soldiers surrounding our camp. There seems to be one behind every tree. Hundreds! Well, a hundred at least. I think we must be very important quarry.

Then a single soldier on a sturdy brown horse trots down the narrow path. He is built to impress with his heavy tabard of leather petals woven with copper wire, his red cloak and the red plume on the helmet that glints in the sun. We are enclosed in the clatter and rustle of men and armour as the soldiers stand up straight away from their trees and their other hiding places. So many of them.

The Centurion (as I suppose he must be) steers his horse right up to us. He bows and speaks directly to Lady Serina. 'With regret, madam, I've orders to come for your son and his companions.' He extracts a document from inside his leather jerkin. 'It's ordered here . . .' I notice one of my bees creeping up the leather petals of the man's jerkin.

'We know what has been ordered,' snaps Modeste. He turns

to Serina. 'Madam, say goodbye to your son and leave, else this condemnation taints you.'

Tib nods and looks towards Peter the seaman who is standing on the edge of the clearing. 'Peter! Take my mother back to Good Fortune. Guard her every step of the way.'

Serina stands up straight, her face cold and hard. Tib reaches up and makes the sign of the fish on her forehead. 'Blessings on you, Mother.'

She bows gravely to Modeste, then to me and to Lupinus before bending down to pick up Misou and following the seaman down the path towards the river. The curtain of soldiers parts to let her through.

The Centurion waits till she's out of sight then coughs. 'Now, messires, madam. We must go to this village and show these ignorant people what happens to those who show no respect for our old gods.'

Modeste steps before him. 'Centurion! The man of Aegyptus here is a slave of her Imperial Highness, sent with us from Nicomedia in gratitude when we cured her grandson. You will have heard of that? This man is no follower of the Nazarene. His name will certainly not be on your document. Let him go.'

The Centurion glances across at Lupinus, checks his paper and nods.

'Go!' hisses Modeste.

Lupinus shakes his head.

'Go!' echoes Tib. 'What else can you do, Lupinus? Go!'

Lupinus frowns and shrugs, then slips away. Now it's just the three of us.

Modeste tries again. 'And the woman! She's no follower of the Nazarene. I tell you! She's from another place. She believes in Mars and Jupiter and reads their messages from the heavens. She's not a follower, I tell you!' I so love him for the sheer desperation in his voice.

The commander shakes his head. 'You're named Florence?' he says directly to me. His eyes are large and brown and set in a network of deep wrinkles.

'I have two names,' I say, my voice trembling. 'But one of them is Florence.'

He nods his satisfaction then glances at two soldiers standing near him. 'Tie them! Take them!' he says.

Later, as I stumble down the path behind Tib and in front of Modeste, I see a coronet of bees buzzing around Tib's head. I can hear them buzzing around me. Bees are strange creatures. Even through all this helpless, numb misery I wonder what they're up to now.

The village, when we reach it, is crowded with pilgrims as well as villagers. The air is rent with shrieks and moans. The soldiers have to batter the crowds away with the flat of their swords as we make our way to the centre of the village. We have to step over a man who is lying in the path, moaning, foaming at the mouth.

In the village clearing, there are soldiers already piling brushwood in a pyre before Cessaro's crudely built little temple. The cry of 'Shame! Shame!' is taken up by many voices. Then the crowd quietens as three soldiers haul a block of wood before the central wooden columns of the temple.

The Centurion reins in his horse, stops our little procession and watches two men roll a second block of wood and position it beside the first. 'The gods will be well appeased today,' he says grimly.

His soldiers hustle us on towards the house of Léance, the biggest in the village. Now I can see my bees. They are hanging in a swarm, like a bundle of wool, from the steep overhang of Léance's roof. The bees in Léance's own hive will be none too pleased by their presence.

Inside the house the soldiers tie us to the central tree trunk post and leave us. There is no sign of Léance or his wife. 'This is it, friends,' says Modeste quietly. 'This is where everything is tested.'

'There was so much more to do,' says Tib, his voice thready and so very young. 'I don't want this, Modeste. What can we do?'

Oh, Tib! Oh, Siri, tied to another tree trunk, hundreds of miles and seventeen hundred years away.

'We can do nothing, Tib,' says Modeste. 'They'll ask you if you will make sacrifices to the old gods, to the God Emperors. If you don't, nothing can stop this thing here today.'

Tib laughs hysterically at this. 'I would never do that.' He sounds so very young.

'Then what happens today, dearest boy, will happen. It's

our time. Don't we know that we will be there today at the side of our own Lord? In Paradise?'

Modeste's tranquil voice makes me angry and I shout, 'Why don't we fight? Why don't we argue? Why do we just have to accept this? You make me sick! The pair of you.' I start to shiver violently.

Modeste lifts a manacled hand, pulls my face closer to his and looks me deep in the eyes. 'Have you learned nothing while you have been with us, Florence? An honest and true life must remain that till the end. And we know – you in your own pagan way know – that the end is not the end. There is no ending.' He repeats the words. 'There is no ending.'

'Modeste is right. That's the point, dear Florence,' says Tib softly, firmly now. 'The end is not the end.'

I'm still shuddering and shaking. Tib hauls on his shackles, comes in close and all three of us stand in a circle, our arms around each other. Tib stares hard at me with those eyes too wide for life. Modeste clutches my hand. My mad panic fades.

Tib bends his neck and allows his fish amulet to fall into his hand. He catches it and throws it towards me. I duck and, awkwardly, manage to loop it over my head. 'This will guard you, Florence. This will keep you safe.'

Then the door swings open and sunlight floods into the room. The three soldiers are black shadows as they move forward and untie us. Each soldier takes charge of one of us and marches us outside, through the shouting, screaming crowd to the square before the temple. At first all I can see are the soldiers, shoulder to shoulder with their backs to the hollow square, facing a grumbling crowd of Cesseroneans and pilgrims. Even in this dire moment I think how brave these people are, not to run away from these murderous men.

Brushwood is piled high around a newly erected post. Whoever built the pyre has left a space for access with crude steps behind and my soldier hustles me up these steps and ties me to the post. The pyre is placed so that I'm looking down on the two blocks of wood where now Modeste and Tib are being forced to kneel. Behind them, their appointed soldiers draw their swords from their scabbards and hold them loosely in front of them.

The Centurion's horse snickers and the bright sun glances off the shining sidepieces of his helmet. The bees are buzzing around his head, clambering from the metal leaves of his armour into the more comfortable fields of his flowing red cloak.

He calls out something to Tib and to Modeste, gesturing to the open doors of the temple. But here is a strange thing: try as I might I can't understand a word he's saying. And – worse – I can't understand the words of their response although their shaking heads tell me their meaning. It's gone, the gift of understanding that miraculously came upon me by the river on that first day at Pentecost.

Now, Modeste and Tib are kneeling and being told to bow their heads and they do so. The soldier behind Modeste turns his neck this way and that, settles his shoulders and grasps his sword firmly with both hands. His comrade follows suit.

My soldier goes off and returns with a long flaring torch. The soldiers behind Modeste and Tib raise their swords, two-handed, above their heads, the tips pointed dagger-like at the napes of Tib and Modeste. I can see the muscles in their forearms flex as they grasp their swords even more tightly. Someone in the crowd shrieks 'No!' and the chant is taken up. 'No. No. No!' At least I recognize this word.

At an order from the Centurion the soldiers facing the crowds in the square draw their swords, their armour creaking and rattling.

I look around in desperation. Somehow Léance and Lupinus have made their way inside the hollow square of soldiers and are standing beside my pyre. In their arms they are holding the great flagons Léance uses for his wine. Behind the cordon are more Cesseroneans with more flagons.

The Centurion sits on his horse, both hands raised and his legs pressed to the horse's flanks. He's ready to make some signal. Then the horse rears and the Centurion's hands come down to control it. Now I see him clawing at the neck of his jerkin, his face red. My bees are at work. Soldiers behind him run to his aid and people run through the cordon, flagons in their hands, and stand by Léance.

At last the Centurion roars an order strangled by a great bellow of pain. The executioners keep their hands above their heads and, with a glance into my eyes, the torch soldier kneels to light the edges of my pyre. The flames leap up as the smoke cuts the air. So although I can hear the half exultant, half despairing roar of the crowd I do not see the executioners' work. All I see is the red cloak of the Centurion flailing about as he fights my bees. I close my eyes and open them as the flames lick closer. I wish I could pray like Tib and Modeste but I can't.

Now Lupinus and Léance raise their flagons, and all the others do the same. All their movements become slow; every action is deliberate and elongated as Lupinus and the Cesseroneans shoot flagon after flagon of water over me: gallons of water slosh over my body, my head, my face, and my neck. I hear the flames sizzle. I cannot see. I cannot breathe: my lungs are full of steam and water is crashing over my face, in my eyes, in my mouth, into my nose.

I am drowning.

THIRTY-FIVE

Into the Now

C harles shook hands with the man from the boatyard, who then set off again down the canal path on his dusty, heavy duty bike. The boat man's verdict had been final. The gearbox was kaput. He'd grinned. 'In the old days you could have rowed or set up sail, Monsieur. But now a new gearbox of a special kind we must discover.' It would take a day to get the new gearbox from Beziers – if they had one – and perhaps another day to fit it.

The gearbox had been complaining crankily since Paris and although for a while it had responded to his tinkering, it had given up the ghost here at Agde where he'd come to witness the famous celebration of Pentecost.

He'd just been warming up the engine for his return journey when the grinding had come to a crescendo and then dissolved into deadly, irretrievable silence. He told himself not to complain. His narrowboat had done such good service, bringing him down the canals and rivers of England, then across the Channel with a volunteer crew who relished the risk of getting a boat with such a shallow draft across the Channel. Then, he was alone again and the narrowboat had chugged on and on down the rivers of France and finally here on to the Canal du Midi. So don't complain, Charles, he'd told himself in one of many conversations he'd had with himself on this long journey.

The boatyard man had shaken his head as he listened to Charles' travellers' tales. He'd wedged the air with his hands. *'Sûrement, monsieur, le projet de ce bateau est trop peu profond pour naviguer dans la Manche?'* The draft too shallow for the English Channel. Still, being a boatman himself the man had admired the boat's rather restrained decoration – dark green with a red trim and a painted castle in landscape. But he'd thrown up his hands in amazement when Charles explained that the castle had been built to house animals. *'Les Anglais, ils sont tellement très fous!'* he said. The English are mad. Very.

Now Charles watched the boatman's bike swerve on the canal path to avoid a couple walking along hand in hand. The afternoon had that baked feeling common this far south and he thought a walk by the river would cool him down. He locked up his boat, checked the padlocks on the chain that secured his motorbike to the deck, pulled on the linen jacket that he wore for its useful pockets and set off into the town and down towards the river.

He'd been right. The river was shadier and cooler than the canal and the walk was pleasant. He stopped now and then to take photographs of the light on the flat green water and the deep shadows of the undergrowth on the far bank. He stopped for a minute on a muddy boat landing to allow more exposure time to compensate for the deep shade. Standing very still, he became aware of some turbulence eight feet from the bank. Could be a turtle, he thought. He's seen a turtle swimming down the centre of the canal yesterday. But later, on his computer screen, the creature had been barely visible.

Now he lowered his camera and watched as the turbulence transformed itself into a hand, a shoulder, a black and white face that spluttered and coughed, spitting out water like a whale. He threw down his camera, threw off his jacket, sat down on the bank and slithered his way into the water. It was deeper than he'd thought and he had to swim a couple of strokes to reach the flailing woman.

When he got to her she shouted and fought, but finally he managed to get one arm under her shoulder and turn on to his back to haul her to the shore. She was a bundle of sodden black rags and smelled of the river and – curiously – of acrid smoke. He pulled her on to the landing place, knelt down and looked at her. She was younger than he'd thought. He leaned down to pull back the thick black hair that was plastered over her face. Sodden, withered flowers came away in his hands. Her face was black with soot and her mascara had run, giving her the look of a clown. Ah yes! he thought. The wild joy in the streets yesterday. Pentecost!

'*Mon dieu!*' A voice came from behind him. '*Elle est morte?*' A diminutive woman had stopped and was standing with her feet astride her bicycle.

She had a straw hat on her head, a blonde pony tail and rope-soled sandals.

He blinked. 'I don't think so, madame.' He leaned down again, felt the woman's throat and found a very faint pulse. Quickly, he turned her on to her side and thumped her back quite hard. Once. Twice. 'Come on!' he said. 'Come on!' Then she retched, her body arched and she spewed out what seemed like gallons of foul-smelling river water on to the ground beside her. Then she started to cough and splutter again. Again he could smell smoke and something like sour cheese.

The cyclist clapped her hands. 'Bravo,' she said. 'She will survive, I think?' she said. He realized now she must be English. She leaned down and took a pink mobile phone from underneath the book in her basket. 'We require a doctor, I think.' She peered short-sightedly at the screen, made a few clicks and rang a number.

Charles looked down. The woman was wearing what looked like sodden fancy dress. All in black, with those funny pantaloons. Pentecost! Perhaps that was how she'd ended up in the water.

The cyclist tucked her phone away. 'I'll be on my way, then,' she said, putting a foot on the drive pedal. She looked at him, her very dark eyes thoughtful. 'Every day I ride here by the river, find a very private place and read my book. It's very soothing.' Then she rode off, a tiny, trim figure exuding energy.

He only realized when she'd gone that he didn't know her name.

The woman at his feet groaned and – desperate to do something – he tucked his coat over her. His hand caught the weight of his camera and keys in his pockets and he transferred them to his shirt pocket. She moaned again. 'Shshsh,' he said. 'The doctor's coming. You're safe now, madame.' He pushed more of that hair away from her face and she looked into his eyes. 'You're safe now,' he repeated.

She blinked. Her lips moved. 'Safe . . .' she said. Her hand reached towards him and she lost consciousness. Charles patted her face but she was dead to the world. He felt her neck and could feel the strong beat of her heart. He tucked his coat more tightly around her and settled down to wait for help.

Help came in the form of a man and woman in uniform. Some kinds of medics, he thought. They clicked and tutted over her body and the woman medic went running off. The man pulled a foil sheet from his backpack and covered the woman's body with it. He felt her pulse and nodded, obviously satisfied. He looked up at Charles. 'This is your wife, monsieur?'

'No, no,' he said. 'I just pulled her ashore.'

The man frowned. 'Are you sure she's not your wife, monsieur?'

Charles was indignant. 'I tell you, I . . .' Then he saw what the man was holding. There was the silver chain around the woman's neck. Dangling from the chain, small and perfectly carved in silver, was a fish. Charles's hand went to his own neck, where its twin hung, perfectly carved, in amber. 'Look! I don't know her. I'm visiting here for the first time. I have a boat on the canal. I just came down here to walk, saw this woman in the canal and dragged her out.'

'It seems *à propos*, monsieur, that a husband and wife would have the same amulets.' The man's tone was severe.

Charles flushed. 'Look, mate, I got this thing on Saturday at the flea market here, in a tray of *bric à brac*. The whole tray cost me five euros.' Did this man think he was an axe-murderer or a wife-beater?

The man beamed. 'Ah. A coincidence, monsieur? This world is full of strange coincidences. *Non?*'

Charles relaxed, but was relieved when he saw the woman medic trundling a kind of wheelchair-cum-stretcher along the river path. The man spoke quickly to her and they both glanced at Charles, who found himself blushing again.

The woman knelt by the unconscious woman and suddenly said, 'Houpla!' She'd found one of those money belts round the river woman's waist. From it she pulled out two items, barely damp from the water: a wallet with some euros and an English passport.

'Estella Warner,' she said. '*Anglais. Et aussi!*' She pulled out a large key and read the luggage label attached. '*Villa d'Estella, rue Haute.*'

She thrust the key at Charles. 'You must go to the house, monsieur, and tell them there we have found their *maman* and she is at the hospital. Say she is breathing well, no injuries. They will make checks and bring her back to the rue Haute.'

After that she and the other medic ignored him, fussing over transferring the unconscious woman on to the stretcher and trundling her away along the river path. Charles slipped on his now damp and dirty jacket and followed them slowly.

He called in at a *tabac* and asked the way to the rue Haute. The man sold him a street map and pointed out the route, upwards towards the ridge of the town.

He made his way from the harbour up through the old town, up the narrow rue Venuste as far as the rue Haute – an alleyway of tall houses which was well named, situated as it was high up above the old town.

The house with the door large enough to fit the key was easy to find. He banged his fist on it twice, three times. When no one answered he inserted the key in the lock and passed through an archway into a shady courtyard. Leading off the courtyard were two glazed doorways, one into a kitchen and one into a salon. The salon door was open when he tried it, so he let himself in.

He looked around. The salon was modest enough in itself, with a long couch and a graceful table, but was dominated by a vast fireplace big enough to roast an ox. A kitchen at one time, he supposed. He peered into the large kitchen next door which led through to another internal courtyard. There was no sign of life.

He listened again. No sound. Then, almost without willing it, he made for the stairs. Every bed except one was stripped. He peered under one of the stripped beds and looped out a Barbie doll. He propped her in a comfortable pose against a pillow on her stripped bed. In another room where the bed was made up there was a laptop case on a table and a single suit-case. Only a few items of clothing remained in the massive armoire: jeans; embroidered blouses; a silk jacket; a knitted shawl; trainers; boots. Not much, all told. Clearly the woman was here on her own.

He backed out of the room in some embarrassment and saw there was yet another wooden staircase rising against the massive grey stone wall. He climbed upwards again and found himself in a room high in the eaves. He could make out a rather messy daybed and a long table covered with books, neat piles of paper and a slim blue laptop.

The light from the narrow window was dim so he fumbled around for a switch and turned on the light. He sat down and turned over some of the papers. Most of them were astrologers' charts scribbled over and marked with different coloured pens. Beside the laptop was a chubby spiralbound notebook. He flipped through it and saw pages of neat writing – people's names at the top with information below neatly organized into bullet points with succinct conclusions at the end. Charles thought that if you discounted the fact that astrology was bunk, here was evidence of an organized, sane mind – not the mind of someone who would throw themselves in a river.

He turned the book over and started again from the back. These pages were full – in a scrawl almost by another hand – of various versions of the word *Siri* written a thousand times – large, small, sideways, backwards. This time it was clear the writer was clearly very hurt, or very angry, or both. These pages were full of madness. They were in the hand of a person who might very well throw themselves in the river.

He placed the notebook by the laptop and tried to put the sheets of paper back in neat piles. His eye dropped to a brown folder at the bottom and he pulled this out. It was full of newspaper cuttings of articles about a single event. The headlines ranged from *Chilling Teenage Killing* through *Girl Slaughtered by Friends* to *Teenagers Sentenced for Savage Killings*. The cuttings were three years old. The girl had been eleven years old and her name was Siri Warner. There was a photo of Siri's mother and father at the funeral. Their grief bled from the page of grainy newsprint.

Charles frowned and shoved the cuttings back into the folder, shoved the folder to the bottom of the file, clattered down the wooden staircases, out through the salon and the courtyard and out into the street.

He looked both ways and decided to go right, back down to the quayside and out over the wide bridge to the canal. He needed to get to his boat, his refuge in recent years when things had been bad in business, bad in life. He couldn't bear to think of a little girl called Siri being killed and a mother so sad that dark swirling water was a positive option.

He would check on the woman tomorrow, but for today he hurried down to the quayside along the narrow rue Venuste which once, according to his guidebook – in 600 BC – had led up to the beautiful Temple of Venus on the brow of the hill in the town they then called Good Fortune.

THIRTY-SIX
Starr Bright

My chest was sore and my eyes were screwed up against the light. I was fighting against the man-handling, thinking first it was Goldenwand's men, then the execution soldiers in Cessero. How much you can think in a flash! I was soaking wet with the water thrown by Lupinus and choking with the smoke from the smouldering woodpile.

At last I opened my eyes to blazing white light and saw Modeste's amber fish pendant dangling from the neck of the stranger. Then blackness, then murmuring voices. Then the roar of traffic and the rattle of a nearby train. So I kept my eyes closed tight and pretended to be unconscious as they poked and prodded and manhandled me on to a stretcher then into a van of some kind.

I knew instantly that I was back into my own not-dreamed life, although most of me was still in that muddy village, watching the soldiers' sinews flex as they brought the swords down on the necks of my dear ones, Modeste and Tib. Then as I was lying there in some clinic, being poked and prodded yet again, my mind struggled with the very hard thought that there was no 'then and now'. Really it was the 'now and the now'.

And now I'm back at the Maison d'Estella, showered and changed and drinking camomile tea made by the nurse who did the prodding and poking and finally brought me home. She tutted and fussed when we found the house open to God and good neighbours – or more particularly the Gitans who lived in the old quarter, whom she didn't trust.

I asked her about the man who rescued me. She didn't know him. 'But he was a boatman, madame. He had a boat on the canal. He was English and I think his name is Charles.' I close my eyes and see Modeste's amber fish dangling before my eyes as the man came close to me there on the river.

*   *   *

Now she's gone, leaving behind a lingering scent of antiseptic.

I sip the rest of the tea and try my very best to make sense of it all. It can't have been a dream. How can I remember it so well? My mobile, still on the kitchen top, vibrates. I take a very deep breath and answer it. It's Philip. 'That you, Starr? Where've you been? I've called you a dozen times this morning. Are you OK?'

It's thrilling, in its own way, to hear his voice. 'I'm OK, Philip. Really. I've been out and about. Talking to people. Eating nice food.' I think of Tib's honey.

'On your own?'

'I met some people. And I did a lot of thinking.'

A silence at the other end of the phone.

I try the usual thing. 'How was the flight?'

'There was a delay. Weather. George was sick and Olga went off with a stranger who bought her a story book and returned her safe and sound. Mae drank a bottle of wine and slept the whole of the journey.'

'Oh, well. You know Mae. Not much you can say, really.'

'Estella,' he says. 'About what was said . . .'

'I'm sorry, Philip, but I think . . .' I pause. 'If I've done anything here in Agde I've realized that I have to let Siri go. I have to set her free from my own sadness.'

'That's so good,' he says his voice tentative. 'You do know that I've always missed her, Stella. And always will.'

'You were a wonderful father for her, Phil. You made our lives better.'

'And now . . .?'

'I think we both have to let go. You have to let me go. I think you should find someone who brings out your sense of fun. As Mae said, I've been trampling on that for a few years now. There has to be someone out there.'

'But it's you I want, the old Stella.' He coughs. 'You know, you sound like the old Stella even from here.'

'That old Stella's not here, Philip. You have to let her go.'

Another pause, which I don't know how to break.

He says at last, 'Are you sure you're OK?'

'I'm sure.' I take a breath. 'I will always be grateful to you, Philip. And I'll always be your friend.'

'There'll be things to sort.' He sounds forlorn.

'We'll do that when I get back to England. Will you do something for me in the meantime?'

'Anything.'

'You know that little attaché case of my mother's? The one I put Siri's bits and pieces in?'

'Of course.'

'Will you put that in a very safe place?'

'Of course.' A pause which I allow to lie there between us like a sword. 'Goodbye then, Stella.'

'Bye Philip.' I hit *end call* to stop it all.

My body is beginning to flood with relief, like the calm-down after an orgasm. I go through to the salon and lie down to reflect on all these events. One version of the truth might be that, cast down by my irreparable loss, I isolated myself and then tried and failed to commit suicide by drowning. Then, the theory would go, the fact that my attempt failed was a relief and will allow me to re-evaluate the rest of my life.

The other, more vital version, is that I've been granted an epiphany, a glimpse of eternal and enduring life, of deep truths buried in history. I've experienced great happiness, terrible cruelty and learned many things that I'll never forget, that will be part of me forever. And I know now that my daughter has a great soul that survives, amongst others, alongside the souls of Tib and Modeste.

But certain things are very clear to me now. One is that I didn't try to kill myself. Another is that my time with Modeste and Tib was no dream. Another is that I was with them for a purpose: to allow the baby to continue on her journey and to be a witness for Tib and Modeste to those last cruel events. Finally, I'm quite certain that Tib has worked his miracle on me. My mind is clear – clear as a bell. Not a touch of madness about me. Not now.

I must have drifted off. When I wake the shadows in the courtyard have deepened. The wall clock tells me I've been asleep for two hours. How refreshing to sleep without dreaming. I am clearly back to that other Starr, *also called Estella*. I check my phone and see I've missed other calls apart from those from Philip: one was from Mae. 'How are you, babe? We're thinking of you. Olga ran away at the airport and George was sick. It's a relief to be home. Billy says you should ring us to say you're OK. But he says you will be OK anyway. I love you, girl, you know that.'

The other calls are from two magazines chasing up late copy. I leap upstairs to the eyrie and grab my laptop. I look around the room. There's something different here. I can't put my finger on it. I run down the hill, past the busy Café Plazza, and get to the library in time to use their broadband to post my copy.

Passing the café on my way back up the hill I see a scooter padlocked to the bollard where Madame Patrice's bicycle once stood. I avert my gaze and hurry back to the house. Once here I have another shower and wash my hair again, blow-drying it straight and tying it back in a loop. In one cell of my mind I remember washing it in the river, with Tib scooping up river water to rinse it and Modeste rubbing it dry with a rough woollen cloth. Now it's as straight and silky as it never was in Cessero, in Good Fortune, or in Nicomedia.

I pull on fresh jeans and a white tee shirt, tuck a hundred euros in my back pocket and pick up the pink silk linen jacket hanging in the *armoire*. Locking the great door of the house carefully behind me I turn right, down towards the quayside. I turn left again and make my way by the rue de la Poissonnerie. The house where Madame Patrice and Louis lived is all boarded up and has a faded old *A Vendre* sign nailed to the door. It looks as though it hasn't been entered for years. I make my way along the rue Louis Bages and buy an overpriced bottle of wine from an *alimentation* and make for the bridge.

On the canal path my fast pace slows. This is a fool's errand – looking for a man called Charles in a boat I won't recognize. I can't even ask in my faltering French. 'Er . . . there was this man called Charles who hauled me out of the water this morning?' They would think I was mad, wouldn't they?

I dawdle on. There are dozens of boats tied up by the canal – large, small, grand, simple, wrecked, glamorous. In this early-evening hour there is quite a lot of activity – couples walking, children playing, people drinking and eating under deck awnings.

Then at last I see the boat and I know it. A tremble of delight passes through me from my heels to my head. I knock on the door to the cabin, once, then again more loudly, to make myself heard over the guitar music inside. Then I stand back as far as is possible on a narrowboat that has a motorbike shackled to its rail. The music dies, the door opens and a figure emerges. And emerges. I'd forgotten just how large he was. He's thinner now but he's still very big. He is wearing long shorts and the amber fish pendant twinkles against his bare chest. His curls are still fair but cropped short and he's wearing rimless spectacles. His face is more sharply boned than I remember.

'Yes?' he says, blinking. His eyes are the familiar sharp pale blue but in no other way does he resemble either Louis or Modeste. But they are him and he is them.

I hold out my bottle of wine. 'I came to say thank you for hauling me out of the drink.'

He frowns. 'You? You don't look like . . .'

'The bedraggled wretch you fished out of the river?'

He nods and smiles a little. I'd forgotten that dimple on his cheek. 'How did you find me?' he says.

I tap the painting on the side of the cabin. 'The *Deer House*,' I say. 'I remember the Deer House.'

'The Deer House? Climbing the wall in the dark? Those years ago? I remember. I looked for you . . .' He blinks again. Now he knows. He knows it's me; he remembers that fateful night so many years ago. 'Come inside,' he says. 'Please.'

I follow him into the narrow space with shining wood walls and crowded shelves with objects lined up in order. It has a kind of tightly packed elegance. He takes two glasses from a shelf and gestures for me to sit down on a side bench and sits on the opposite side to open the bottle. Here we are, face to face. 'I left your house open. I'm sorry,' he says calmly.

He tells me that he found the Maison d'Estella and went exploring. We are on our second drink when he asks about Siri. 'She was your daughter? I saw the news cuttings in your top room. Sorry, I shouldn't have been so nosy . . .'

'You more than anyone have a right to know about Siri.'

I *will* tell him all about Siri. And Louis, and Modeste and Tib. But there will be plenty of time for all that. First . . . 'Your name! The nurse said you were an Englishman called Charles something . . .'

He grins and moves to sit beside me on the narrow bench so we are sitting tightly, shoulder to shoulder. 'My ex-wife preferred Charles, but really it's Ludovic. Do you remember,

your friend compared me to a board game? So it's Ludovic.'
He takes a long sip of his wine and turns to look straight at
me with those big blue eyes. *Louis. Modeste.* 'My friends now
call me Luke. A work thing,' he says, holding up his glass in
a toast to me. Or both of us, perhaps.

'Hello again, Ludovic,' I say. 'Hello Luke.'

THIRTY-SEVEN
And in the Beginning

I found out the truth about Tibery and Modeste the day before Luke and I set off on the *Deer House* to begin our journey back to England. The days since he dragged me out of the river had been a tumble of catching up, explanation and exploration. Luke was desolate to hear about Siri, knowing her and losing her in an instant, concerned about my grief and faintly disbelieving about my stories of Louis and Madame Patrice, Tibery and Modeste. Odd, that – Luke smiling in disbelief, looking at me with Modeste's eyes.

On our last day in Agde we went on Luke's motorbike to a place called St Thibery, a mile or so from the city. There by the river we found a small dusty town whose streets circled in an odd fashion around the remnants of a beautiful medieval abbey. We kept getting lost. We found the one *tabac* then lost it again. We found the one *boulangerie* then lost it again. Somehow there was no way of knowing our left from our right. It was a shapeshifting kind of place.

We sat in the one café and I tried to tell Luke about the Cessero I knew. We wandered around again, hand in hand. I tried and failed to see *my* Cessero. Only its location near the river told me it was the place I wanted it to be: that and the dusty plaque linking the medieval abbey to the martyred boy. Saint Thibery.

We called in the tiny tourist shop and I asked the woman for information about the village and its history. She rooted in a store cupboard and fished out a sheaf of papers. '*Seulement un document, Madame*,' she said, smiling.

The document is single-spaced, seven pages long, in faded typescript and unsigned. It speaks of Tib and Modeste. So, as Luke and I made our way north through the locks on the Canal du Midi and then up the great rivers on our way to Paris, I used his old doorstep Harrap's dictionary to translate the pages of the document one by one. I worked very hard to get it right,

careful not to add my own remembered truths, the truths of
my own experience.

I was sitting with my back to Luke's bike on the deck of
the *Deer House* when I wrote the last words on my pad and
read my translation right through again. Looking up at the
night sky over Paris I could see Virgo twinkling above us. And
across the sky, steady as ever, the Great Bear sat secure in its
proper place.

Afterword

Extract from Starr Warner's translation of her 'found' paper:

The Greeks, the Gauls and the Romans called this place Keppero, then Cessero. Only after the Merovingian age, when the Christian era began, was it called Saint Thibery . . . There was a child called Thibery who in the fourth century AD was found guilty of embracing Christianity and martyred in this place . . . As legend has it, the boy could cure a sick man of his mental demons with a single touch. His noble and inspiring acts made people respect and admire him. And apart from his physical beauty he possessed the highest intelligence and a loving heart. Even at eleven years old he was sensitive to the flaws in the human heart and was particularly skilled at curing those ill in the mind . . . Thibery was born in Agde – then called Good Fortune – in 301 or 293. His father Helée, governor of the city of Agde, was a devoted servant of Rome . . . He appointed, as tutor for his son, a wise and literary man called Modeste, who bestowed on his pupil the sacred fruits of knowledge gathered throughout his life . . . The fact is that in secret, Modeste was following the new religion of Christianity. His pupil witnessed his commitment and – like his tutor – was drawn to Christianity and secretly began to participate in the rites of that religion . . . Although he cured his father of blindness and also cured a relative of the Emperor Diocletian of a degenerative sickness, Thibery and Modeste's religion made them traitors and, with their companion Florence, they were executed on 10th November 304 AD. The executions took place on the landing stage at Cessero. The three of them were buried at their place of execution . . .